Also by Claire Boston

<u>The Texan Quartet</u>
What Goes on Tour
All that Sparkles
Under the Covers
Into the Fire

<u>The Flanagan Sisters</u>
Break the Rules
Change of Heart
Blaze a Trail
Place to Belong

<u>The Beginner Writer's Toolkit</u>
Self-Editing

Place to Belong

The Flanagan Sisters #4

Claire Boston

BANTILLY
PUBLISHING

First published by Bantilly Publishing in 2017

Place to Belong: The Flanagan Sisters 4

EPUB format: 978-0-9953918-2-6
Mobi format: 978-0-9953918-3-3
Print format: 978-0-9953918-4-0

Cover design by Amygdala Design
Edited by Julia Knapman
Proofread by Grammar Smith Editing Services

DEDICATION

To the LGBTQI community of Australia.
Because it's about damn time same-sex marriage is legal here — love is love.

Chapter 1

Sean Flanagan's stomach rolled as the plane descended.

He shouldn't have come. He shouldn't have given in to the urge, the desperate desire to meet the family he had never known. He should have been happy with his life as it was. Being a bartender in a small Irish town wasn't bad. It was a steady job and he had his own apartment. He shouldn't want more. Besides, chances were high that his half-sisters weren't really as nice as they seemed online — they couldn't possibly be.

He breathed deeply and shifted in his seat, his foot tapping on the floor.

He'd disembark and find the next flight back home. If he was lucky, his sisters would give up waiting for him and go home and he'd never have to see them. Maybe they hadn't even come to the airport to pick him up like they'd promised.

The plane touched down and the roar of the wheels on the tarmac filled the plane as it slowed. Sean closed his eyes, his heart beating rapidly, his skin hot. Around him, people unclicked their seatbelts and stood. He stayed where he was as overhead lockers were opened, carry-on bags were lifted down and the aisles filled with people eager to be off the plane.

He couldn't move.

Would the cabin crew notice if he stayed here?

He could stay where he was and take the plane to wherever its next destination was.

"Excuse me, sir. You need to leave." The gentle female voice was above him.

He opened his eyes to the concerned expression on the flight attendant's face. The plane was empty. "Sorry." He reached for his backpack under the seat in front of him, and then stood, his legs a little shaky.

"Are you all right? You're a little pale."

He forced a smile to his face. "Just my Irish pallor, love."

The woman blushed and he walked past her, off the plane and followed the signs to customs.

He had to get a grip, otherwise he'd attract the attention of customs officials. He really didn't need that. He got his iPod out of his backpack and chose his favorite playlist, taking a moment to listen to the first verse of an upbeat song. He breathed out as some of his anxiety receded. He wasn't walking to face a firing squad, he was meeting three sisters he hadn't known existed until five months ago. It had staggered him to receive the social media message out of the blue from Zita, who had been looking for information about their father. But when it had finally sunk in that he had three sisters, he'd been cautiously hopeful. Perhaps this was his chance to have a family.

Arriving at customs, Sean shuffled forward with the rest of the people. Several planes had landed at the same time, and he was more than happy to wait.

Carly, Bridget, and Zita had seemed pleased to meet him. He'd had some fun Skype sessions with them over the last few months, getting to know them, but people weren't necessarily honest online. He hadn't been. He hadn't dared tell them the whole truth.

The situation was so much more difficult because he was here for his sisters' weddings. He didn't know how to behave at family events. He'd never had any practice.

He should have refused. He should have said he couldn't get time off work, or couldn't afford the flight. Not that the last one would have worked. Carly, the oldest of his three sisters, was a billionaire and had offered to pay for the flight and his accommodation. Not wanting to owe her anything, he'd paid for his own flight, but had agreed to stay with his sisters during his time there. He hoped he wouldn't regret the decision.

And then there was Carmen, his sisters' mother. How was she going to react to the illegitimate son of her dead husband? He'd only spoken to her once online and she'd been distant. He couldn't blame her. It had to have come as a shock to discover her beloved husband had another child.

Finally, he reached the front of the line and was fingerprinted, photographed and his passport was scanned. Americans sure were paranoid. He moved on to the luggage carousel where the crowds had already thinned. His backpack was there so he grabbed it and went through the final checks before he was allowed out to where people were waiting for passengers.

He took his time attaching his smaller backpack to the larger one and shrugged it on, adjusting the straps. Then there was nothing else he could do to delay the inevitable. It was time to meet his sisters in person.

He steeled himself and walked into the public area.

He spotted his sisters immediately. It was hard to miss them. They were holding a huge welcome sign with colorful helium balloons coming off it. He had no time to prepare himself as Zita, his youngest sister and the one who looked the most like him with her strawberry-blonde hair, dropped the sign and flung herself at him, wrapping her arms around him and squeezing him tightly. "Welcome! It's so good to see you."

Sean's heart lodged in his throat as he hugged her back.

"Move over, Z, let me have a turn." Bridget nudged her sister out of the way and grinned at him. "I thought you were never going to get here." She wrapped her arms around him. She was about his height, with the same blue eyes, but her curly brown hair and darker skin came from her Salvadoran heritage.

He had no words, wouldn't have been able to get them through the lump in his throat even if he had.

Bridget stepped back to allow Carly to greet him. She was every bit of her Salvadoran heritage with dark eyes, dark hair, and so short he had to bend over to hug her.

"How was your flight?" Carly asked.

He swallowed and forced out the words. "Fine. Long."

"We're going straight to my place," she said. "We thought you'd like to stay in the city for the first few days at least, so you can explore."

He honestly hadn't considered sightseeing in Houston while he was here. Hadn't thought much past the fact he was meeting his family. Still, he nodded. "Thanks."

He followed them out of the airport where the humidity smothered him. He stopped to adjust — it was unlike anything he'd ever known.

"You'll get used to the heat," Zita said, taking his arm. "It's always humid in July."

This wasn't humid, this was like syrup. His skin flushed and sweat sprang to the surface, adding to the already overripe feeling of his clothes after being on the go for over twelve hours. He'd kill for a shower.

They reached a brand new white station wagon and he put his backpack in the trunk. It wasn't the Aston Martin he'd pictured for a billionaire, but Carly's fiancé was an artist, so perhaps it was his car.

Zita joined him on the backseat. "What time did you leave Dublin?"

"Nine a.m.," he replied, holding his hand up to the air conditioning that was blaring through the outlets.

"That's pretty reasonable," Bridget said. "Hopefully you won't be too jet-lagged."

"I'm fine. Where are the guys?" He was kind of glad his sisters' fiancés weren't here.

"They're at my place cooking dinner," Carly said. "We didn't want to swamp you at the airport." She glanced in the rearview mirror, met his eyes and smiled.

Zita squeezed his hand. "If it's too much, or if you're tired, just say the word. We won't be offended. It must be kind of hard for you when you don't know us that well."

He smiled at her. His sisters were already trying to take care of him. The hope that they may actually become part of his family for real stirred and he gently pushed it back down. He knew not to get his hopes up. "It'll be great to meet them properly." He'd seen a little bit of Evan, Jack and David online when he'd spoken with his sisters, but they generally left after saying hello. Each of his sisters had met their partners within the last twelve months, and from the way they spoke, they were already one big happy family. Something he'd never had.

Was he going to mess it all up?

He ignored the fear as he made small talk with his sisters and took in his surroundings. They drove on the opposite side of the road than he was used to, and a couple of times he had to stop himself from calling out to Carly to change lanes.

By the time they arrived at Carly's penthouse apartment, he was starting to flag. It was about midnight in Ireland even though it was only six in Houston. He followed them into the open plan living area with floor to ceiling windows looking out over the city. There was a meaty smell in the air, perhaps a roast cooking. Three men sat on the antique-looking sofas drinking beer and wine. They stood up when his sisters walked in.

Sean scanned the faces as each woman greeted her partner with a kiss. His sisters really knew how to pick them. Evan, the painter, had black hair that was slightly past his collarbone; Jack, Bridget's partner, was tall and fit with short brown hair; and David, Zita's man, was the typical blond-haired, blue-eyed all-American. Introductions were made and he shook each man's hand, looking for judgment. He couldn't find any. They appeared to be genuinely pleased to meet him.

"Something smells fantastic," Bridget said.

"We cooked a roast," Jack replied. "Thought it might be homey for Sean." He smiled.

Sean nodded his thanks. No one had ever cooked a roast for him. If they'd wanted to remind him of his childhood, a can of baked beans would have done the trick.

"Why don't you dish up and I'll show Sean his room?" Carly said.

He followed Carly down a short hallway to a bedroom. He stared. It was the most luxurious room he'd ever seen. The queen-sized bed was covered in pillows and a thick quilt that made it ever so enticing. There was a window giving him a bird's-eye view over the city and a walk-in closet for his clothes.

"Make yourself at home," Carly said. "The bathroom is through there." She pointed. "You'll have it to yourself as Evan and I use the one in my bedroom. Did you want a shower first? I can delay dinner."

His desire to shower warred with his fear of being a

nuisance. "No…it's fine. I'll have one later."

"Why don't you freshen up and then come out?" She reached out and squeezed his hand. "I know this might be a little overwhelming for you, but we're so glad you came." She left and he stood there, staring after her.

She had no clue how overwhelmed he was. He wanted to lock himself in his room and cry for sheer relief that they had even been at the airport to pick him up. Instead, he went into the bathroom, splashed some cold water on his face, sniffed his armpits and then dug out his spray deodorant. Finally, with a deep breath to fortify himself, he went to have dinner with his sisters.

***

It was midday by the time Sean woke the next morning. He lay in bed and listened for sounds that anyone was home. It was silent. Carly had mentioned it was her last day of work before the wedding, but Evan hadn't mentioned his plans. He got up and took his time in the shower, washing away the last of his fatigue. After he dressed, he wandered down the hallway to the living area. Evan was painting by the windows.

McClane, Evan's Australian bulldog, jumped down from the couch and trotted over to greet him.

Sean smiled and patted the dog. "Morning," he called.

There was no response.

Sean frowned. Was this how it was going to be? Polite while Carly was around and ignore him when she was gone? Perhaps Evan wasn't as genuine as he'd seemed the night before. He took a couple of steps closer, moving so he was in Evan's field of vision. "Mind if I make a cup of tea?"

Still nothing.

He hesitated, running a hand through his mid-length hair. This was awkward. Should he try again or just help himself? He stepped closer and said, "Evan?" He waved a hand to get his attention.

Evan jumped, swore and turned to him with his paintbrush raised. When he saw Sean, his breath released with a whoosh. "Damn."

"Didn't mean to startle you."

"No, my fault entirely. I tend to get caught up when I'm painting."

No kidding. "Sorry for interrupting."

Evan put his paintbrush in a jar of liquid and scrubbed his hands on his shirt. "It's fine. I was only planning to paint until you got up." He smiled and walked toward the kitchen. "Want a cup of coffee?"

"Tea if you've got it." Sean followed him, not certain whether the man was telling the truth. Was it possible to be so involved with your work that you didn't hear someone speak?

Evan filled the kettle and asked, "How did you sleep?"

"Like a log."

"Carly doesn't skimp on things. If your bed's anything like ours, it's like lying on a cloud."

Sean smiled. "Exactly."

Evan made the drinks and then dug around the fridge. "You want a sandwich?"

"Sure."

Sean sipped his tea while Evan pulled out ingredients. "If you're feeling up to it, Carly said she'd show you around her company, Comunidad, this afternoon."

"I'd like that."

"Great." Evan pushed a sandwich over to Sean and then handed him a SIM card and a piece of paper. "Carly wasn't sure whether you'd have international roaming on your phone, so she got you a US SIM card. The paper has all our numbers on it."

Sean looked at the card. His finances were limited. "How much is it?"

"It's nothing."

There was no way he was taking more from his sisters. They were already letting him stay with them. The more he took, the more he would owe them. "It's fine. I've got my own phone." He tucked the list of numbers into his pocket.

Evan looked at him for a long moment. "We barely know each other, but let me say something," he said. "Carly and her sisters are the real deal. They give everything they have generously, without wanting anything in return." He took a sip of his coffee. "They're all so excited to have an older brother and to make up for lost time. Part of that is going to be taking you places and buying you things. Don't reject it because you're too proud to accept gifts, or you feel like you will owe them. It comes with no strings attached."

Sean was silent. How could Evan know what he was thinking?

"Unless you decide to make hour-long phone calls to a girlfriend in Ireland, the phone costs are going to be negligible."

Sean forced out a laugh. "There's no girlfriend."

"Then I'd recommend you take the SIM." Evan took a bite of his sandwich.

Sean hesitated. He'd been planning to get a SIM card when he arrived at the airport but had forgotten. "All right. Thanks."

"I'll give Carly a call and check when she's free," Evan said.

Sean ate his lunch while Evan called Carly. The way his face lit up while he was talking with her was kind of sweet.

"Great. We'll see you then." Evan hung up. "She's got a few things to tie up, but she'll be ready at three. Did you want to check out downtown Houston?"

He glanced over to the window. "I don't want to interrupt if you've got work." He wanted a little more time to adjust to where he was.

Evan chuckled. "I can always paint."

"To be honest, I don't think I've got the energy yet," Sean admitted. "I'm happy to read until it's time to visit Carly."

"If you're sure," Evan said.

He nodded. He was three-quarters of the way through a crime novel and wanted finish it.

"Then let me set an alarm." Evan grabbed his phone and entered something. "If this goes off at half past two and I don't stop painting, give me a shake or something."

"Sure."

"Oh, and help yourself to anything."

"Thanks." Sean wandered back to his room to get his book, and by the time he'd returned, Evan was painting again. It was kind of nice that he wasn't treating him like anything special. It made him more comfortable, more at home than if he'd been hovering.

Sean settled onto the couch to read.

"Evan, it's time to stop painting." The slightly annoyed timbre of Carly's voice made Sean look up. He hadn't heard her return.

"Evan, it's time to stop painting."

The voice came from over near the window. Sean grinned as Evan stepped back and reached for his phone. "Nice alarm."

Evan's smile was slightly bashful. "Carly's voice is the only thing that really breaks through." He washed his brush. "Give me ten minutes to clean up and we'll head off."

Sean got to his feet and returned his book to his room.

When Evan came out, he said, "I almost forgot to give you this." He handed Sean a key. "That way you can come and go as you please."

Sean's breath caught. It was such a show of trust. "Thanks."

"No problem."

Sean tucked the key into his pocket and followed Evan downstairs. After introducing him to the doorman, they went outside. The heat was even worse than it had been yesterday. Instantly his skin was covered in a film of sweat. "*Feck.* How do you stand the heat?"

Evan laughed. "You get used to it. If you want we can drive instead of walk."

"How far is it?"

"About ten minutes down the road."

He could handle that. He'd be damned if he'd let a little bit of humidity stop him. "Lead the way."

They walked down the shaded side of the sidewalk, not that it did anything against the thick humidity. By the time they arrived at the Comunidad building Sean felt like a wilted weed. Stepping into the air-conditioned lobby was a huge relief.

"Welcome to Comunidad," Evan said.

He wiped his brow. "Does Carly own this whole building?"

Evan nodded. "She rents out a couple of floors."

It was one thing knowing his sister was rich, but another seeing the proof.

"I'll take you up to her office."

The elevator bank had a dozen elevators and it wasn't long before they were whisked to the top floor.

Evan stepped out of the elevator first and led Sean down a corridor. "Hey, Hayden, is Carly ready?"

"She's just arrived back." The man's voice was like triple-distilled whiskey — smooth and smoky. "Let me call her."

Sean stepped to the side to see who was talking and froze. He was an African-American Adonis. His hair was curly and cropped short, and his body fit the navy blue suit he was wearing to perfection. Sean snapped his mouth closed as Hayden met his eyes. The man looked him up and down with a smile as he picked up the phone.

Sean's body stirred and his head screamed NO. *Feck*. There was no way he could be attracted to someone over here. No way he could let his sisters know about his sexuality. Quickly, he glanced away as if fascinated by the artwork on the wall.

"Carly, Evan's here." There was a pause. "I'll send them right in." Hayden hung up and said, "Go right through."

"Hayden, this is Carly's brother, Sean." Evan turned to Sean. "Hayden is Carly's executive manager."

Hayden stood and held out a hand. "Nice to meet you."

"Likewise." With no real choice, he gripped the man's hand. It was warm and firm and the spark that shot through Sean was definitely unwanted. He quickly let go and followed Evan into Carly's office, not daring to look back.

He did *not* need a complication like this.

Chapter 2

Hayden Johnson watched the hot Irish man walk away, admiring the way his denim shorts molded to his butt. The lightly defined muscles in his arms and calves were damn sexy. He caught Carly's eye and grinned, fanning himself. He gave her the thumbs up and returned to his desk. Carly hadn't mentioned how good-looking her new brother was. If he wasn't mistaken, Sean had seemed attracted to him as well. It would be proof there was a God, if Sean played for the same team.

Hayden smiled. Maybe he could offer to play tour guide while Sean was in town.

Then he'd find out for sure.

Evan came out of the office a few minutes later alone. "I've left them to it," he said as he walked past. "You're coming to Casa Flanagan on Sunday aren't you?"

Hayden smiled. "Of course. We've got to go through the final details for the wedding."

"Great. I'll see you then."

Hayden waved and then glanced at the closed office door. What excuse could he use to get another peek at Carly's sexy brother? Before he could come up with anything, the phone rang and he answered it.

"Hayden, is Carly still here?"

It was Frederick, Carly's PR Executive. Hayden hesitated.

She hadn't said to hold her calls. "She's with someone."

"It's important. I need a response before she goes on leave."

He sighed. "Hold on." He put the man on hold and called Carly. "You've got Frederick on line one."

"All right."

He hung up and a few minutes later she came out with Sean. "I'm so sorry, Sean," Carly said. "I have to deal with this."

"No trouble at all. I can find my own way back."

"I wanted to show you around the building."

Grabbing the excuse, Hayden said, "I can do it."

Carly and Sean turned to him and Sean frowned. Hayden smiled. "I'm happy to give Sean the tour."

Carly hesitated.

He anticipated her next words. "It's no trouble. I've finished the report I was working on and could do with a break."

"That would be great." She turned to Sean. "Hayden knows this place almost better than I do. He'll show you everything."

"I don't want to interrupt." His Irish accent was divine and warmed Hayden's body.

"Not at all. I need to get away from my desk."

The man didn't seem all that thrilled by the idea. Maybe he wasn't gay, but one of those guys who felt threatened by homosexuals. Some of Hayden's enthusiasm waned. It wouldn't be the first time he'd got it wrong.

"Wonderful. I'll hopefully be done by the time you finish the tour and we can walk home together," Carly said and went back into her office.

A little less certain now, Hayden got to his feet and smiled. "This level is for the executives," he said, leading the way to the elevators. "The next couple of floors are for administration: finance, human resources and marketing." He hit the down button.

"I guess Comunidad employs a lot of people," Sean said.

"Globally we have a couple of thousand employees," Hayden replied, enjoying the way Sean's eyes widened. They got into the elevator and Hayden hit the button for the tech floor. "Aside from the social network, Comunidad, we maintain several different software systems, have a games division and dozens of apps."

"I never realized."

Hayden turned to him. "You didn't google Carly?"

He shrugged, the movement fluid and almost unconscious. "Only a little. Most of the stuff online was about her work and that wasn't what I wanted to know."

They arrived at the first tech floor and got out. "What did you want to know?"

Sean frowned. "I wanted to find out what kind of person she was." He avoided Hayden's gaze.

Was he uncomfortable?

Perhaps Hayden shouldn't pry, but he loved Carly and wanted to make sure this guy wasn't going to take advantage of her. "By the time you've finished the tour, you'll know more about her. The way Comunidad is run represents who Carly is."

Sean glanced at him, obviously curious, and Hayden flashed him a smile. "This is one of the Comunidad floors. The people here deal with the technical aspects of the social media platform, making sure it's always up and running, fixing bugs and helping users with questions." He led him through to the kitchen. "This is the break room."

"They're sitting on bean bags."

Hayden nodded. "Carly believes in making her staff comfortable. All the drinks are free and she provides areas where people can get away from their desks for a while. There are sofas in the brainstorming rooms." He was so conscious of Sean next to him, his body heat and his earthy scent.

"Brainstorming rooms?"

"Instead of meeting rooms. No one has their own office, so if people want to discuss ideas, they go into one of the brainstorming rooms so they don't disturb the others."

"Don't people take advantage of it?"

"Rarely," Hayden said as they walked back to the elevators. "Anyone who does doesn't last long." He hit the button for the next floor and stepped back next to Sean. Sean shifted away.

Damn. The guy was either homophobic or so far inside the closet, he couldn't see the doors. He'd dated a guy who wasn't open about his sexuality and it had led to heartache on both sides. He didn't want to go there again.

It was a shame. Sean was seriously fine.

When the doors opened, he said, "This is the advertising floor. Companies can advertise in Comunidad, but every company gets assessed before their ads are approved."

"Why?"

"Comunidad is predominantly used by migrants and refugees. They're vulnerable and sometimes ignorant. Carly doesn't want anyone taking advantage of that. Therefore, everything gets checked to make sure it's legitimate."

"That's gotta be a lot of work."

"She believes it's worth it." It was one of the many things he loved about her.

"So why migrants and refugees?" Sean asked.

"The platform is designed like a community," Hayden replied. "There are forums where people can ask questions and notice boards with upcoming events. Users can connect with people who are living in the same area. It aims to make the transition to their new country easier." He paused. "Comunidad also recycles computers and laptops, giving them to people who can't otherwise afford them, so they can connect."

Sean nodded and asked the occasional question — interesting questions, not calculating ones — as they continued the tour. He didn't appear to be assessing the company's worth, which was a relief. Hayden would hate it if he turned out to be a gold digger.

"Another tech floor?" Sean asked as they stepped out at the final stop.

"No, this is the indie hub. Carly rents space out to independent developers at a nominal price. Part of the agreement includes a Comunidad developer coming down once a day to mentor."

"Why would she do that?"

"She's been there herself. Without her own mentor, she never would have got where she is. She believes in paying it forward." He greeted a couple of the developers before taking Sean back upstairs. "Do you know Carly a bit better now?"

"Yes, thanks." He smiled politely.

As the elevator doors opened, they both walked forward at the same time. Hayden's arm brushed Sean's and Sean jumped back as if stung.

Hayden couldn't help himself. After an hour next to this man, being so conscious of him, he wanted to know his sexual inclination. "Sorry, honey." He winked.

Sean's face turned red, but there was something in his eyes — was it desire? Before Hayden could figure it out, the shutters had come down. Sean pushed past Hayden and hurried toward Carly's office.

Hayden watched him go, admiring his walk, even as disappointment filled him. He still didn't know if Sean was gay.

What he did know was that Sean was an interesting puzzle.

But did he want to solve it?

****

Relief filled Sean as he approached Carly's office and he saw her inside. He had to get away from Hayden. The man had such a presence and being next to him for an hour had kept every nerve in his body alert and twitching. But there was no way he was going there.

He stopped at the doorway and knocked on the frame. Carly looked up. "Come in. Have you finished the tour?"

"Yeah."

"What did you think?" The question was casual, but there was a little bit of vulnerability to her tone.

"It's amazing, Carly. Looks like a great place to work."

"Thanks." She beamed at him. "I'm just about finished here. Why don't you take a seat?"

Sean sat, pleased Hayden had gone back to his desk. He wouldn't see Hayden again after this. The man was dangerous for his peace of mind.

He turned his attention to Carly's office. She had two paintings on the wall. One was a farming scene, with workers in the field. The other painting was of a woman in a lush tropical garden. "Is this you?" The signature at the bottom was E. Hayes.

"No, it's Mama," Carly said. "Evan painted it."

The man was good.

"I'm ready." Carly stood and hefted a laptop bag onto her shoulder.

"Let me take that for you," Sean said, hurrying forward.

"Thank you." She handed him the bag and they walked out. Carly stopped by Hayden's desk. "You have everything you need, don't you?" she asked. "I'll have my phone with me for the rest of the week and while on honeymoon."

"And it won't ring once," Hayden said, with a gorgeous smile. "We'll manage without you and you'll have an awesome vacation."

Carly twisted her hands together.

Hayden stood and kissed her cheek. "Trust me, Carolina."

She smiled then with real affection. "Always. I'll see you later."

Sean couldn't prevent the twinge of jealousy. It was stupid. She'd known Hayden for far longer than she'd known him. Sean was the odd one out, the stranger here.

They walked to the elevators and then out of the building. The humidity hadn't lessened any, and Sean's skin immediately flushed. He tried to think of something to say as they strolled along the pavement.

"Is there anything in particular you want to do while you're in Houston?" Carly asked.

"No."

"The Space Center is interesting."

Could he be honest with her? Would it make him too vulnerable? "I just want to get to know you and Bridget and Zita." This was his last chance at having any family.

Her smile was huge and she hugged him. "And we want to get to know you."

The easy affection was surprising and soothing. He was so pathetic, soaking it up like a thirsty plant. He had to stop — that way led to pain. "How long did it take you to build Comunidad?"

"I sold my first software program when I was sixteen."

He stopped walking. "Sixteen?"

"Yeah. All I had was a secondhand laptop and an idea, but my mentor helped me sell it."

"You must be pretty smart." He began walking again.

"Determined and shy," Carly told him. "I was too socially awkward to socialize so I coded instead. What about you? What were you doing at sixteen? Chasing girls?"

"No." He looked away. How could he answer? Should he tell the truth?

She placed a hand on his arm. "You don't need to answer if you don't want. I didn't mean to pry."

Damn. The whole idea of coming here was to learn about each other, which meant he should open up as well. But he didn't want their pity. He cleared his throat. "Working."

Carly frowned at him. "At sixteen?"

He shrugged. "I was tired of school, so I got a job," he lied.

"Doing what?"

"I worked on a farm for a while, then when I turned eighteen, I got a job at the bar where I work now." They arrived at Carly's apartment building, and the interior was a blessed relief from the heat outside.

"What did your mother think?"

The bitterness swept through him. "She never had a problem with it."

"It's great she was so supportive."

Sean didn't bother to correct her.

As they entered Carly's apartment, Evan was painting. "We're home," Carly called as she shut the door behind them.

He smiled, putting down his paintbrush. "How was the tour?"

Carly sighed. "I had to get Hayden to show Sean around. Frederick had a last-minute interview for me to check."

"I'm sure Hayden was thorough," Evan said. "He loves that place almost as much as you do."

Sean didn't want to think about Hayden being thorough. It conjured all kinds of inappropriate images involving a bed and a bottle of lube.

"I know. If he wasn't there, I'd be anxious while we're away."

Sean frowned, shutting down his thoughts. "Why?"

"She's a little obsessive about Comunidad," Evan explained.

Carly screwed up her face and nodded. "He's right. I'm getting better though. Hayden showed me I could delegate more."

Sean was pleased Carly had someone she could trust, even if Hayden made him uncomfortable.

"I don't feel like cooking tonight," Carly said, taking some menus from the cupboard and throwing them on the breakfast bar. "What do you want for dinner?"

Sean hesitated. He was going to offer to pay his way as much as he could while he was here, but if he had to buy dinner every night his budget wouldn't stretch very far. "Carly, I've got a couple of hundred dollars to put toward bills and food, but I don't have much more than that."

She frowned at him. "Don't be silly. I don't want your money. I want your company."

"I don't want to be a burden."

"You're not a burden, you're my brother." She stood on her tiptoes to kiss his cheek. "It's my treat. Now what do you want for dinner?"

She was so accepting, so welcoming. He didn't deserve it.

But he wasn't going to tell her that.

Chapter 3

On Saturday Sean spent the day with his sisters and they'd taken him to the Space Center. They were so genuinely happy to spend time with him, but he wasn't used to being so social and it was tiring.

He slept late on Sunday morning and wandered into the kitchen to find Carly and Evan kissing. "Oops, sorry," he said, pivoting and walking out.

Carly laughed. "No need to apologize. Come back."

He peeked over his shoulder to see Evan getting something out of the fridge and Carly looking a little bashful. "I'll be noisier next time."

"Good idea." She laughed again and handed him a box of cereal before feeding McClane.

"What have we got planned today?" he asked, pouring himself a bowl.

"It's family lunch day at Mama's."

Sean froze for a split second before saying, "I'll amuse myself then." He'd not been brave enough to ask his sisters what Carmen thought about him.

"You don't get out of it that easily," Evan said lightly. "You're invited too."

Sean looked to Carly for confirmation.

"Of course you're invited." She placed a gentle hand on his arm. "You're family."

His heart jumped. "Not to Carmen."

"Nonsense. Mama's been dying to meet you, but she wanted to give you a chance to spend time with us first. She didn't want to scare you off when you see how crazy Casa Flanagan is."

"Crazy?" That didn't sound promising.

"Busy," Carly said.

"Vibrant and mad," Evan told him.

Carly laughed and swatted him.

Sean frowned. "Isn't Casa Flanagan the name of your charity?"

"Yes. It started with Mama fostering migrant children from Central America and so it's named after her house," Carly said. "She's got five girls at the moment plus Julio and the Garcias, so that's an extra four. It's pretty noisy."

"The more, the merrier," Evan said.

Not in his experience. He really wasn't ready to meet Carmen. Not when everything was going so well. "Are you sure?"

"Absolutely. Mama wouldn't forgive me if I didn't bring you."

"All right." He couldn't think of a gracious way to get out of it. Maybe he could fake a stomach upset before they left.

Before Sean knew it, he was in the backseat of Evan's station wagon as they drove to Casa Flanagan. His lap was being used as a pillow by McClane. It was nice to be the focus of the dog's adoration.

Sean stroked McClane, hoping it would soothe some of the anxiety inside him. He was going to meet his father's wife. He was the boy his father hadn't known he'd had, the child Brendan had left behind in Ireland when he'd gone to El Salvador. Carmen had to hate him for existing, hate him for ruining the memory she had of her dead husband, hate him for being proof her husband had been intimate with others before he'd met her.

It was inevitable.

His heart beat so loudly in his chest, he was surprised Carly and Evan couldn't hear it. McClane lifted his head and licked Sean's hand as if sensing he was tense. It was a shame he couldn't hide out with McClane over lunch.

Finally, Evan pulled into a driveway. Sean gaped at the huge two-story house that was almost hidden amongst the lush tropical plants surrounding it. Two dogs raced out to greet the car, barking. McClane stood up, wagging his tail furiously. It was a real home. His heart pinched.

Sean opened the car door and McClane leaped over his lap, one foot landing directly on Sean's crotch as he scampered out of the car. All the breath left Sean as pain seared through him.

"Are you all right?" Carly asked.

Sean nodded, sucking in the air. "McClane trod on me on the way out."

"He's heavy isn't he?"

"That too," Sean agreed, forcing himself out of the car. There were three other cars in the driveway: a very nice black mustang, a pickup truck and a red four-door sedan. The nerves returned and he took long, quiet breaths as he followed Carly and Evan into the house.

The living room was crowded. Sean wanted to hide behind Carly and Evan, but they were both shorter than he was, so he could see over their heads anyway. He spotted Bridget and Zita immediately, and they both moved forward to hug him. Relieved to see the friendly faces, he hugged them back. When they moved to the side there was an older, even shorter version of Carly standing there. Carmen.

Her eyes glistened with tears and she put her hand over her mouth.

"*Dios mío*," she breathed. "So much like my Brendan." She stepped forward. "Welcome." Her fierce hug shocked him and it took him a second to respond, to wrap his arms around the small woman who was now shaking as tears ran down her face.

He couldn't breathe, he couldn't speak. She was hugging him, *welcoming* him.

Carly shooed the rest of the people into another room as he stood there being hugged by his stepmother.

"Mama, you need to let him go eventually," Zita said with a laugh and placed her hands on her mother's shoulders.

"*Sí*. I know." Carmen stepped back. "It is too much. Brendan's boy. He would have loved you." She stroked his cheek with a tenderness he'd never known, and then took his hand and led him to a sofa. "Sit down. Tell me all about yourself."

Sean didn't know what to say, or how to react. This wasn't a scenario he'd ever imagined — and he'd imagined plenty, mostly involving rejection and accusations.

"Mama, there will be time for that," Bridget said. "Let's give Sean a chance to get used to Casa Flanagan, have some lunch, and then you can show him your garden and talk."

He shot Bridget a thankful glance.

"Of course. I am impatient, but you are right. Food first." She wiped the remaining tears from her face. "I shall finish preparing. Why don't you have a look at some of the photos in here?" She gestured to the walls before leaving.

He looked at his sisters, still not able to speak. Zita took his hand. "We don't have many photos of Papa, but some of them are up here." Photos were hung from the wall, but what caught Sean's attention was the picture of the Virgin Mary and the wooden cross with Jesus on it. Worry stirred in his gut. Religion had never been his friend. He'd been right to keep his sexuality a secret. He pushed his trepidation aside as the women showed him the evidence of how happy they had been as a family. There were a few pictures of his father and then as the girls grew older, he disappeared.

Would this have been his life if his father had known about him? Would he have come back to Ireland to claim him? Would Sean have grown up with these women as true sisters? Or would he have viewed Sean as a burden like his mother had?

There was no point playing *what if.*

He cleared his throat. "Thank you."

"It's our pleasure," Bridget said and they gave him a group hug.

He turned away and wiped his eyes with the heel of his hand. He had to get a grip on his emotions.

"Lunch is ready," Carmen called.

Carly smiled at him. "Ready to meet everyone else?"

He nodded. "As I'll ever be."

***

The dining table was huge and there had to be over a dozen people sitting at it. Sean scanned the faces, noting most of them were Hispanic teenaged girls. They must be the foster sisters. Then his eyes met familiar brown ones which were looking at him with compassion. His stomach jolted. Hayden.

What the hell was he doing here?

Carmen made the introductions and he barely heard the names as he fought to ignore Hayden's presence.

"Why don't you sit next to Hayden?" Carly said.

Sean forced a smile and nodded. "Great." His arm brushed Hayden's as he sat and there was that electric zap again. The man was far too sexy for his own good, but Sean couldn't deal with him right now. Not when his emotions were already reeling from this roller-coaster ride he was on.

"You're in for a treat," Hayden said quietly. "Carmen's gone all out today because she wasn't sure what you'd like."

There were myriad dishes on the table. "She did this for me?"

"She wants to make a good impression."

Sean frowned. How did Hayden know? "Do you come over a lot?"

"Carmen and I became friends after Carly and Evan got engaged. We've been planning the weddings together."

"All of them?"

"Absolutely. I was researching everything for Carly, so Bridget and Zita decided to use the information as well."

"Isn't that a bit outside your job description?"

Hayden's eyes narrowed. "Carly's not paying me to do it. I'm doing it for fun." He brightened. "I love weddings."

He was so enthusiastic it was hard not to smile at him.

"What about you?" Hayden asked. "Do you like weddings?"

"Carly's will be the first I've been to," Sean admitted.

"Really?" His disbelief was clear.

Sean nodded, not letting his normal defensiveness take hold. He didn't need to explain he had no close friends. It was none of Hayden's business.

He bowed his head as they said grace, and then Bridget passed him a plate of pasteles and he turned away from Hayden and began dishing up.

***

Hayden wasn't sure what to make of Sean Flanagan. There was something odd about him, something he was hiding. When Sean had walked in the door, the fear on his face had been clear and he'd physically flinched when Carmen had hugged him as if he was expecting to be hit. A thousand emotions had flashed across his face and tears had welled in his eyes. It was as if he was expecting to be rejected, or as if he'd never been hugged before.

Hayden's empathy kicked in and he wanted to ask Carly about it, but now wasn't the time.

Now he was sitting next to Mr. Delectably Different, trying to weasel some more information out of him, but he was being remarkably taciturn. "How long are you in Houston?"

"Six weeks."

"So you'll go home after Bridget's wedding?"

Sean nodded.

"What are you planning to do while you're here?"

"No plans."

"If you want some recommendations, let me know. I planned an itinerary for my aunt when she came to visit last year."

"Thanks."

Wow, a monkey would be chattier. Hayden resisted rolling his eyes. So much for Irish hospitality and gregariousness. He couldn't help himself, couldn't resist teasing. "I can show you some great gay bars."

Sean was taking a sip of his drink and he choked, slapping his hand over his mouth to swallow before coughing, his eyes wide.

"Are you all right?" Carmen asked.

Sean didn't look at Hayden. "Just swallowed down the wrong pipe."

When everyone was back to eating, Hayden whispered, "Don't worry, it's not contagious."

Sean's ears went red, but otherwise he didn't respond.

What was it about the man that made Hayden want to get a response from him? He was used to men feeling uncomfortable around him. He wasn't what he'd call flaming gay, but people couldn't doubt it after spending a couple of hours with him. He refused to hide who he was and had been open about his sexuality since he was a teen. The world could take him as he was, or not at all.

It was disappointing Sean was one of the haters. Carly had been so excited to meet him, all of the Flanagans had been. They'd spoken about him constantly in the lead-up to his arrival and Hayden had had high expectations.

It didn't really matter. It wasn't as if he was going to spend much time with Sean. He'd see him at the weddings and that was it. He wouldn't mention to Carly that her brother was homophobic.

After the lunch dishes had been cleared, Hayden sat at the table with Carly, Carmen and Evan to run through the program for the wedding on Wednesday.

He went through his list, confirming things until he came to the last point. "How is Sean getting to the wedding?" Salvadoran tradition had the bride being picked up by seven white cars, so there was room for Sean, but he wasn't sure where Sean was staying the night before.

"I didn't think of that," Carly said. "Do we have a spare bed here, Mama?"

Carmen shook her head. "No. Evan's family is staying in the cottages."

Carly wrung her hands together.

He didn't want her to worry. "I can pick him up from your apartment," Hayden said. "I'm bringing the flowers here anyway."

"Thank you, Hayden," Carly said. "You're wonderful."

He waved away her compliment. "I'll discuss the details with him before you leave." He made a note.

"I really appreciate your help," Carly said, squeezing his hand. "You've made this so easy for me."

"My absolute pleasure." He kissed her cheek. He would do anything for the woman who'd given him a chance. After he'd graduated college, he'd had a couple of jobs in quick succession. When his bosses had discovered he was gay, the dynamics had changed and while he wasn't asked to leave, it had been fairly obvious he wasn't wanted. He'd never felt unwanted at Comunidad. His sexuality had never been an issue.

"I'll tell Sean about Wednesday," Hayden said, getting to his feet.

"He's in the living room," Carly told him.

Hayden found him sitting between Zita and Bridget, chatting. Sean stiffened when Hayden walked in.

Nice.

Ignoring the pang of rejection, he forced himself to smile. "Sean, I'll be picking you up before the wedding on Wednesday."

Sean glanced at his sisters. "All right."

Carly moved over to Sean. "I'm so sorry. Evan's getting ready at Bridget and Jack's place because it's close to the venue, and I'll be getting ready here, but we don't have a spare bed."

"It's fine." Sean didn't look enthused by the proposition, but he'd just have to suck it up.

"I'll pick you up at a quarter to nine," Hayden said.

"Thanks," Sean replied, not looking at him.

The others didn't seem to notice Sean's reticence. Was it just him?

"Sean, I must show you my garden." Carmen held out a hand.

Sean smiled. "That'd be great." He kept his distance from Hayden as he followed Carmen out of the room.

Hayden sighed. He'd only have to put up with Sean for a couple more days.

He could do that.

Chapter 4

Sean was so relieved to get away from Hayden that he didn't comprehend what he'd agreed to until he reached the back door. His heart pounded. He was going to be alone with his father's wife. Was this the moment Carmen was waiting for? Was she going to turn on him and tell him to go back to where he came from, that he wasn't wanted here?

They walked outside and the heat hit him. Some of his tension disappeared as he stared at the pure beauty of the garden. There were tropical plants climbing over each other in competition and garden beds full of vegetables and flowers. It was serenity.

"There is a nice place to sit this way," Carmen said and led the way down a path.

He wasn't used to such color, such lushness. He lifted his hand and brushed the leaves of some of the plants to make sure they were real. The leaves were smooth against his skin. Reaching the garden bench, he said, "Your garden is beautiful, Carmen."

She smiled. "Thank you. It is my little hobby."

There was nothing little about it. The property had to be a couple of acres in size and aside from the sprawling garden, they'd walked past several little cottages behind the main house.

She sat and patted the space next to her.

The nerves leaped back into being. Slowly he sat next to her.

Carmen was silent and Sean couldn't think of a thing to say. His skin was tight, waiting for the accusations, the hatred, the derision. Finally, he couldn't handle the silence any longer. "I'm sorry for coming. I know this must be awful for you, having your husband's illegitimate child come here."

Carmen stared at him.

"I'll stay out of your way as much as possible," he added.

She shook her head. "No. It is *I* who must apologize to you." She placed a hand on his knee. "It is my fault Brendan didn't return to Ireland. Because of me, you didn't know your father and I'm so deeply sorry."

Sean's jaw dropped. "What?"

"If he hadn't met me, he would have returned eventually, he would have learned about your existence." She sighed. "When we decided to leave El Salvador, he wanted to return, but I didn't want to go so far from my family. If I had agreed, he would still be alive and we would have found you. You would have known your father and grown up with your sisters."

Sean's mind raced. He could barely process what Carmen was saying. Finally, he said, "But I'm not your child." Why would she want him?

She frowned. "I loved your father with all of my heart. He was everything that was good and kind." She patted his leg. "You are Brendan's child, and so you are my child." Her smile was uncertain. "You do not know me, and you have your own mother, but I would like to be your friend if you would have me. Over time you might even be comfortable enough to call me Mama."

He couldn't breathe. Was she kidding? No one had ever wanted him. He wanted to say yes, wanted to pull her close and hug her tightly, but he couldn't. She didn't know him. When she discovered he was gay, she would retract her words – being gay was a sin. He didn't dare get attached.

"I have made you uncomfortable. I'm sorry." She got to her feet.

"No." He grabbed her hand. He didn't know what to say, but he didn't want her to feel bad. "It's a surprise. I wasn't expecting everyone to be so welcoming." He would be as honest as he could. "I expected you to hate me. I thought my existence would ruin Brendan's memory for you."

"Never," she said fiercely, squeezing his hand. "I could never hate anything of Brendan's. He always wanted a son."

Sean's skin was being peeled back and all his insides exposed. Everything she said was part balm and part sorrow. He couldn't afford to get attached, to let his guard down. If he did, her later rejection would destroy him. "That's nice to know." It was the master of all understatements, but he couldn't tell her how he really felt.

"If you have any questions about your father, you can ask me. I will tell you everything."

He nodded. He longed to hug her, but he wasn't brave enough.

She wrapped her arms around him.

He relaxed, hugging her back, drawing comfort from her.

She stepped back. "Would you like to see the rest of my garden?"

"Yes, please."

She tugged him to his feet. "This way."

***

On Wednesday, Hayden was on the phone all morning, making sure the cars were on their way and answering last-minute questions from the reception venue. He was running a couple of minutes late by the time he pulled up in front of Carly's apartment building to pick up Sean. He parked illegally in the loading zone and dialed Sean's cell number as he hurried into the building. Then he spotted Sean.

Damn, he looked fine. The charcoal gray suit he wore was sublime, and the blue tie brought out the color of his eyes. Hayden's body stirred as he hung up the phone and walked over to him. "Sorry I'm late," he said, giving what he hoped was a friendly smile.

Sean's eyes widened and he did such a quick up and down check-out of Hayden that Hayden would have thought he'd imagined it if Sean hadn't flushed.

"You ready to go?" Hayden asked. He was tired of the mixed messages, but he was determined to be on his best behavior today, and that included not baiting Mr. Might-be-gay-or-not.

"Sure."

Sean's accent sent shivers down Hayden's spine. Quickly he

moved outside and opened the car door for Sean. The man hesitated and, annoyed, Hayden left him to it and went around to the driver's side.

They had a whole hour's drive before they arrived at Casa Flanagan and he should clear the air with Sean. He didn't want to irritate the man and have him moody for Carly's wedding. He'd try small talk first. "What have you been up to?" he asked as he pulled into the traffic.

"Not much."

"Are you comfortable at Carly's?"

"Yeah."

"Have you seen much of Bridget and Zita?"

"A bit."

Hayden sighed. "Are you always this chatty or is it me?"

Sean was silent for so long Hayden didn't think he'd reply. "Sorry. I'm not much of a talker."

Hayden frowned. "Don't you work in a bar? I thought all Irish bartenders had the gift of the gab."

He chuckled and the sound was kind of musical. "Our regulars like a chat, but that means they talk and I listen."

"Are you their confessional?"

"Sometimes. Mostly they just like to have a yarn." Sean's shoulders relaxed and his hands unclenched.

"What's the bar like? Do people break into song all the time?"

He snorted. "No. We have music on a Friday and Saturday night."

"Sounds cozy."

"It's nice enough."

"Have you worked there long?"

Sean stiffened. "Twelve years."

Hayden frowned. It was an innocuous question. Why was he so tense all of a sudden? "So what do you do in your spare time?"

"Not much."

He sighed. Back to short answers. "Play any instruments?"

"The tin whistle."

"What's that?"

"It's a six-holed woodwind instrument – kind of like a

recorder."

"Oh, right. Are you any good?"

"I can hold a tune."

"Know any good Irish songs?"

"A few."

Hayden glanced at him. "Zita wanted to have a mix of Irish, Salvadoran and American traditions at her wedding. Could you play something?"

"I don't know."

Hayden had never met a more reticent guy. "Do you play at the bar's music nights?"

"Sometimes."

Hayden pushed. "You'd be doing me a huge favor if you could play a song. Zita would love it."

"If she wants me to, I will." Sean's response was a little reluctant.

Perhaps he wasn't any good. He'd have to get a demonstration. "I'll ask."

Silence fell, but it wasn't as tense as it had been when Sean first got into the car.

"What do you do for fun?" Sean asked.

The question was so unexpected that Hayden looked at Sean. He glanced away, obviously uncomfortable. Well, the guy was trying. "I hang out with my friends," Hayden told him. "We go dancing."

"Sounds like fun."

"You like to dance?" Color him surprised.

"I used to when I was younger."

"You don't have much dancing in the pub?"

"No." He smiled.

Sean's smile really was quite something. It was only small, a slight upturn at the edges, but it made him far more approachable.

Hayden debated for a split second and then said, "You're welcome to come out with me on the weekend."

"To a gay bar?" The tension was back.

"Doesn't have to be."

"I'll think about it."

Geez, the guy really knew how to make him feel like a leper.

Exasperated, Hayden didn't bother continuing the conversation. It wasn't often that his sexuality was an issue. Everyone at work accepted him or did a good job hiding it, and he didn't tend to hang out in places that shunned his kind. He made a conscious effort to push the annoyance away. He didn't want to be upset. Carly was one of his favorite people in the world and she was getting married. He wanted to be happy and celebrate.

Why should his sexuality matter?

They arrived at Casa Flanagan, and the white cars were already in the drive. Zita's dogs were nowhere to be seen, which meant they were probably inside. Hayden parked out of the way and then got the first bouquet of flowers out from the backseat. Sean grabbed another couple without needing to be asked and they walked to the front door. Hayden walked inside.

"Shouldn't you knock?" Sean asked.

"No need. They know me." Carmen had scolded him the last time he'd knocked, telling him he was family. To appease the Irishman, he called, "The men have arrived."

"We're upstairs," Bridget called.

Hayden placed the flowers on the dining room table before moving upstairs with Sean. There was a gaggle of women hovering outside Carmen's bedroom all dressed in their finest.

Elena, one of the foster sisters, turned to him. "They're helping Carly into her dress." She grinned.

Hayden stopped where he was. "We'll wait here then." He didn't need to see his friend and boss in her underwear.

A few minutes later Carly came out.

She was exquisite. The white dress was strapless with a sweetheart bodice that clung to her curves before flowing in a wider skirt to the ground.

"You look stunning, honey," he said, kissing her cheek.

"Thanks." She beamed at him and then glanced at Sean.

He smiled. "You're like a shining star in the night's sky."

Hayden softened toward the man as Carly's eyes watered. If he kept this up, he'd be all right. Checking the time, he said, "I'd better get the rest of the flowers."

"I'll help," Sean offered, surprising Hayden.

"Thanks."

Together, they went downstairs, and it didn't take them long to bring the bouquets inside. Everyone was crowded into the living room and the photographer was getting a couple of photos.

Sean stood at the edge of the group, shifting his feet, seemingly engrossed by the photos on the walls.

"I'll be off," Hayden told Carly. "I've got to get the boutonnieres to the guys."

"No problem. I'll see you there."

He turned to go when Sean stopped him. "Could I go with you?"

Though surprised, he said, "Sure. Too much estrogen?"

He nodded.

"Carly, I'm taking your brother," he called.

"Oh, wait a second. I want a photo with all my siblings." She grabbed Sean and dragged him over to Zita and Bridget.

Hayden saw the disbelief on Sean's face before he hid it. Sean seemed constantly amazed by any form of affection.

When they got back into the car, Hayden asked, "Do you have any siblings in Ireland?"

"No."

"Must be hard, coming from being an only child, to suddenly having three sisters." He was prying, but he couldn't help it.

Sean let out a whoosh of air. "They keep surprising me." He ran a hand through his hair, and then pulled down the sun visor to check it. "That was my first family photograph."

"You don't have any photos with your mom?"

"No."

What did that say about Sean? Hadn't Sean's mother cared enough to take photos?

It would explain the absolute shock on Sean's face when Carmen had hugged him on Sunday. Hayden's heart went out to him. He'd be more sympathetic to the guy.

"I imagine you'll be in a whole heap more photos by the end of the day," Hayden said. "You'll be sick of smiling."

"That'd be nice." There was a wistful look on his face.

Damn, maybe he'd misinterpreted Sean completely. He wanted to ask him more questions, but he resisted the urge. He didn't want to upset him.

They arrived at the reception venue, which was a beautiful

big building surrounded by a couple of acres of lush gardens, and went inside. A lot of people were milling in the foyer, but not the groomsmen. Hayden went into the ceremony room where he found Evan talking with the celebrant, his three groomsmen next to him.

"Hi Hayden, Sean," Evan said.

"Got your boutonnieres here," Hayden said, handing out the flowers and then helping them pin them properly.

"Have you seen Carly?" Evan asked.

"Yes, and she looks stunning," Hayden told him. "They were having photographs when we left, but they won't be too far behind."

"Should we get people seated?"

"Let's wait until the cars arrive. The girls are going to want to have a seat close to the front." Hayden turned to Sean. "You'll be in the front row with Carmen."

Sean's eyes widened and he nodded.

Hayden left Sean with the guys and went to check everything was in place. He found the venue's consultant in the reception hall.

"I was wondering when you'd turn up," she said.

He laughed. "I trust you've got everything organized, but I need to check."

She smiled. "Take a look and let me know."

She wasn't upset. They'd formed a good relationship while he was organizing Carly's wedding. He did a quick walk through and everything was as he'd planned. He wandered out to the foyer as the first of the seven cars pulled up outside.

"Can everyone take their seats now, please?" he called, and when people started moving, he went out to the cars to see if anything else was needed. Aside from the drivers, it was a sea of women. He walked over to Carly.

"Oh, Hayden, I'm glad to see you," Carly said.

"What can I do?" he asked.

She twisted her hands. "I wanted to ask Sean a favor. Could you bring him out here?"

"Of course." Carly was worried about something. He hoped Sean would do whatever she asked of him.

He hurried inside.

***

A hand on Sean's shoulder made him flinch. Someone was going to ask him to move from the front row. He glanced up to Hayden's gorgeous face above him. The man was distinguished and delectable in a navy blue three-piece suit.

"Carly wants you outside," Hayden said.

Crap. This was when she'd say there'd been a mistake, that they'd invited too many people and he had to go home. She'd say she didn't really want him here. With a heavy heart, he nodded and followed Hayden outside to where Carly, Bridget, Zita and Carmen were waiting. Bridget and Zita both looked gorgeous in cherry-red knee-length dresses. He approached the group and Bridget, Zita and Carmen moved away. He braced himself and forced a smile to his face. "Hayden said you wanted to see me."

Her smile was a little uncertain. "I wanted to ask you a favor."

"Anything." He didn't want to make this hard on her.

Her smile grew a little brighter. "I don't want you to feel you have to, not if it makes you uncomfortable."

She was nervous. Protectiveness swept over him, surprising him. "What do you need?"

"I was wondering whether you might walk me down the aisle. You and Mama together." There was such hope on her face.

Sean froze, sure he'd heard incorrectly. "You want me to walk you down the aisle?"

She nodded.

Was he ever going to get used to the shock of actually being wanted? He swallowed hard. "I'd be honored."

"Thank you." She hugged him.

"You're most welcome," he managed to say.

She turned to the others. "He said yes."

"Wonderful," Carmen said. "We should go inside. We don't want to keep Evan waiting."

Sean offered Carly his arm and together they walked inside. Hayden cued the music and took his seat. When the music began, Zita walked in first, followed by Bridget and then, with

Carmen on the other side, he walked Carly down the aisle.

The expression on Evan's face when he saw Carly was breathtaking. There was love, admiration and affection all in the one look. Sean couldn't imagine anyone ever looking at him like that. He handed Carly to Evan when the time was right and took his seat next to Carmen. She took his hand, squeezing it tightly, and dabbed her eyes with a tissue.

Sean barely listened to the service. He was too busy soaking up the experience and the energy. He cheered along with the rest of the crowd when the couple kissed and walked out of the room as husband and wife.

By the time the photos had been taken, Hayden's premonition had come true. Sean was sick of smiling and sick of the crowd. There were about seventy people there and he'd been introduced to all of them. He needed five minutes of peace. There were too many people around, all wanting to speak with him.

The MC finally announced that lunch would be served and Sean breathed a sigh of relief. At least he would only have to speak with the people at his table. He checked his allocation. He was sitting next to Hayden. *Damn.* Hayden was a genuinely nice guy, but Sean couldn't let down his guard around him. He didn't want to be a blip on Hayden's gaydar.

"How are those cheeks?" Hayden asked as he sat.

"Sore."

"Told you." He smiled. "You can relax and rest them now. Lunch is going to be sensational."

The person on his right sat and he got a waft of sweet perfume. He screwed up his nose and turned to say hello.

"I'm Amy, Evan's cousin," the brunette said. She was in her mid-twenties and perky.

"Sean. Carly's brother." It felt so weird to say that.

"Ooh, that's a sexy accent you've got there, Sean. Where are you from? Australia?"

Hayden chuckled and Sean tried not to smile. "Ireland."

"Even better," she purred, placing a hand on his arm. "How long are you in town?"

Hell. This was all kinds of awkward. "Not long," he lied.

"Me neither." She winked at him. "Sounds perfect."

He cleared his throat. He wasn't used to women hitting on him. The average age of his pub regulars was fifty. Before he could come up with a suitable response, the first course was served.

Hayden was right. The food was sensational. His was some kind of shrimp dish with a light, tangy sauce. Completely different from his usual pub grub.

"So, Sean, how do you like the States?" Amy asked, and took a long swig of her champagne.

"It's hot."

Amy laughed. "Houston's the worst. You should check out New York. It's much nicer."

"Is that where you're from?"

"Sure am."

Sean relaxed a little. She was just being friendly. He could handle friendly. "What do you do there?"

"I'm a teacher."

They chatted for a while, but her enthusiasm and energy was exhausting. He needed some fresh air. He drained his glass and said to her, "I'll just find a refill." He got to his feet.

"I'll show you where," Hayden said with a smile.

Not able to refuse, Sean nodded and gestured for him to lead the way. Waiters were beginning to bring out the main course. They'd reached the foyer before Sean realized Hayden wasn't showing him to a drinks table. "Where are we going?"

Hayden opened a door that led outside to a small courtyard. "You looked like you needed a break."

Sean stared at him and Hayden gestured for him to go in. "Honey, if you sat any stiffer than you were, you'd have snapped in half."

Too relieved to deny it, Sean walked onto the pavement and took a deep breath. Even the heat didn't bother him. "Thanks."

"You're not one for crowds are you?"

He shook his head.

"Doesn't that make your job difficult?"

"No. They stay on the other side of the bar."

Hayden nodded in understanding. "Take your time. I can get them to reheat your lunch when you come back in."

He was so incredibly sweet and perceptive. Sean didn't want to be attracted to him, but it was hard not to be. The man knew what he wanted. "I appreciate it."

Hayden smiled and left, shutting the door behind him.

Sean sat on the stone bench and breathed deeply. The murmur of voices and clattering of cutlery was background noise. Here he was alone.

He was better when he was alone. No expectations, no need to pretend to be someone he wasn't, no pressures. He closed his eyes to center himself. He'd learned the technique from one of his workmates when she'd realized he was having a panic attack.

He needed time to absorb the moment. He was at his sister's wedding. He'd walked her down the aisle. Five months ago, he hadn't known his sisters existed, and now they wanted him to be part of their lives. He couldn't express what that meant to him. They were so welcoming and honest. But he was lying to them, pretending to be someone he wasn't. If he was being honest, he'd be flirting with Hayden, hoping they'd hook up while he was here.

But he couldn't be.

He had to hide his attraction, ignore it, pretend he was straight so his sisters would still like him.

To be rejected again when he'd finally found family would be too much.

He breathed deeply. They never needed to know. He'd be back in Ireland in a few weeks, back to his normal existence where he hid who he was. The thought held no appeal.

He sighed. His food would be getting cold.

He walked back inside and as he approached his table, Hayden spotted him and gestured to a waiter. By the time Sean sat down, he had a hot plate of food in front of him. "Thank you," he said to Hayden.

"My pleasure. You feeling better now?"

He nodded.

"They're not using the courtyard today, so you can go out as often as you need." His smile was gentle and understanding.

Sean's heart thudded in his chest as he gazed into Hayden's eyes. He'd never felt this level of attraction for anyone before. Usually, he hooked up for a night, but Hayden was someone he

wanted to get to know.
That was a very bad thing.

Chapter 5

After lunch and the speeches, the dancing started. Amy tried to get him to dance with her, but Sean politely refused.

Men don't dance.

Only gays do.

His mother might have been sitting right next to him — her voice was so clear in his head.

He scowled. He wasn't ten anymore and telling her he wanted to join the town musical society.

Everyone was having a ball on the dance floor. Sean tapped his foot in time with the music as Bridget and Zita shimmied with Jack, David and Hayden. Hayden sure knew how to dance. The man was insanely rhythmic and the way he moved his hips made Sean think of sex. He blocked the thought and scanned the room. At least he wasn't the only one not dancing. Carly had only danced the bridal dance before sitting back down.

Hayden glanced over at him and then said something to Zita. Zita grinned and made a beeline to him.

Sean tensed.

"Why aren't you dancing?" she asked, holding out a hand.

"I don't dance."

"Hayden said you used to dance as a kid."

He'd forgotten he'd mentioned it. "I'm out of practice."

"Well, now's a good opportunity," she said, and tugged him to his feet. "I want to dance with my big brother."

His heart tugged at the word *brother.* He couldn't refuse her. One song, and then he'd sit back down. He let the beat flood his body and he began to move. Bridget grinned at him and gave him a thumbs up. It was so good to feel the music and let go. When the song ended, he wanted to keep dancing, but he'd risked enough. He didn't want any attention. Jack and David had left the floor to get drinks, and now he and Hayden were the only men left there. He turned to go.

"Not so fast," Bridget called and grabbed his hand. "You haven't danced with me yet."

Not able to say no, he danced with his other sister. Then the music slowed and he moved off the floor. Carly intercepted him. "This one's my dance," she said.

She led him back onto the dance floor and put a hand on his shoulder. "I'm a hopeless dancer, but I wanted to dance with you."

His heart swelled and he gently led her around the dance floor. She was kind of awkward, not able to pick the rhythm, but she just laughed. He laughed with her. "Ready? One, two, three, four. One, two, three, four." Even counting the steps didn't help. When the song ended, she kissed his cheek. "Thank you."

The music changed to an upbeat Latin tune and he accompanied her back to where Evan was chatting to someone from his family.

"My turn," a voice said behind him.

It was Carmen. She did a little salsa step and held out her hand. Sean had always loved Latin music. He put his hand in hers and let her lead him to the floor. She showed him the basic step and they went from there. Or rather he continued to do the step she'd taught him and she danced around him, spinning and moving with the beat. He relaxed, added a shoulder shimmy to match Carmen and anticipated her next twirl. The song ended and Carmen dipped into a curtsy. His heart was racing as he brought her hand up to his mouth and kissed it. "Thank you."

"No, thank you," she said. "You are good. Have you had lessons?"

He shook his head.

She put a hand to her heart. "Imagine what you could do with lessons! I can teach you. Then we can dance at the other weddings."

He glanced around. No one cared that he was dancing. "I'd

like that." He met Hayden's eyes and they were dark, intense. Sean knew exactly what they meant. Attraction.

Feck.

He couldn't go there. As much as he wanted to keep dancing, it was too dangerous. "I'm going to get a drink. Would you like one?" he asked Carmen.

"No, thank you."

He walked over to the small bar and got a glass of water. He needed to get away. Wandering out of the reception hall, he went into the courtyard and sat down, sipping his drink.

Nothing good would come of his attraction to Hayden. His first gay experience had taught him that. From then on, he'd kept his sex life completely separate from the rest of his life. He worked at the bar, kept his regulars happy, listening to them talk about their lives, and when he needed a release, he'd go to Dublin for the weekend and spend his time at the gay bars there.

It worked for him.

"Thought I'd find you here."

Sean tensed and looked up straight into Hayden's eyes. Damn. He glanced away so Hayden didn't see his desire. "Taking a break," he said, holding up the glass of water.

"You've got some pretty good moves for someone who doesn't dance."

"It came back to me."

Hayden raised an eyebrow. "That was lucky."

They both knew he was lying.

"If you want to check out some clubs while you're here, the Sizzle Bar and Beach Bar are good places to go."

Were they gay bars? He didn't dare ask. "Thanks."

"No problem. A guy who can dance like you should be showing it off." Hayden smiled and then walked away.

Sean let out a deep breath and adjusted himself. He couldn't go there. No matter how much he wanted to.

***

It was early evening when Carly and Evan left the reception. They were heading to a hotel for their wedding night before flying out for their honeymoon. The guests began to leave and

Hayden transferred the few wedding gifts into his car. He was going to drop them at Carly's apartment when he took Sean home.

Carmen and the girls were saying goodbye to everyone and the boys were gathering up the few things they'd brought with them.

"Need a hand?"

Hayden paused. Just Sean's accent could stir him. He slowly turned. Hayden had done his best to avoid Sean for the rest of the afternoon. Watching Sean dance had made him throb, and he hadn't wanted to be walking around in a constant state of semi-arousal. What he did want was to clear up the question of Sean's sexuality, but he wouldn't ask. He didn't want to make things awkward for the rest of Sean's stay and he knew better than to chase someone who wasn't out of the closet.

But damn if the man wasn't intriguing.

"I'm taking the gifts to the car," he said. "You can help if you want."

They worked in silence, Hayden aware of Sean's presence at each moment. When they were done, he had a few words with the venue's consultant to make sure everything had been dealt with and then checked to see if Carmen and the girls were ready to go.

"*Sí*," Carmen said, kissing his cheek. "Thank you for your help. Are you giving Sean a ride home?"

"Yeah."

"Wonderful." She kissed Sean as well. "Do you have plans tomorrow?"

"I think I need a day to recover," Sean said with a smile.

"You have my number if you need anything," Carmen said. "I wish you weren't staying there alone while Carly's away."

"I'll see the girls most days anyway."

She nodded and said goodbye.

Hayden waited until they were in the car before he asked, "You're not moving in with Zita?"

"No. I'm taking care of McClane and the fish while Carly's away." He didn't sound like he minded. "Zita has most of my days planned anyway. She's not starting college for another month, so she's got time now that the woman she rescued from

El Salvador has taken over at Casa Flanagan."

"Johanna," Hayden supplied the name for Sean. "How did you like your first wedding?"

"It was amazing. Carly and Evan suit each other, don't they?"

"Yeah, they're pretty special." He glanced at Sean. "Have you got anyone in Ireland?"

"No. I don't do relationships."

That was a warning sign. Still, Hayden was intrigued. "Not at all? You don't want to get married?"

Sean shook his head.

"Why not?"

Sean shrugged, turned away. "I wouldn't know how to behave."

Hayden frowned. "You'd be yourself."

His laugh was bitter. "That doesn't work."

There was such pain in his voice that Hayden's heart went out to him. "When you find the right person, it's easy to be yourself. Carly showed me that."

"Maybe." He'd tensed up again and was hunched over in the corner, so Hayden let it be. When they arrived at the apartment, they took a couple of trips to get the gifts upstairs and then Hayden stood in the hallway. "Thanks for your help today."

"No problem." Sean wouldn't look at him, and Hayden was acutely aware they were completely alone. No one was going to walk in on them here. Should he say something? Ask if he was gay? Invite him to go dancing?

No. He wasn't that desperate, wasn't a glutton for punishment. "I'll see you around."

"Yeah."

Hayden walked out, closing the door behind him. There was something about Sean that got him all hot and bothered. He needed to let off some steam before he saw him again.

Hopefully, it would help.

On his way down in the elevator, he called his friend Max. "Want to go out tonight?"

"Didn't you have a wedding today?" Max asked.

"Yeah, but I need this."

"I'll meet you at the Cider House at nine."

Hayden let out a deep breath. Max never let him down.

There was a good crowd already at the Cider House when Hayden arrived. He'd stopped at home to change into skinny leg pants and a cute green top. Hayden waved to a few people he knew while scanning the room for Max. He was at the bar flirting with the bartender, Terry.

Hayden smiled as he walked over. "You don't waste any time."

Max fluttered his eyelashes at Hayden. "Just making sure Terry hasn't forgotten me."

"How could I?" Terry responded, handing Max his cocktail.

"Isn't he sweet?" Max fanned himself before taking a sip.

"What'll it be, Hayden?" Terry asked.

"Martini."

Max gave him his full attention. "Was the wedding that bad?"

Hayden shook his head. "It was lovely. It's something else."

Max glanced around. "There's a table in the corner of the mezzanine. I'll grab it."

People often underestimated his friend because he was all of five foot three, wiry build and effeminate, but Max always saw right to the heart of matters. Hayden paid for his drink and carried it over to the table Max had nabbed. The mezzanine floor was more of a raised section of the bar which allowed patrons to easily view the dance floor and check out who had arrived. It was amazing that there was a table free.

"So spill," Max said as Hayden sat down.

Now he was here, he wasn't sure what to say. "The wedding was gorgeous. Carly and Evan are so happy together."

Max gave him *the* look. "So why did you call me?"

It was so stupid now that he thought about it. He was lusting after a guy that was most probably straight. He knew what Max was going to say about that.

"Hayden." Max put a hand over his.

"I told you about Carly's brother, didn't I?"

"The one she's only just discovered she had? Her father got some woman pregnant in Ireland before he went to El Salvador and met her mother, right?"

Hayden nodded.

"Is he cute?"

He sighed. "No. He's incredibly hot."

Max clapped his hands together. "Is he gay?"

"I don't know."

Max frowned. "Your gaydar's usually spot on."

"Right now it's going haywire."

"Tell me everything."

So Hayden did. He told him about the mixed signals and how attracted he was to Sean.

"My lovely, this isn't going to end well." Max used his stern voice. "If he is gay, he's in the closet and that will only bring heartache to you. He's here for what, a few weeks?"

Hayden nodded.

"It's not worth it, my friend. What we need to do is find you someone to hook up with so you can forget about him." Max perused the floor below. "Oh, how about the cutie by the bar? The blond."

Hayden scanned the bar and his heart leaped. He squinted, sure his eyes were playing tricks on him. "*Damn.*"

"I know, right? I sure can pick them." Max grinned.

"No. *That's* Carly's brother."

Max's eyes widened. "There's your answer then."

Hayden shook his head. He couldn't get his hopes up. "Maybe he wandered into the wrong bar."

Max raised an eyebrow.

"He's from Ireland."

"I'll go and talk with him." Max stood up. "If he flirts with me, you know he's one of us and you can come and say hello."

Hayden hesitated. Sean was likely to freak out if he saw Hayden. But damn, there was something about the man that made his body throb.

Max squeezed himself into a place at the bar next to Sean and gave him his patented "I think you're hot" look.

Sean actually smiled at him, didn't seem the least bit uncomfortable. Then he ordered Max a drink. Max waved Hayden over and gave a thumbs up.

Hayden's heart raced.

Well, that answered that question.

Now, what the hell was he going to do about it?

***

Sean walked into the Cider House and every muscle in his body relaxed. These were his people, this was the place where he could be who he really was. There were quite a few people there, some sitting at the bar, others dancing to the latest hits on the small dance floor, and some sitting at tables together. The music wasn't overly loud, but it didn't inhibit the people on the floor. After a quick internet search, he'd chosen this place because it was some distance away from the other bars Hayden had mentioned — which *had* been gay bars. He didn't want to risk bumping into the man.

He received a few interested glances as he moved to the bar and inwardly he smiled. He had no problem being checked out here. Here he could be gay and no one was going to judge him. He ordered a cider and as it arrived, someone squeezed in next to him.

"Hello, handsome." The African-American guy was slim and a good six inches shorter than Sean. His obvious scan of Sean's body made Sean smile.

"Hello."

"I'm Max. You're not from around here." He held out his hand and Sean shook it. It was a little limp-wristed for Sean's taste, but the guy was cute.

"Sean. I'm from Ireland."

"How long have you been in Houston?"

"About a week."

"A tourist, huh? Well, Sean, honey, I've made this mistake before, so I need to confirm — you know you've walked into a gay bar, don't you?"

Sean laughed and glanced around at all of the men in the room. "Yeah, I figured. Can I buy you a drink?"

Max positively beamed. "Yes, please. A cosmopolitan."

Sean ordered the drink from a very butch man who smiled at him broadly. He was glad he'd come. This was what he needed to take his mind off Hayden. He needed a night to be himself so he could put the mask back on tomorrow. He'd be able to resist Hayden if he took this time now.

The drink was placed in front of Max and Sean paid.

"I got a table over there," Max said. "Want to join us?"

There was someone sitting at a table on the raised section of the bar, but it was too dark to make out their face. "Sure." He grabbed his glass and followed Max. The floor was quite crowded and he carefully maneuvered around people and furniture, his eyes on Max. He was about six feet away when he glanced at the table. He froze.

Hayden.

Feck. All the blood drained from his face and the glass slipped from his hand, smashing on the floor. The drink splashed on his jeans and his heart pounded like a death march in his chest.

"Don't move, honey," Max said. "I'll get Terry to clean it up." He hurried off.

Sean couldn't move.

Hayden sat there, a half smile on his face. He twitched his fingers in a wave.

What the hell was he going to do now? He couldn't deny who he was anymore.

Hayden got to his feet and reached out a hand. "Why don't you sit down before you faint?"

That voice was sin. He automatically took hold of Hayden's hand and let himself be led to the table. As he sat, he put his head in his hands. "*Feck.*"

Hayden rubbed his back. "I won't tell anyone."

Sean squeezed his eyes shut, trying to ignore the comfort of Hayden's touch. He couldn't hope Hayden was telling the truth. He didn't know the man well enough. He was Carly's executive manager, her friend, why would he keep something like this from her? He panted, his breath coming in short bursts. He was going to start hyperventilating, he could feel it.

"Breathe, Sean," Hayden said. "Slow breaths. It's all right. Really, it is."

"Honey, don't panic." It was Max and he wrapped his arm around Sean's shoulder. "You're safe here." There was a pause and then, "My friend Hayden here doesn't normally get such a bad reaction. I mean, I know he's not as pretty as me, but he can't help that."

Sean couldn't stop his bark of laughter. This *so* wasn't funny.

"Here, I got you some water." Max pushed a glass against his folded arms.

He had to look up. Hiding wasn't going to change matters. He glanced at Max. "Thanks." He took a sip and then braced himself and looked at Hayden. "Hi."

Hayden's smile was warm and slow. "Hi, Sean. Fancy seeing you here."

Damn the man was the sexiest thing he'd ever seen. Was it no wonder he was having such a hard time? He needed to make it clear, he needed to make Hayden understand why it was so important that he say nothing to Carly, or any of the Flanagans.

"I don't want my family to know."

Hayden nodded. "They won't care. Carly's never had a problem with my sexuality."

"But you're not related to her."

Hayden raised an eyebrow. "None of my family care I'm gay."

Max took Sean's hand. "You know you're one of the lucky ones," he said to Hayden. "Not everyone's like your family."

Hayden frowned. "Do you believe Carly would care?"

Max shook his head. "No, but I haven't met the rest of her family."

Sean squeezed Max's hand. He had someone who was on his side. Maybe between the two of them, they could convince Hayden to keep quiet. "Please, Hayden."

"I won't tell them," Hayden assured him. "I'm not going to out you if you're not ready, but you need to know your sisters won't have a problem that you're gay."

He couldn't risk it. Not now when their relationship was still so new, so fragile. Not when past experiences had taught him otherwise.

"You can trust him," Max said.

He let out a breath. "Thank you."

"Well, that was a little bit more excitement than I was expecting," Max said. "I'm going to dance."

Sean wanted to ask him to stay or to go with him, but he had to face Hayden sooner or later.

"Your mom didn't take the news very well." It was a

statement more than a question from Hayden.

"No."

"Want to talk about it?"

"Not right now." Not ever.

"All right." Hayden finished his drink. "Come on. We both came here to let our hair down," he said, holding out a hand. "Let's dance."

Sean took his hand and let himself be pulled onto the dance floor. The music was good and he felt the rhythm, moved his body. Hayden was right. He needed to forget about the outside world for tonight. That was why he came here. To be himself.

A song came on which was primal, sexual. Watching Hayden dance made Sean throb. He moved closer, wanting to hold on to Hayden and press himself against him.

Was he that brave?

Hayden opened his eyes and grinned at him. He pulled Sean close and then they were together, dancing, grinding up against each other in time with the music. His body was hot, hard and wanting, and the rub of his crotch against Hayden was almost too much.

Hayden wrapped his arms around Sean's shoulders and then his lips were on his.

Instant fire. The man's lips were thick and hard and so *fecking* right. Sean pulled him closer and matched him kiss for kiss, tasting him, and the flick of Hayden's tongue left Sean panting.

The song ended, but the kiss didn't.

Sean didn't want it to ever end. There was so much want and need, and it was everything Sean had been fantasizing about since he'd met Hayden.

Hayden broke the kiss first and stared at him, his breath fast. There was surprise in his eyes as if he was stunned by the intensity between them.

"My house isn't far from here," Hayden said.

Sean hesitated for only a split second. This was his fantasy, he would give himself this night. "Let's go."

Chapter 6

After a quick goodbye to Max, they caught a cab to Hayden's place. Hayden took Sean's hand and kissed it, needing to touch him, to taste him.

"None of that stuff while you're in my cab," the driver said.

Sean flinched as if he'd been struck and snatched his hand back. Hayden wanted to curse the driver, but it would only get them kicked out. He stayed silent until they arrived and got out.

"Ignore him," Hayden said, meeting Sean on the sidewalk and taking his hand again.

Sean pulled away once more. "Can we get inside first?"

The hurt was sharp, but the misery on Sean's face was enough to temper it. It appeared that gay bars were the only safe place to be openly gay. He led the way up the steps to his house and opened the door. Did he want this hookup, would he be happy with a quick fuck and then to go back to pretending they weren't attracted to each other?

He wasn't sure.

Once they were inside and the door was locked, Sean backed him against the front door. The kiss was desperate, and Hayden ignored his concerns, swept up in Sean's taste and the way his lips moved against his own. Perhaps this was all he needed, perhaps it was all either of them wanted. Sean was a damn good kisser. Imagine if they'd had the chance to sneak off to that hidden courtyard today and kiss.

Sean cupped Hayden's crotch and desire shot through him, but Hayden broke away. If Sean wasn't out, how experienced was he? "Honey, we need to talk."

"Later."

The raw need on Sean's face was almost enough to make Hayden forget his worries. He kissed Sean's neck as he murmured, "Have you done this before?"

"Are you saying I'm no good?" Sean asked, stepping away, hurt on his face.

"No. Definitely not." To prove it, Hayden kissed him again, taking his time, enjoying the passion. He ran his hands down Sean's back and grabbed his ass. "I just thought if you're not out, you might not have much experience."

"I go to Dublin every few months."

Hayden looked at him. "And that's the only time you get to be yourself?" It was sad. Why did Sean feel he had to hide from everyone?

Sean shrugged. "The town where I live is conservative." Then he kissed Hayden again and slipped his hands under his shirt and Hayden forgot to be concerned. Sean clearly knew what he was doing.

Hayden grabbed his hand and pulled him toward the bedroom. "When were you last tested?"

"After my last trip to Dublin. I'm clear. You?"

"Me too." Hayden heeled out of his shoes before running his hands under Sean's top. The man was ripped. "Hello, gorgeous," Hayden breathed and sucked on Sean's nipple. Sean groaned and pushed Hayden onto the bed, then stripped his own shirt off and undid his pants.

Hayden wasted no time unzipping himself, but the skinny-leg pants got stuck halfway down his thighs. Sean growled and ripped them off.

Hayden was going to combust. The man was pure sex. How could he ever have doubted he was gay?

Then they were both naked and his penis rubbed against Sean's. Hell, he wasn't going to last at this pace. He wanted to slow things down, explore Sean's body, discover what made him moan. He dragged Sean's mouth back to his and kissed him, all the while the friction between them built.

"Come for me, Hayden."

The demand shattered what control he had left. He yelled, coming hard, and a moment later, Sean did too.

***

After they had both cleaned up, Sean lay on the bed next to Hayden. Sex had been fast, ferocious, and just what he needed. Hayden's body was better than his fantasies.

Hayden ran a hand over Sean's chest, playing with his nipple, and Sean stirred again. "Give me a minute." He laughed and stilled Hayden's hand. He definitely wanted more. That had been the first course.

Hayden shifted onto his elbow and leaned over, kissing him slowly. The passion was like nothing Sean was used to. He yearned to lose himself in the kiss, but he was feeling emotions he didn't associate with sex. Dangerous emotions — wanting more than a quick release.

"Why don't you stay the night?" Hayden asked. "I can drop you back at the apartment on my way to work tomorrow."

Sean froze as his mind yelled *yes, yes, yes.*

No. That wasn't why he was here. Staying the night made it more than a hookup, didn't it? Sleeping together was more than sex. "You want me to stay?"

"Yeah. We'll probably be seeing a lot of each other over the next few weeks."

Sean sat up, shifted away. No, this had to be a one-off thing. "You said you wouldn't tell."

Hayden huffed out a breath. "I won't. I was talking about the other weddings." He frowned. "Did all of your family disown you?"

He wasn't going to go there. "I don't want to talk about it."

Hayden sat up as well, tentatively reaching out and taking hold of Sean's hand, rubbing it. "Maybe you should."

Sean closed his eyes. The temptation to confide his whole sorry story to Hayden was strong. Too strong. It made him way too vulnerable. People couldn't be trusted.

Hayden shuffled closer, put his arm around Sean's shoulder. "I'm a good listener."

No, he couldn't do this. He opened his eyes. "We can talk later." He kissed Hayden hard, running his hand down Hayden's body, to where his cock was already standing to attention. This was what tonight was about. Sex.

And he was going to take full advantage of it.

***

It was early morning when music blared out and a cheery tune wished him good morning. What the hell? Sean groaned and pulled the pillow up around his ears.

Someone next to him moved and he was suddenly wide awake. He opened his eyes as Hayden slapped a button on the alarm.

He'd spent the night at Hayden's.

He hadn't meant to. It was meant to be just about sex, but somewhere along the way, he must have fallen asleep. His shoulders tensed as Hayden rolled over and pulled him close.

"Morning." Hayden kissed his forehead and ran a hand possessively down his side. "Regrets?"

"No." He'd needed the release. But this was the one man who could out him to his sisters.

"Then what are you so tense about?"

He debated what to say. "What's it going to be like when I see you with my sisters?"

"I can't answer that for you. I'm going to want to drag you off into a dark corner and kiss you senseless." Hayden's grin was wicked.

Sean grimaced. "That doesn't help. Now I'm going to be thinking about you doing that to me." And what a delicious thought it was.

For a moment Sean let himself fantasize that he could be open about his sexuality, that he and Hayden could sneak off and kiss, but the thought of Carly walking in on him like he'd walked in on her and Evan froze his bones. He shook his head. He couldn't. He just couldn't handle the rejection now.

"I'm not going to say anything, but I want you to think about it," Hayden said. "Consider telling your sisters the truth. They're wonderful women, and it won't change how they feel about you."

Every nerve in his body screamed no, but looking at Hayden's hopeful expression he said, "I'll think about it."

"That's all I ask." He rolled over and got out of bed. "Do you want to have a shower with me?"

Sean smiled. "Sure."

When Hayden dropped Sean off in front of Carly's apartment, Sean squeezed his hand in lieu of a kiss, and Hayden didn't seem to mind. On his way up to the apartment, his cell rang.

"Hi, Zita."

"Sean, I wasn't sure you'd be awake yet," she said. "I've got to go to the college to pick up some books and register for a few things. Do you want to keep me company?"

He was damn tired and he wanted some time alone, but he couldn't prevent the glow inside at the fact she wanted to spend time with him. He tried to be cheerful. "Sure."

"Great. Meet me downstairs in an hour."

Sean unlocked the apartment and headed for his bedroom. McClane jumped off the sofa and trotted after him. Crap. He'd forgotten about the dog. Some pet-sitter he was. Sean gave him a quick pat before getting changed and then wandered into the kitchen to feed him.

What was he going to do about Hayden?

If he was openly gay, he'd love to get to know him better, spend his holiday having fantastic sex, have something more than a one-night stand. But he wasn't.

So he couldn't.

He didn't have a choice about seeing Hayden again, but his heart pounded at the thought. Could he hide his attraction from his sisters?

He had before. He should be able to do it again.

Except now every time he thought of the man, his cheeks heated. The sex had been more than a quick shag. And the intensity of it... He was going to need a damn good poker face.

He sucked at poker.

He couldn't deny the yearning that one day he could be like Hayden, true about who he was, with the acceptance of others, but his whole life had been proof it was a pipe dream.

Besides, Hayden may not want to see him again. He might have got it out of his system and not be interested in more.

Especially with someone as anxious as Sean.

He was high maintenance.

He was useless.

He wasn't worth the hassle.

The familiar cloud of judgment and self-doubt hovered over him. He stood up. He couldn't let it rain down on him. Checking the time, he grabbed McClane's lead. Taking the dog for a quick walk would help clear his mind.

***

Sean arrived back at the apartment just before Zita was due. He took McClane upstairs and returned to the foyer as Zita's yellow SUV pulled up. He hurried out into the heat and climbed inside.

"Morning!" Zita said as she pulled back into traffic.

"You're cheerful this morning," Sean said, putting on his seatbelt.

"It's a gorgeous day, my sister got married to the love of her life yesterday, and I'm due to marry David in a little over two weeks — what's not to be cheerful about?"

"Well, when you put it like that…" He smiled. "What do you need to do at college?"

"I've got my book list and I want to familiarize myself with the campus."

"This is your first time to college?"

"Yes. I've been helping Mama with Casa Flanagan since I was in high school. Now there's Johanna to help her, I'm going to become a lawyer." Her breath was a little bit shuddery on her exhale. "I still can't believe it."

"Why the change?" He knew about her work fostering child migrants from Central America, but was curious why she didn't want to do that anymore.

"I never knew what I wanted to do when I grew up," she said. "A few years ago, I started taking my foster sisters to court for their hearings, and I realized that's what I wanted to do. I wanted to defend them and fight for their freedom."

It was such a worthwhile cause.

"What about you, Mr. Bartender? Do you have any long-term goals?"

Nothing as worthy as hers. He didn't let himself dream big. "I dunno."

She glanced at him. "Really? Will you be happy as a bartender for the rest of your life?"

He hesitated. She was going to laugh at him.

"Sean?"

He took a breath. "It would be nice to own my own pub."

"That's a great idea. What would it be like? An Irish pub?"

In his wildest fantasies, it would be a gay bar, but he couldn't say that. "Well, if it's in Ireland, it would be an Irish pub."

She laughed. "Smart-ass. You know what I mean. Would it be hip and trendy, or comfortable and casual?"

"Comfortable and casual. Everyone welcome."

"What kind of decor?" She sounded genuinely interested.

He glanced at her and she smiled in encouragement. "It would have a big chunky wooden bar that was full of stories—you know, scratches and dings, but smooth from being cared for."

"That's a beautiful image. What else?"

"A well-stocked bar. Guinness of course, with other beers, ales and ciders, but a good wine cellar and a great cocktail list."

"Do you make a mean cocktail?"

"Not much call to at my bar. The regulars are Guinness or ale drinkers, with the occasional house wine. We've got a good scotch and brandy selection, but people drink them neat."

She screwed up her nose. "Sounds a little boring."

"They like the familiar, aren't big about change." And certainly not a change like discovering their local bartender was a fairy. He'd be sacked before he could scare the customers away.

"OK, so what else would you have? Music?"

"Something different every night," he said. "Folk music, bands — a chance for people to play music, to jam together. At ten o'clock, we'd clear back the tables to make room for a dance floor and dance the night away."

"I thought you weren't much of a dancer."

He stiffened. He'd said too much. "People like to dance."

"They sure do. I'd come to your pub." She parked the car and they got out. Zita hooked her arm through his and he flinched.

"Sorry," she said, letting go.

"No, it's fine." He took her arm back. "Just caught me by surprise." He wasn't used to being touched.

"I'm going to ask you a real personal question." She smiled cautiously. "I don't want to offend you though."

He braced himself. "Go ahead."

"Do you have many friends?" She glanced at him and then hurriedly added, "It's just that you seem uncomfortable with any affection. But maybe that's what Irish guys are like. Or maybe it's because you don't know us so well. Or maybe I should think before I speak."

He was silent while he considered how to answer her. "I usually open the pub about ten thirty in the morning and close after midnight. That doesn't leave a lot of time for socializing."

"But you must get time off."

"Most people I know work during the day."

Zita was silent for a while as they walked through the college grounds. "No girlfriend?"

His insides shriveled. "No."

"Do you see much of your mother?"

"No, we don't live near each other." Not that he knew where his mother was living at the moment.

"I can't imagine what it would be like not to visit Mama regularly," Zita said.

"You get used to it. Besides, there's always the telephone."

Zita let go of his arm as they entered a bookstore. "I'll try to be quick."

Relieved at the chance to avoid the topic of his mother, he said, "Do you want to give me some of the titles, and I'll help find them?"

She nodded and together they gathered her books for college.

As they walked back to the car, Zita said, "On Saturday we're going to make decorations for Bridget's wedding. Do you want to come?"

He loved the idea of being able to help. "Sure. What are we making?"

She laughed. "I'm not entirely sure. I'm just an extra set of hands. I think there's going to be bunting, or lanterns or something, and there was talk about Bonbonniere."

He raised an eyebrow.

"You know the little gifts people give to guests at weddings? Hayden and Bridget have it all sorted out."

"Hayden's going to be there as well?" He wasn't sure whether that was a good thing or not.

"Of course. He's the wedding planner extraordinaire."

"He seems to be doing a lot of work for you all."

"He is, but he and Mama loves it. And with us all getting married close together, it made sense to use the information he'd put together for Carly."

Sean smiled and then thought of something. "Isn't your wedding next?"

"Yeah, but everything's figured out."

"Weren't you having difficulty with David's parents?" He tried to remember the details of one of their earlier conversations.

"Yes. Fay wanted to invite half of Houston. In the end, we agreed on a set number of guests for both sides of the family." She sighed. "I didn't want anything fancy or over-the-top, but it meant so much to Fay to have all the bells and whistles. And since she and Bob insisted on paying, I went with it."

He frowned. "It's your wedding. You should be able to do what you like."

"It's not a big deal. I just want to be married." She grinned. "But I will admit that even though Fay insisted on certain things, I chose what we had. It wasn't quite the white and gold theme Fay had envisioned."

He grinned. Zita was definitely his most colorful sister, with bright, quirky clothing. He couldn't wait to see what it all looked like.

"I'm starving," Zita said. "Let's go to lunch."

His cell phone rang as he got into the car. There was no caller ID. "Hello."

"Hello, gorgeous."

Hayden. Sean's body warred with itself as the pleasure of hearing his voice fought with the anxiety of having Zita in the car and the chance she would overhear.

"Hi. Zita was just telling me about the plans for Saturday."

He kept his voice casual, hoping Hayden would understand.

"Are you with her?" he asked.

"Yes."

"All right, I'll get straight to why I'm calling then." He sounded disappointed. "I'm taking some teenagers to a baseball game tomorrow night and I've got a spare ticket. I thought you might like to come."

He had been planning to keep his distance from Hayden, but none of his sisters would be there. He'd be safe, and the idea Hayden wanted to spend more time with him made him smile. "Sure."

"Great. I'll pick you up after I finish work."

"I'll see you then." Sean hung up.

"Was that Bridget?" Zita asked.

"No. Hayden." He tried for casual. "Said he had a spare ticket to a baseball game tomorrow night and invited me along."

"That's nice of him," Zita said. "I didn't consider that you might like to watch some sports while you were here. Bridget would have taken you to a football game, but it's the off-season."

Sean shrugged, relieved she didn't think it was weird that Hayden was inviting him out. "It's fine. I don't know a lot about baseball."

"Me neither. I'm sure Hayden will be able to explain it." She glanced at him. "We really should be giving you a better taste of Texas," she said. "Let's have Texas barbecue for lunch."

He nodded.

And ignored the sharp stab of guilt from not being completely honest with his sister.

Chapter 7

Time had slowed to a crawl. Normally Hayden loved his job, but today he couldn't help watching the clock, waiting for five o'clock to roll around.

At five to five, he started packing up.

"Hayden, have you got a minute?" It was Frederick.

Hayden forced a smile onto his face. "Sure, what's up?"

"I need to get a hold of Carolina."

He frowned. "What's so important?"

"I've got a huge deal in the works to do a television special on Comunidad and in particular on Carolina. I need to get this contract signed ASAP and I need her approval first."

It could wait. "No. She's on her honeymoon."

"These aren't people who will wait. They'll find someone else for their special."

Hayden wasn't sure Carly would agree to a TV special. She didn't like the attention. "Explain that she has just got married and will be available in another week." There was no way he was giving out Evan's cell number to Frederick for this. He'd promised he would only contact them for emergencies, and that promise meant Evan had convinced Carly to leave her cell phone at home.

"Hayden, be reasonable. This is a great opportunity."

"Then I'm sure there will be other stations willing to do a similar interview if Carly is interested when she returns. The answer's still no."

Frederick scowled at him, but Hayden ignored him. The man had no perspective on what was urgent.

Hayden tucked his cell phone into his pocket and made sure he had everything in his leather satchel. "Now, if that's everything, I've got an appointment to get to."

Leaving work so he could pick up his new lover — now *that* was urgent.

He grinned and headed out.

Arriving at Carly's apartment, he parked in one of the spots designated for visitors and, after greeting the doorman, he headed up. If he'd called Sean to meet him in the lobby, he'd miss out on his hello kiss, and he didn't want that. He knocked on the door and his smile faltered slightly when Zita opened it.

Damn.

"Hayden!" She gave him a hug. "You're taking Sean to the baseball game, right? Sorry, we were talking and lost track of time. He's gone to get changed." She invited him in.

If only he could slip down the corridor and watch him. With an internal sigh, he said, "We're meeting at Casa Flanagan at ten tomorrow, aren't we?"

"Yeah. I was going to pick up Sean on my way. Do you want a ride too?"

His vision of spending the night with Sean was slowly disappearing. "How about I pick up the pair of you instead?"

"Oh, no. Don't be silly," she said, picking up a couple of glasses on the coffee table and taking them into the kitchen. "You'd have to double back for me. You're both on my way anyway."

Sean came out wearing denim shorts and a sleeveless top that showed off his lean muscles. He looked good enough to eat. Hayden blew him a kiss.

Sean stiffened and his gaze darted to Zita, whose back was turned to them.

Hayden's smile faded. That's right, no affection unless they were alone.

Zita came out of the kitchen. "Are you ready to go? I'll go down with you."

Hayden nodded. He was going to have to wait for that kiss, if he even got one at all. "Lead the way."

Downstairs, Hayden waited for Zita to leave so he could greet Sean properly, but she was in her car fiddling with her phone. She looked up, realized they were still there and waved them away.

Damn. He started his car and drove off. When they were a block away Hayden said, "It's good to see you."

"You too." Sean smiled at him, but it was kind of forced.

Hayden's good mood deflated further. "I knew Zita wasn't looking when I blew you that kiss."

Sean ran a hand through his hair. "Sorry, this is all new to me. I can't be so blasé."

Hayden reminded himself to be patient. Sean wasn't ready to come out to his sisters. He ran a hand along Sean's thigh. "I'm sorry. I've been fantasizing about kissing you all day and then Zita answered the door."

"I was trying to get her to leave, but she wouldn't take the hint." Sean's smile was genuine this time.

"Well, at least that proves we're not being obvious," Hayden said, hoping to put Sean at ease. "If she'd got an inkling about how I really wanted to greet you, she would have made herself scarce."

Sean shifted in his seat, adjusting himself.

"Yeah, it had something to do with that," Hayden said, enjoying the way Sean blushed. Damn, he was going to combust if he didn't at least get to kiss him soon. It was the worst possible time of day, during rush hour, so it was taking forever to get to his place.

"So who are we taking to the baseball?" Sean asked.

Hayden adjusted his focus. "I do a bit of work with a homeless shelter for teens. A couple of the kids are huge baseball fans, so I got them tickets. Max had to pull out at the last moment, so I thought of you."

Sean was silent for a time. "What's the shelter like?"

"You can see for yourself. We're picking the kids up from there."

"They don't have a problem with you being gay?"

Hayden frowned. He really wanted to hear Sean's story, find out what made him so scared to come out, but he would have to gain Sean's trust. "No. Some of them are gay as well."

Sean's eyes widened.

"They came out to their parents and found themselves chucked out on the street. The shelter does what it can to support them, gives them the opportunity to keep going to school, but it's hard. Some of the kids have turned to drugs, many of them suffer from depression and anxiety."

"I get that."

It was said so quietly that Hayden almost didn't hear it. Was that what had happened to Sean?

They pulled into Hayden's driveway and he checked the time. "I've got about five minutes to get changed before we have to leave."

Sean followed him inside and the moment the door was closed, Hayden pulled him close. "Just one kiss first."

The moment their mouths met, Hayden was lost. One kiss wasn't going to be enough. He wanted to keep kissing Sean, wanted to strip him naked and go down on him. He ran a hand between them to touch Sean, and his phone alarm started to sing.

"Shit." He stepped away and pulled it out of his pocket, silencing the reminder to make sure he grabbed the tickets. His breath was fast as he looked at Sean. "Stay here tonight."

Sean shook his head. "Zita's picking me up tomorrow."

There had to be a way they could work this. "I'll call her, tell her I'm taking you out on the town after the game, that we're meeting up with my friends." He saw the refusal on Sean's face. "I have straight friends as well." He ran a hand through his hair. "I'll tell her you're going to crash here in my spare room, to save time in the morning."

Sean was considering it.

Hayden stepped forward, kissed him softly. "We could have all night. We'll stop by Carly's apartment on our way back here so you can get a change of clothes." He kissed him again, running his hands down Sean's back and over his butt. "Please."

"I can't leave McClane there alone. He'll need to be fed in the morning." Sean's eyes were closed and he pressed himself into Hayden's hands.

"He can come too. Carmen won't mind him going to Casa Flanagan tomorrow."

Sean nodded. "All right."

The victory was sweet. He didn't want to question why he was so eager, but he needed Sean tonight. He whipped out his phone and dialed Zita. "Hey, Z. Change of plans tonight. After the game, I'm heading out with some friends, so I thought I'd show your brother how we party in Houston." He dumped his keys on the bench next to the tickets.

"Sounds like fun."

"Should be. Since we'll be out late, Sean's going to crash at my place. That way you only have one stop to make to pick us up tomorrow."

"Oh. Sure." She paused. "I'll pick you up about nine."

"Great. Later." He hung up and checked the time. "Damn, we're running late." He tossed his phone with his keys and hurried into his bedroom to change. Sean followed him.

"Zita was fine with that?"

"Yeah. She didn't question it." He stripped off his jacket and hung it in his wardrobe before undoing his shirt.

Sean leaned up against the doorframe, his gaze intoxicating.

"You keep watching me like that and we're going to miss the first innings," Hayden said, turning his back as he threw the shirt into the hamper and started unbuttoning his pants.

"I've heard baseball's not a fast sport. We won't miss much will we?"

Hayden grinned. The man was temptation itself. "Probably not, but the kids will be disappointed."

"Ah, yes. I'd forgotten. I'll leave you be." He left the room.

Quickly Hayden hung up his pants and changed into a nice pair of chino shorts and a polo shirt, before heading out to the living area where Sean was waiting.

"You do know how to make clothes look good," Sean said.

Hayden flushed, grabbing the tickets, keys and phone. "Thanks." He gave Sean one more quick kiss before heading to the door. "Let's go."

"I'm already looking forward to coming back." Sean's grin was wicked as they climbed into the car.

So was Hayden.

***

Sean had to think about something aside from the sexy man next to him, otherwise, he was going to embarrass himself when he got out of the car. "How many kids are going tonight?"

"Five. Three guys, two girls. The shelter has a van we can borrow to get to the ballpark."

"Have the kids been homeless long?"

"It varies from a couple of months to a couple of years."

Sean was silent. He knew what that was like. "What kind of volunteer work do you do there?"

"On Tuesday nights I run a couple of sessions. One is to help them get jobs — how to write resumes, dress for interviews, that kind of thing. The other is a support group for those who are homosexual. Help them deal with being gay for those who are struggling and to answer any questions they might have."

Sean closed his eyes. What would it have been like if he'd had somewhere like that to go to when he'd been young?

They pulled up to a red-brick building that had a sign outside saying "Teen Shelter". There was a small gray van parked outside.

Sean followed Hayden inside where a group of teenagers was waiting in a lounge room. Seeing Hayden, they got to their feet.

"Hi Hayden." The African-American guy's clothes looked trendy and brand new, which was kind of odd if he was homeless. He smoothed out his black shorts as he got to his feet.

"Hey, Bruno. How's things?" Hayden replied, walking over to him.

"You're late," the other African-American guy complained.

"We'll make it in time, Deon," Hayden said, doing some kind of elaborate handshake and slapping them on the back. Then he turned to the Hispanic man who was sitting behind a desk doing paperwork, "Hey, Alberto."

"Hayden, glad you're here. These kids have been bursting out of their skin for you to arrive."

Hayden laughed. "We'll be on our way. I'll bring them straight back after the game."

"No problem."

Hayden introduced Sean to the kids who all looked about

fifteen.

"Is he your boyfriend?" Angela, who was heavily pregnant asked.

Sean wished the answer was yes, but that was crazy. They weren't dating and never could. He wasn't brave enough to out himself even to these kids.

"He's a friend," Hayden said and walked toward the door.

"Yeah, with benefits I'll bet," Bruno said.

"I'd hit that," Deon said and they gave each other a high five.

Sean's face flamed as he quickly got into the front seat of the van. Was it obvious he was gay, or was it because he was with Hayden? What was he letting himself in for?

"Hey, show some respect," Hayden told them. "He's not a piece of meat." He turned to Sean. "I forgot to mention, the kids like to tease."

"Is that what that is?"

It was a rowdy ride to the baseball stadium. Once inside, Sean was surprised by the size of the place. It had to seat about forty thousand people. It was pretty humid and the first stop was at the refreshment bar to get drinks and food.

Hayden bought whatever food the teenagers asked for, and they each ordered extra non-perishables to shove in their backpacks. Hayden didn't blink an eye.

Sean remembered what that was like. Grabbing whatever food he could when it was available.

With arms loaded with snacks, they made their way to their seats in one of the upper levels. Sean glanced down at the baseball diamond and then at the crowd. There were quite a few empty seats, but it was still early. He sat between Hayden and Angela and took a bite of his hot dog, which, like most food in the US, was oversized and full of trimmings. It was delicious.

He turned to Angela, who had to be close to nine months pregnant. "When's the baby due?"

"Are you saying I'm fat?" she asked, her face outraged.

Feck. He opened his mouth to apologize, but nothing came out.

Angela laughed. "Just kidding. I'm due in four weeks."

Sean let out a breath and smiled weakly. "It's got to be hard, being pregnant and living on the streets."

She nodded. "Alberto's reserved one of the beds in the shelter for me permanently for the next month."

"What are you going to do afterward?"

She shrugged, her face a bit wistful. "I keep hoping that when my parents see the baby, they'll take me back."

"What happened?"

"Usual story. Fell in love with the wrong guy. He just wanted to get in my pants and won't have anything to do with me now. His parents didn't believe me when I told them he was the father — said the father had to be some other guy. As if I was sleeping around."

"And your parents?"

"World War Three. Mom was hysterical, Dad called me a whore — told me to get out."

The story was far too similar to his mother's experience. "How do you feel about the baby?"

She wrapped her arms around her belly. "She's mine. I'll do whatever I can to protect her. It's not her fault that her mom was naïve."

Sean's heart filled. "You're going to be a wonderful mother."

Her eyes filled with tears. "Do you think so?"

He nodded. "You already care for your child. My mother never did."

"She got kicked out too?"

Sean glanced at Hayden, but he was talking to one of the other kids. "Yeah. She made it work, but she didn't much care for me."

"I'll make sure my baby always knows she's loved."

"That's the most precious gift you can give her."

She smiled at him, brushing away the tears. "Thank you."

He hugged her, not sure who was most surprised by the gesture, and Angela clung to him. Sean's heart broke for her. There had to be something he could do to help.

But what? He was only in Houston for another five weeks. He might not even be here when the baby was born and he didn't have a whole lot of money to splash around.

He'd have to think about it.

He didn't want Angela to struggle the way his mother had.

Throughout the game, the kids moved seats, all wanting an opportunity to sit next to Hayden and chat to him about some issue they had. During the last inning, Sean was sitting next to the Hispanic boy, Gil, who was slouched down in his chair scowling at the infield despite the fact the Astros were up by two runs.

"You're not an Astros fan?" Sean asked.

Gil glanced at him and shrugged. "Doesn't really matter who wins," he said. "It's not going to change my life."

"Might be something to cheer you up for a while."

Gil grunted. "What would you know?"

Sean stopped with the soda halfway to his mouth. He lowered it. Should he tell Gil the truth? He looked at the boy, saw the weariness on his face, the complete lack of hope. Checking Hayden wasn't listening, he said, "I lived on the streets for a while when I was your age."

Gil looked at him. "Oh yeah?" His expression was faked disinterest.

"Yeah. Mam kicked me out when she found out I was gay."

"You told her?" He sat up straighter, paying attention now.

"Nah. I knew she wouldn't accept it. She caught me kissing another guy."

"Ouch." Gil winced. "Was it bad?"

"Yeah."

"What did you do?"

"Caught a bus out of town and tried to find a job."

"Did anyone hire you?"

"Eventually. I spent a few weeks on the streets until I found someone willing to give me food and board in return for some work."

"Lucky."

"What about you? How long have you been on the streets?"

"Six months."

No wonder the kid was low. "Are you still going to school?"

"No, it's too hard. I miss it though. I wanted to go to college."

"And study what?"

"Computer programming."

Was that something Carly did over at Comunidad?

"I didn't know that, Gil," Hayden said. "What kind of programming?"

Sean froze. How long had Hayden been listening?

"Computer games."

Hayden pulled his wallet out of his pocket and handed Gil a business card. "Come and see me at work on Monday afternoon and I'll see if I can find you something."

Gil took the card and his eyes widened. "You work at Comunidad?"

Hayden nodded.

"Oh man, Carolina Flanagan is the bomb." He grinned, the first sign of real enthusiasm Sean had seen from him. "Do you know her?"

Hayden chuckled. "She's my boss. And she's Sean's sister."

Sean stiffened. Damn, he shouldn't have admitted he was gay. He frantically tried to figure out how to tell Gil not to say anything, without making it appear he was ashamed of his sexuality.

"Aren't you like Irish or something?" Gil asked.

He nodded.

"Sean's got a different mother," Hayden said. "He hasn't come out to his sisters yet."

"Roger that," Gil said.

Sean exhaled.

"Is she homophobic?" Gil asked.

"Not at all," Hayden told him. "She knows I'm gay."

Gil thought about it a moment. "Yeah, I'd probably be wary about telling someone again." He glanced at the business card. "Thanks for this." He settled back in his seat to watch the game, a smile on his face.

Sean didn't dare look at Hayden. Didn't want to know how much Hayden had heard.

Gil was still a kid, trying to find acceptance and understanding in the world. He wanted to believe things were going to turn out all right. Sean wanted that too. He wanted to help Gil and the other kids here. Though he wasn't comfortable asking Carly for money, maybe there was something the company could do.

He steeled himself and turned to Hayden. His attention was on the game. "Does Comunidad support a lot of charities?"

Hayden glanced at him. "We're having a fundraiser to raise money for the shelter soon. But Carly also offers a lot of scholarships for both high school and college students and we've been talking about setting up an apprenticeship or intern section."

"That would be good for Gil," Sean said.

"Yeah. Each department is going to get involved because people are always looking for experience in different areas."

"Whose idea was it?"

"I suggested it after chatting with Alberto. He was searching for mechanic apprenticeships and the like for some of the kids. I thought we could do something similar but there's a bit of paperwork involved."

"And Carly liked the idea?"

"She was all over it. Couldn't believe she hadn't thought of it herself. She likes to support the community and those less fortunate than herself."

Sean smiled. He really liked his sister. It made him feel so good that she hadn't forgotten where she came from.

Hayden squeezed his leg and Sean glanced at him. There were questions all over Hayden's face, but Sean wasn't willing to answer them just yet.

Chapter 8

After dropping the kids back at the shelter with promises he would visit with Hayden next week, they made a quick stop at Carly's apartment so Sean could pick up a change of clothes and McClane. Then they headed for Hayden's house.

Sean couldn't stop thinking about the teens. It wasn't right that the people who were meant to protect them had turned their backs on them.

"How often did you say you go to the shelter?" he asked Hayden.

"At least once a week. Sometimes twice. Max introduced me to it. He lived there for a while when he was younger."

"What do they need?"

"More rooms and more money," Hayden told him. "It's filled to capacity every night and there are more kids who need beds. There's an outdoor area which is set up with tents and mattresses to make more room, but in hurricane season it's no good." He sighed. "They need money for food and to pay for any medicine the kids need."

"Does Alberto work there full-time?"

"Yeah, he's the only paid person. The rest are volunteers. He does his best to find the kids work, but not all of them are in the right head space to accept the help they're offered. Some are on drugs, others are still too angry at the world to hold down a job."

"Are they allowed to do drugs on the premises?"

Hayden shook his head. "No, but when it's bursting at the seams, Alberto doesn't always catch them. And what's he supposed to do if he does? Kick them out on the streets so they can get into more trouble while they're high?"

It was a mess. Sean had never turned to drugs, never been tempted.

"Some of them, like Gil, just want to be self-sufficient. If I can get him an apprenticeship at Comunidad where he earns enough to live on, he can leave the shelter and get on with his life."

"But he'd need more support than that."

"The kids who get jobs and move on know they can get help from Alberto if they need it. Plus, if he was working at Comunidad, I'd be there for him."

Sean was silent. The idea of staying in Houston flitted through his mind. If he stayed, he'd be able to do more to help. Plus, he would be close to his sisters.

He shook his head. He was being fanciful.

They pulled into Hayden's driveway. Inside, Hayden put on the coffee machine while Sean set up McClane's bed in the living room. "Want a drink?" Hayden asked.

"Tea, if you've got it. I'm not a fan of coffee."

"Sure. Why don't you put your bag in my room?"

Sean did as Hayden suggested. The relaxed, casual vibe was nice. After the passion of earlier, he'd half expected Hayden to jump him at the door, but Sean needed more processing time.

He wandered back to the living room.

"Do you have milk or sugar?" Hayden asked.

"No, black's fine."

Hayden grinned and put a hand on his hip. "Damn straight it is."

Sean laughed. He'd smiled and laughed more times this week than he ever had before. At least not with this happy glow inside. He took his mug from Hayden and they sat on the sofa next to each other.

"Do you get many homeless teens in Ireland?" Hayden asked.

He shook his head. "Not in my town. There might be more in Dublin, but I don't go there regularly."

"Do you enjoy working in a bar?"

"It's a job." Sean shrugged. "I'm comfortable. The bar in

itself is its own little family."

"They know you're gay?"

He shook his head.

"So you're not really yourself."

He'd never had this yearning to be out before. He'd come to accept that this was his lot in life. He had somewhere to live, food on the table and a steady job. He'd be greedy to ask for more. He'd leave the dreams to those who had the ability to achieve them. "I am who I need to be."

"Really? You don't feel constricted? You're not suffocating when you're not able to be who you really are?"

Annoyance sparked. "And what do you know about who I really am?"

"I don't," Hayden said. "But I'd like to get to know you." His gentle smile dissolved Sean's anger. "You're more relaxed when it's just the two of us or when you're with people who know you're gay, like tonight with the teens. When you're with your sisters, there's a tension there, as if you're afraid."

"I am afraid," he admitted and the truth lifted some of the weight off his heart. "The only time I've come out, I ended up on the streets."

"Want to tell me about it?"

He did, and that was a surprise in itself. Hayden was easy to talk with. "I only had my mam." He paused. No. That wasn't the right place to start. He tried again. "I knew I liked boys when I was about ten," he said. "I also knew it would make me more of an outcast than I already was, so I tried hard to like girls instead."

Hayden took hold of Sean's hand and kissed the back of it. "What made you an outcast?"

"I was a bastard. Mam was a single parent and Dad was still considered a terrorist even though it was proved he wasn't. No one wanted to know me."

"Terrorist?" Hayden asked.

"It was in the eighties when the IRA was really active. There'd been a bombing and Dad had been accused of accessory. That's when he fled to El Salvador. A year later, the true culprit was found, but people still believed he was guilty because he didn't come back."

"What about your grandparents?"

"Dad's parents had died and Mam's parents disowned her for getting pregnant out of wedlock."

"You couldn't tell your mother you were gay?"

"No." His laugh was bitter.

"So what happened?"

"When I was fifteen, I was working on a group assignment with a cute guy in my class. He was one of those guys that everyone called a fag, but he denied it."

"No one thought you were gay?"

Sean shook his head. "I hid it well."

"So what happened?"

"We were at the kitchen table working and he came right out and said he was gay." Sean glanced at Hayden. "Shocked the hell out of me."

Hayden smiled. "So what did you do?"

"I seized the chance. We were alone, Mam wasn't due home for a couple more hours and there was no one to see, so I told him I might be gay too." He laughed. "We kind of dived at each other and started kissing. I thought I'd died and gone to heaven. I damn nearly came in my pants." He fell silent, remembering the short-lived joy.

"Then?"

"Mam walked in. She'd had a migraine and had come home from work early."

"Damn."

He nodded. "She screamed, started abusing the both of us. The guy grabbed his things and fled."

"And you?"

"She hit me, told me I was an abomination, that I was going to hell and I had to get out."

Hayden pulled him closer and hugged him, and Sean drew comfort from it.

He sighed. "I was bigger than her, so I ran upstairs, stuffed a backpack full of things, grabbed my money and left."

"Did you ever go back?"

"Yeah. The next day I thought she might have calmed down. The lock on the door had changed and when I knocked she said she'd kill me if I ever came back, if I ever breathed a word about being gay to anyone."

Hayden swore.

"It was a tiny town and she was already on the lowest rung of society."

"What did you do?"

"I caught the next bus out of town. I eventually found a farmer who needed help on his farm and in return he gave me food and somewhere to sleep."

"He didn't pay you?"

Sean shook his head. "Beggars can't be choosers. It suited me fine until I turned eighteen and could get some identification and sign for my own things. I moved into town then and got a job in a pub."

"And you never told anyone you were gay?"

"I didn't dare. Not long after I started work, one of the guys at the bar was sacked for being gay. I was twenty before I went to Dublin for the first time and that's when I discovered a gay bar. I was blown away."

"Pun intended?" Hayden asked.

Sean laughed. "No. It was so amazing to be around people who were open about their sexuality, not having to hide or be worried about being judged."

"Did you move to Dublin?"

He shook his head. "I wasn't brave enough then, and was barely making ends meet. I didn't want to have to start from scratch again. Then a couple of years later, Ireland went through a recession and there weren't jobs available. I stayed where I was."

"In the closet."

"Yeah." Sean sighed. "I don't want to talk about it anymore."

"You know your sisters won't care you're gay," Hayden said.

"No, I don't know that." His chest squeezed at the very thought of coming out. "I can't risk it. Our relationship is so new, so tentative, plus Carmen is Catholic, so she might think I'm a sinner." He took a breath and exposed his heart. "It would break my heart if they rejected me now."

"They won't reject you." Hayden shifted and wrapped an arm around his shoulders, pulling him closer. "Trust me."

"I can't. Not yet. Maybe not ever." The very idea made nausea swirl in his stomach.

"All right." Hayden kissed his head.

The gesture was so comforting. Sean turned to him, kissed him slowly. "I don't know what you see in me. I'm a mess." He wasn't fishing for an answer, but Hayden gave him one anyway.

"You're incredibly handsome," he said, kissing him again. "And you're kind. Two of my most favorite things."

Sean didn't say anything. No one had called him kind before. He didn't want to think about that now. He wanted to take full advantage of having this wonderful man all to himself for the night.

"I think it's time to go to bed."

Hayden grinned. "You took the words right out of my mouth."

***

There was a loud banging coming from somewhere, and a dog barked. Hayden kept his eyes firmly shut, hoping it would go away. Eventually it did, but then a cell phone started ringing. It wasn't his.

He opened his eyes and squinted at the brightness. Sean reached for his phone as Hayden checked the time. Shit, it was nine o'clock. That had to be Zita. Hayden jumped out of bed and threw on some shorts and a T-shirt.

Sean answered the phone and the blood drained out of his already pale face. "Sorry Z, I'll be right there. I forgot to set my alarm." His voice was remarkably calm considering the panic on his face. He hung up. "*Feck!*"

"I'll get the door," Hayden said. "You grab your things and take a shower."

"But there are no blankets on the couch." His breath was coming in short bursts.

"Calm down. I have a spare bedroom. Go, take the time to compose yourself." He hated the full-on anxiety on his lover's face and the tremble in his hands. He gripped Sean's shoulders and Sean took a deep breath in.

"All right."

Hayden headed for the front door, checking to make sure

Sean was in the bathroom before he opened it. "Sorry Zita."

She was standing there looking fresh and adorable in a green fifties-style dress and flat shoes. "Late night, huh?" she asked as she walked inside and placed her purse on the kitchen counter.

"Yeah," he lied. He turned the coffee machine on. "Sean's taking a shower."

"No rush. Bridget and the others will get started without us. Where did you go?"

Hayden frowned. "Go?"

She laughed. "Last night. You took Sean out on the town."

Shit. He wasn't alert enough to be thinking straight. "Whitewash," he said, making a coffee. "Do you want one?"

"No, I'm good. Did you have fun?"

"Yeah." He didn't want to go into detail, not without Sean here to hear what he said. They should have come up with something to tell Zita. He hated lying. He poured Sean a black tea when the shower stopped running.

Sipping his coffee, he tried to wake up his brain. "I'd better get my wedding file," he said. What else did he need to take to Casa Flanagan? Bridget had all of the decorations, so that was it. He walked down the hallway as Sean came out of the bathroom, his hair damp. Hayden longed to kiss him, but he couldn't risk it. "I made you a cup of tea."

"Thanks." Sean gave a half smile, the nerves still obvious in the slump of his shoulders. He walked down the corridor and greeted Zita.

Hayden quickly dashed into the bathroom to shower, and then dressed in record time. He didn't want Sean having to deal with any questions Zita might throw at him about his night.

On the way back to the kitchen, he grabbed the wedding file.

"You guys must have had a hell of a night," Zita said when he walked in. "Sean's really hazy about the details. I'm not sure whether I approve of you getting my big brother so drunk." She laughed.

Sean's expression clearly said *help me*.

"That rumor about all Irishmen being able to drink like fish isn't true when it comes to Sean." He smiled and grabbed his keys and wallet from the bench and whistled for McClane. "Shall we go?"

***

Casa Flanagan was its usual bustling hub when they arrived. The foster girls were in the living room arguing over which show to watch, and Bridget and Carmen were in the dining room setting out everything. Bridget was having little boxes filled with rocky road for her Bonbonniere and the boxes needed to be made up and then tied with ribbon. But they also had to make the rocky road.

Hayden greeted Carmen and Bridget as well as Beatriz, one of the foster girls, who was only eleven and wanted to help.

Carmen hugged him tightly. "I hear you took my boy to a baseball game last night."

"I sure did. The Astros won."

"Thank you. I did not consider the sporting things he might like to do. I am not used to having boys."

He glanced at Sean, whose face had got that stunned expression on it that Hayden had come to recognize.

"He also took Sean out on the town, and Sean can't remember much of that," Zita said with a grin.

Carmen arched an eyebrow. "I'm not going to have to tell you off, am I?"

"No ma'am. I took care of him." He smiled.

"Good," she said. "Jack's mother should be here soon to show us how to make rocky road." As if on cue, Zita's dogs started barking.

Hayden had been careful to involve Jack's mother in all of Bridget's wedding plans because she'd missed out when her youngest son had eloped last year.

It didn't take long before the kitchen smelled like chocolate and he and Sean were sitting at the dining room table, folding the boxes into shape.

"She called me her boy," Sean murmured.

"She did," Hayden agreed. "Are you all right with that?"

"She barely knows me."

"She knows you're her husband's child. For someone like Carmen, that's enough."

He was quiet.

"I guess it might feel odd, but she's genuine."

He shook his head as if he couldn't quite believe it. "I never expected it. Not in my wildest dreams."

Sean didn't dream big enough. What had his childhood been like? Sure, his mother had kicked him out of home at fifteen, but before that, what had their relationship been like? He wanted to ask, but perhaps now wasn't the best time. Not when people could walk in on the conversation.

In the kitchen, Zita and Bridget were laughing and arguing about how much chocolate to use.

Beatriz yelled, "As much as we're allowed."

Sean smiled. "Beatriz seems right at home."

"Do you know her story?"

He nodded. "Zita told me about all her foster sisters. They'll be getting another child when the Garcias move into their own home."

"Yeah. They move next week. Johanna has been working for Casa Flanagan since she arrived in February, so she has a little bit saved."

They finished putting together the boxes, and then Hayden grabbed the instructions for the paper lanterns that would decorate Carmen's garden. It seemed easy enough. All they had to do today was insert the batteries.

"Bridget's getting married in the garden, isn't she?" Sean asked.

"Yes." He grimaced.

"What's wrong?"

"The weather at this time of year can be stormy," he said. "We don't have a backup plan if it's rainy or windy, plus you've experienced the heat." Bridget was adamant that she wanted to marry in Carmen's garden, but he'd talk to her again about an alternative. He needed to phrase it in terms of reducing risks. As a safety person, she'd understand that.

Bridget came into the dining room. "First batch is finished. Want a taste test?"

He smiled. "Sure." He let Sean take the first piece of rocky road before he took one. It was delicious and chewy.

"It probably needs to set a little longer," Bridget said. "Then you can pack it up."

"Great."

"Do the lanterns work?" Bridget asked.

"Let's see." He took one of the blue lanterns and inserted the batteries before pulling it into shape. He switched it on and it glowed brightly.

"That's gorgeous!" she said. "They'll look so pretty strung up in the garden. Thanks so much for all your help." She hugged them both and went back into the kitchen.

"I've never been hugged so much in my life." Sean chuckled. "It's kind of nice."

Hayden's heart hurt for Sean. Just what had his childhood been like?

***

Sean needed a break. He'd been at the dining table for a couple of hours now and it had been nice talking with Hayden, but then everyone had crowded in and he needed some space. "Is it all right if I take five?" he asked.

"Of course," Carmen said. "It's almost time we had lunch."

He followed her into the kitchen and glanced out at the garden. It was incredible. "Can I go outside?"

"Certainly. *Mi casa es tu casa.* My house is your house."

There it was again. That casual, almost unconscious, generosity. He didn't have to prove himself to her, she didn't want anything from him. He could be who he was and she wouldn't care.

Well, that wasn't entirely true. He had no idea how she would react if he told her he was gay.

Sure, she might accept Hayden, but he wasn't related to her.

Though Sean wasn't either. Not really.

He pushed open the back door and took a second to adjust to the heat, before walking outside. It was so peaceful out here. He strolled down one of the paths, past the bench where he'd sat and spoken with Carmen last weekend. There were little cottages out here, at least half a dozen. They were really cute, and there couldn't be more than a couple of rooms inside, but the garden grew right up to the front door, making them appear like a secret hideaway from the world. That would be nice.

"Sean!"

He turned at Carmen's voice.

"Lunch is ready."

Walking back toward the house, he found Carmen looking for him.

"There you are. I thought you might have gotten lost." She smiled.

"No, I was exploring." He hesitated and then asked, "What are the cottages used for?"

"They're for the foster girls when they're old enough to move out of home — when they want some privacy and independence. Sometimes we have refugee families stay there as well, but they're not really big enough for a whole family. Just a bedroom and a little living room with a kitchenette and bathroom."

"Do they move there as soon as they turn eighteen?"

She frowned. "No. They go there if and when they are ready. They don't need to move out of the main house, but many like to."

He'd offended her. "I'm sorry. I didn't mean to imply they weren't welcome."

She patted his hand. "I know. You do not know me so well." He opened his mouth to protest, but she continued, "The girls choose what they want to do. I believe choice is very important for them. Some live in the cottages, but still eat at the main house, and others like to be fully independent. I think Alejandra will move out there with Julio when she's a little older. She wants her own space."

He thought of Angela. "Are all of the cottages full?"

"No. Only two at the moment."

"Do you ever let others rent them for a time?"

"There is no need for rent. We do not need the money."

"But could someone who isn't a refugee live there?"

"You know of someone in need?"

He told her about Angela. "She's hoping her parents will take her back when the baby is born."

"But no guarantee." Carmen nodded. "It is tricky. We're away from most public transport and it's not easy to get to places. But you should bring her here. Introduce her to me. I'll see what I can do."

Sean blinked. "Really?"

"Of course. I like to help others where I can."

Sean hugged her. "Thank you."

She squeezed him tightly. "You are most welcome. Now let's go and get some food."

***

On Monday, Sean spent the day with Zita as she showed him around Houston. His youngest sister was so full of life as she chatted, telling him about the city and about her childhood. Sean loved her vibrancy, but he was exhausted by the end of the day. It was a relief when she dropped him off at Carly's apartment.

"Are you sure you don't want to come over for dinner?" Zita asked.

"Thanks, but no. McClane's not used to being alone all day," Sean said, thankful he had the bulldog as an excuse.

Zita frowned. "It's a shame David's not allowed animals in his apartment, otherwise you could have brought him with you."

"Yeah." He hoped he appeared disappointed as he got out of the car. "I'll see you tomorrow?"

"Yes. We'll go to Casa Flanagan. Mama wants to teach you how to salsa. I'll pick you up at nine."

He grinned. He was looking forward to it. "See you then." He shut the car door and walked into the apartment building. On his way upstairs, his phone rang.

His pulse jumped as he saw the caller. Hayden. "Hi."

"Sean. Do you have any plans for tonight?" Hayden's voice was smooth like velvet.

"No."

"Would you like to go out to dinner?"

Was Hayden asking him on a date? He couldn't possibly do that. What if he ran into Zita? He fought back the panic. He didn't want to leave the apartment. He'd had enough of the world for today. Except the thought of seeing Hayden was appealing. "I've been out all day," he said. "McClane needs some company." He opened the apartment and McClane came waddling over to greet him, tail wagging.

"Oh, all right. Perhaps some other time." Hayden's

disappointment was clear.

"I was going to get takeout," Sean said, trying to be casual. "Do you want to join me?" He held his breath.

"Sure. Sounds like fun. Do you want me to pick something up on the way over?"

Sean let out the breath. "That'd be great." He dumped his key on the kitchen bench. "Whatever you want."

"All right. I'll see you soon."

Sean smiled as he hung up, already feeling more energetic. There was something about Hayden that made him want to forget about the world and enjoy who he was. He squatted down and gave McClane a rough pat. He needed to take him for a walk, but he'd wait until Hayden arrived.

He got out the dog food, whistling while he did so. He left McClane eating and went to his bedroom, making sure the bed was made and his clothes were put away. Then he went back into the living room and flitted around, plumping pillows, straightening his book on the coffee table. He let out a deep breath as the anxiety crawled along his skin.

This was ridiculous. He was safe here. Carly and Evan were on their honeymoon and no one was going to drop around. No one but Hayden.

He'd never had a man around for dinner, never had a man around at all.

Maybe it wouldn't be as easy as it had been the other night. Maybe they'd have nothing to talk about and would decide not to see each other again.

Sean hoped not. He'd never had someone to talk with, to share his sexuality with. He wanted it so badly — probably too much. He'd only end up hurt.

He should call Hayden now and say he'd changed his mind. He shouldn't be getting involved with someone when he was only here for a few weeks. It was stupid. It couldn't last, and it would hurt all the more when he went home to Ireland and was alone.

He fetched his tin whistle. Music always soothed him, took away some of his negative thoughts. He closed his eyes and played an upbeat tune, the rhythm relaxing him. When there was a knock on the door, Sean placed his instrument on the bench and opened the door.

Hayden looked sensational in a deep green suit with a mint green shirt. He wore suits like they were made just for him, every line hugging his figure and making Sean want to ruffle him up. Hayden's smile was slow and warm. "Hi. Was that you I heard playing?"

Sean's body responded and he smiled. "Yes. Come in." He reached for the bag of food Hayden carried and showed him through to the kitchen.

"You're really good."

Placing the bag on the bench, Sean turned to find Hayden right behind him. Before he could react, Hayden was kissing him; long, languid kisses that set his whole body on fire. He grabbed Hayden's ass and pulled him closer, needing whatever Hayden was willing to give him.

Hayden stepped back. "I've wanted to do that all day."

Sean's body throbbed. He wanted to be inside of him. He slipped his hands under Hayden's jacket and peeled it off, his eyes not leaving Hayden's.

Something bumped against his leg and he looked down at McClane panting happily at their feet. "Bedroom?"

"Absolutely." Hayden grabbed a paper bag out of his satchel. "I might have been a bit presumptuous, but I bought a couple of things that I wasn't sure you'd have." It was a bottle of lube and condoms.

"Great idea." Grabbing Hayden's hand, he pulled him toward the bedroom. Dinner could wait.

Chapter 9

It was some time later before they returned to the kitchen to have dinner. Hayden wore a pair of Sean's shorts and one of his T-shirts. They weren't a bad fit and they smelled deliciously like him. He sat at the table while Sean reheated the Thai food and opened the bottle of wine Hayden had brought.

"So what did you do today?" Hayden asked.

"Zita showed me some more of the sights of Houston." He poured them both a glass of white wine. "I swear she didn't stop talking the whole time we were together. It's like she was reciting a travel guide."

Hayden chuckled. "She was so excited you were coming that she read up about Houston. She figured she'd be spending the most time with you."

Sean looked shocked. "Really?"

"Yeah. The Flanagan sisters were more excited about meeting you than they were about their weddings."

He shook his head and pushed a wine glass across to Hayden. "That's nuts."

"That's the Flanagans," Hayden corrected him, taking a sip of his wine. "Weren't you excited about meeting them?"

"More like terrified," Sean said, taking the first dish out of the microwave. "I nearly didn't leave the airport terminal."

Hayden frowned. "Why not?"

"I was worried I'd disappoint them, or they'd disappoint me.

86

I didn't let myself hope that they were really as nice as they seemed online."

Wasn't that a sad indication of the level of Sean's self-confidence? Had he spent his whole life hiding away from the world, not letting anyone get close to him?

"They *are* as nice as they seem," Hayden told him, reaching for a plate and piling some red curry on it.

Sean smiled but didn't comment as he put the rice on the counter and heated the stir fry.

Hayden wanted to know more about Sean. "Tell me about life in Ireland. You live in a small town?"

"Yeah. Working in a pub means I know most of the people."

"What do you do in your spare time?"

"Not much. Read or play the tin whistle."

"So why the tin whistle?"

"We had to learn it during music class at primary school and it was cheap enough that Mam could afford to buy me one."

"Play any sports?"

"Nah, Mam couldn't afford it."

How poor had Sean's mother been? "What about friends?"

"I didn't have any. We didn't have the money for me to do after-school activities, and none of the parents wanted their children hanging around with me." Sean shrugged. "Besides, I had to cook dinner, so there wasn't much time for playing." He sat down next to Hayden and started dishing up his own food.

Hayden paused. He'd actually been referring to current friends, but this was a glimpse into Sean's past, and he wanted more. "Why did you have to cook dinner?"

"Mam had two jobs. She'd eat at work and so I had to get my own food and keep the house tidy."

Hayden frowned. "How old were you when you started cooking dinner?"

Sean thought about it. "About six, I guess. At that age, I'd heat up some baked beans or make toast."

Sean didn't seem to think there was anything odd about it, so Hayden fought to keep his surprise hidden. "Wasn't there anyone you could go to?"

"No. It wasn't so bad. When Mam was at home, she'd be tired and I had to be quiet, so it was better when she wasn't there. I'd be in bed before she finished work, so it was just in the mornings and Sundays at church that I had to be careful not to bother her."

It sounded like a horribly lonely existence. No wonder he was so anxious about coming out to his sisters, so anxious about everything. He'd never had any affection at all. Before Hayden could ask more, Sean asked, "Do you have any siblings?"

"Two sisters and a brother."

"It must have been nice having someone to play with."

Hayden smiled. "Most of the time. There were days when we'd fight and Mom would send us outside to sort out our differences."

"Are you close?"

He nodded. "They all still live around Houston so we get together about once a month and I call them regularly."

"They never had an issue with you being gay?" Sean sipped his wine.

"No. I think they knew from an early age. My sisters and I would fight over the posters of male celebrities in the teen magazines and my brother got all the female ones." He laughed at the memory.

Sean's lips twitched.

"My parents were always supportive."

"That must have been nice," Sean said. He got to his feet. "Do you want any more food?"

"No, thanks." He helped Sean clean up and they walked over to the sofa where McClane was sprawled.

"I should take McClane for a walk," Sean said. "Do you want to come?"

Hayden glanced at his outfit. "Got a spare pair of shoes?"

"Yeah, you can check if they fit."

They were a bit on the large size, but they would do for a short walk. Sean grabbed McClane's leash, called for the dog and they headed downstairs.

The evening was still warm and the pavement was empty. This part of town didn't have the same amount of foot traffic in the evening as it did during the day. Hayden directed Sean around the block to where there was a small park. A few other people were walking their dogs as well.

Sean was silent, but he looked content, relaxed. Hayden debated holding his hand as they walked, but he didn't want to stress Sean out. Maybe they would get to a stage where Sean would be happy to be openly gay in public, but Hayden doubted it. He wished he didn't care so much. Sean was only in Houston until Bridget's wedding — a little less than five weeks away. That was enough time to have some fun, but Hayden had sworn to himself that he wouldn't date anyone who was in the closet again.

At first he'd been thinking about Sean purely in terms of sex, but seeing him at the baseball with the kids and talking to him afterward showed a whole other side to Sean. He liked Sean — a whole lot.

"Are we going to the shelter tomorrow?" Sean asked as they turned to head back to the apartment.

He'd forgotten Sean had promised the kids he'd visit them. He grinned, pleased he had an excuse to see Sean again. "Yeah. I'll pick you up on my way home from work. You can bring McClane if you like. The kids will love him."

"Thanks, I will."

Hayden shouldn't be worried. Five weeks wasn't really dating, it was more like a holiday fling. It didn't matter that Sean wasn't out because it wasn't going to last.

He ignored the tiny part of him that asked if he could be happy with that.

***

The next morning, Hayden was gone well before Zita arrived. Sean had loaned him his one business shirt, so Hayden didn't have to wear the same shirt for two days in a row. Then he'd gone through the house to make sure all evidence of Hayden being there was gone. All the dishes were done and put away, there were no clothes left lying around and he plumped the cushions on the sofa just in case two indentations could be seen. His phone rang. Zita.

"I'm running late," she said. "Can you meet me downstairs in ten minutes?"

"Sure." He hung up and checked the apartment one last time, before calling McClane and heading downstairs.

At Casa Flanagan, McClane greeted Zita's dogs with enthusiasm.

The day was muggy and hot, and all the girls were sprawled in the living room under the air conditioning watching television or reading books. Some were still in their pajamas. Summer vacation had never looked like this for Sean. Sure, the temperature never got as hot in Ireland, but his mother would leave him lists of things he had to do around the house each day. When he got old enough, he also took odd jobs like weeding and lawn mowing. He managed to hide some of the money he earned from his mother, but most of it was handed over to her each week to help with living expenses.

"Where's Mama?" Zita asked the girls.

"In the garden," Beatriz answered.

Zita stopped in the kitchen to fill up a bottle of water and then Sean followed her out into the beautiful garden. Carmen was in the vegetable patch, a huge straw hat on her head. Her bucket was full of weeds so she must have been at it for some time. Zita handed her the bottle. "*Hola.*"

"*Mis hijos,*" Carmen said. "Is it that time already?" She took a long sip from the bottle.

"Do you want a hand?" Sean asked.

"No. I am finished for the day." She took her hat off and wiped her brow. "Let's go inside where it's cooler." She picked up her bucket and threw its contents in a large bin near the gardening shed. Then she put her tools away and accompanied them inside. Zita put the kettle on.

"Did you have fun yesterday?" Carmen asked Sean.

"Yes. Zita's a great tour guide."

Zita laughed. "I think I wore him out."

"You did," Sean admitted.

"We do not need to do salsa lessons today if you're tired," Carmen said.

"I'd like to. I slept well last night."

"Carly's got comfortable beds, doesn't she?" Zita asked.

He nodded. There was no way he was going to tell her the real reason he slept so well. His body warmed thinking about Hayden.

"Have you done much formal dancing?" Zita asked.

"None." His mother would have never approved.

"You're a natural then," Carmen said. "Your salsa moves were perfect."

"Have you been dancing long?" Sean asked.

"All my life," Carmen said. "I did traditional dance when I was a girl, and when we moved here I learned Latin dance from some of the migrants. Music makes all your problems disappear, if only for a short time."

He was curious about their life after his father died. Sean hesitated for a moment before asking, "How hard was it when you first moved to Houston?"

She took the mug of coffee Zita handed her and sighed. "Any move is difficult. I was not expecting to migrate without Brendan, and so my English was not so good. I will admit that for the first year I lived on government handouts, too caught up in my grief to take care of my girls. Carly took care of her sisters, but it was a hard burden for her at only eight years old."

Sean was intrigued. He wouldn't have thought Carmen would give up.

"The world was scary and foreign, and anytime I went out I came back frustrated at my inability to communicate. I felt so stupid." Carmen's smile was sad. "But Carly kept pestering me to learn English and suddenly I realized almost a year had gone by. My Carly had been taking care of us for that whole time." She shook her head. "I found a job in a plant nursery, and I worked hard, determined to show them they had made the right choice. I practiced my English with customers and co-workers and I learned everything they could teach me." She took a sip of her drink. "I loved that job."

He smiled. "When you do something you love, it's not work."

She nodded. "That's right. Do you love what you do?"

He sat back. "The folk are nice. It's not hard pouring drinks for a living."

"Is that all you do?"

"I order stock and do accounts as well."

"That can be tricky, knowing how much to buy," Carmen said.

"The bar's predictable. There are a few days a year like Saint

Patrick's Day when orders need to increase, but day-to-day it's all the same. The guys come in for their pint or two and a yarn each day as regular as clockwork."

"How interesting. Do they order the same thing?"

He nodded. "I could probably recite the whole night's drinks if you wanted me to."

"Is it boring?"

Sean thought about it for a moment. "No, it's comforting. Nothing changes, there are no surprises." He frowned. Is that what he wanted out of life — no surprises?

"Some people underrate the comfort of routine because they have never known anything different," she said. "Life can change in an instant." She got to her feet. "Let me freshen up and then we will dance." She left the room.

Sean sat there, sipping his tea. Zita slung an arm around him. "Our life certainly changed when I found you," she said. "One of my best days ever."

His chest expanded and he couldn't speak. He nodded.

"Come on." She slid off her stool and took his hand. "We need to make a dance floor."

She dragged him into the living room where the television program was finishing. "It's salsa time."

A couple of the girls groaned and headed upstairs, but Beatriz, Elena and Alejandra got up and helped push the furniture back to make room. Zita went over to the stereo and flicked through the playlists to find the right music as Carmen walked back in.

"There are only a few steps you need to begin," Carmen said, standing in the middle of the room. "Forward one step, back to the middle and then back one step and return." She demonstrated the move and they lined up behind her to practice. Sean remembered the step, so he helped Elena, who was having difficulty.

"When you have the steps, add a bit of hip movement," Carmen said, wiggling her hips in emphasis.

Sean copied her and she pressed play on the stereo.

The music was upbeat, and Sean moved his hips in time with it. Then Carmen counted them in and they began to dance. He closed his eyes to feel the rhythm and moved his feet in the steps Carmen had taught him.

He loved to dance. Every fiber in his body shimmied to the beat as the music flowed through him. Music was his escape. Opening his eyes, he smiled at Carmen. She nodded with approval and came over to take his hand.

"To turn with your partner, you adjust your feet like this." She showed what she meant.

He gave it a go, pleased when he got the footwork right.

Carmen grinned. "In this, you do not take after your father," she said. "While he had the enthusiasm, he had no rhythm."

He absorbed the information. All of these little tidbits he was learning about his father were slowly giving him a picture of the kind of man he had been. The picture was bittersweet.

Carmen stopped the music and taught them more steps. Sean took turns dancing with everyone, delighting in their enthusiasm and their eagerness to dance with him.

After a couple of hours, Carmen called a halt. "It is time for lunch."

Sean went to the bathroom to wash up before going into the kitchen. Carmen was rolling out some dough on the bench. "Can I help?" he asked.

"We are having pizza," she said. "You can get the toppings out of the fridge."

He pulled out various things which could work on the pizza — cheese, olives, ham, salami, pineapple, onion.

Carmen nodded her approval as she divided the dough onto various pizza trays. "You can chop it up."

He found the cutting board in one of the cupboards and grabbed a knife from the knife block. He felt so at ease here, almost part of the family. Zita came in from the garden carrying some herbs and tomatoes.

"I'm starving," Zita said.

"The dancing has given me an appetite," Sean agreed.

"Are you eating properly?" Carmen asked. "Did Carly leave you enough food before she left?"

Sean chuckled at her concern. "Yes, Carmen. There's plenty of food, and if it runs out, I can find a supermarket."

"Tell me if you need more food. I can buy it for you."

"Thank you, but it's not necessary." But damn if it didn't feel good that she wanted to take care of him.

"Call me if you need anything," Carmen insisted. "What are you having for dinner tonight?"

"I'm not sure yet." If Hayden was picking him up after work, they might have dinner together.

"You can come to our place," Zita said. "There's always plenty."

He couldn't use McClane as an excuse today, not when the dog was happily sprawled across the floor having his belly rubbed by Beatriz. But he wasn't sure what their reaction to Hayden would be. "I, ah, promised the kids from the shelter that I'd visit them again tonight with Hayden. He goes every Tuesday," he said. "They want to hear about Ireland."

"That's so nice of you," Zita said.

"This is the homeless shelter?" Carmen asked.

He nodded.

"You were going to bring the pregnant girl to see me."

"I'll hopefully see her tonight," he said.

"What's this?" Zita asked as she chopped up the tomatoes.

Sean told her about Angela and she pursed her lips.

"Mama, maybe we can help. When the weddings are over, we won't need the cottages for accommodation and perhaps we can give these kids somewhere safe to stay."

"Doesn't Casa Flanagan just help migrants?" Sean asked.

"That's our core goal, but there's no reason why we can't expand. It's still a couple of years before any of the girls will be old enough to use the cottages. There's no point in them sitting empty."

Carmen nodded. "We can talk with Hayden when we see him next."

Sean looked at the two of them. They didn't even hesitate to offer to help. It was incredibly generous. "Thank you."

Zita smiled. "*De nada.* Helping people is what we do."

***

Hayden's pulse quickened as he knocked on the door of Carly's apartment just after five. Sean opened it, looking entirely delectable in fitted black shorts and a T-shirt that hugged his chest. "Hi." Hayden pulled Sean close, kissing him hard. There was something about the man that was addictive. Sean dragged him inside and shut the door behind him. The bang of the door made Hayden step back. He couldn't get caught up — they had to go to the shelter.

The intensity in Sean's gaze almost made Hayden forget his good intentions. He forced himself to walk into the living area. "How was your day?"

"Great. Carmen taught me to salsa."

The image of Sean dancing made him hard. He needed to get a grip. Quickly he dug into his satchel and drew out the gift. "The photographer from Carly's wedding put up a couple of photos online," he said, giving him the photo frame. "So I called her and bought this one for you."

Sean stared at him for a long moment, the surprise clear, before glancing down at the photo. It was Sean with his sisters and they were all laughing. Hayden had to buy it as soon as he'd seen it. It was gorgeous, so full of fun.

Sean's eyes glistened. "Thank you."

Hayden ran a hand over his arm and kissed him quickly. "You're most welcome. Why don't you put it in your room and we'll get going?"

Sean nodded.

It killed Hayden that Sean seemed surprised by every small bit of kindness he was shown. Sean's mother deserved to rot in hell.

When they arrived at the shelter, McClane was a big hit. Hayden introduced Sean and the dog to the kids he knew and then went over to Alberto. "Am I in the usual room?"

"Yeah. There are five kids who want you to review their job applications."

"Great."

Sean walked up. "Is Angela around?"

Alberto shook his head. "She ran into a girl she knew from school and they've gone to the movies."

"Damn."

"What's wrong?" Hayden asked.

"I wanted to talk to her about Casa Flanagan. Carmen wants to meet her, said she might have somewhere Angela can stay."

Hayden raised his eyebrows. "Where?"

"In one of the cottages out the back. They'll be empty after the weddings."

"What's this?" Alberto asked.

Hayden explained about Casa Flanagan. "Carmen has had a few pregnant teenagers over the years. It would be perfect for Angela." He should have thought of it himself. It was nice that Sean had.

"I'll tell her," Alberto said.

Gil wandered over to the group. "Any news?" he asked Hayden casually.

Hayden swallowed his smile. Gil had met him at Comunidad the day before and they'd gone through his resume before Hayden had taken him to the tech floor to be assessed. The developer had been impressed by Gil's skills and wanted to hire him right away, but HR had to be notified. Hayden had called in a couple of favors to get everything processed quickly. He reached into his satchel and pulled out an envelope. "I've got this for you."

Gil's eyes widened as he took it and ripped it open. "It's an employment contract," he breathed.

Hayden nodded. "You can start as soon as you sign it."

Gil whooped. "Give me a pen!"

Hayden grinned, but stopped Alberto from giving Gil a pen. "You've been to one of my sessions. You know you need to read everything to make sure you understand and agree with it."

Gil swore. "Are you saying Comunidad aren't trustworthy?"

"No. I'm saying you need to get into the habit of checking paperwork before you sign, no matter how excited you are. So sit down, read through it and tell me if you've got any questions." He'd checked the contract himself, but it was good for the teenager to do so as well.

"All right." Gil moved away.

"Good advice," Alberto said. "I should go to one of your sessions." He laughed.

Hayden smiled. "I'm doing one now." He turned to Sean. "Want to come?"

"Sure."

Hayden walked into the small meeting room where he

helped the kids put together job applications. "Take a seat," he said to Sean.

"What's this session about?" Sean asked.

"Most of the kids are looking for work, so I check their applications against the wanted ads and help them improve it if I can. But first I give a general information session about some aspect of searching for work."

When they had all arrived, Hayden began his talk. Today was about the importance of behaving professionally. He fielded questions and then reviewed the applications. The final person was Bruno. Once again, he was dressed in the latest fashion, each piece stylishly mixed together and Hayden didn't dare ask where he'd got the clothes from.

"I shouldn't bother," Bruno grumbled. "No one's going to give me a job."

"Why not?" Sean asked.

"I'm black, I'm gay and I'm homeless." Bruno gave him a *duh* look.

"Hey, I'm black and gay and have a great job," Hayden said. "So, what do you want to do?"

Bruno shrugged.

"Come on, man. Work with me," Hayden said. "Where do you want to be in five years' time?"

"Not dead."

Hayden wanted to sigh. Before he could say anything, Sean said, "That's a good start. Do you want to have somewhere to live?"

Bruno stared at him. "Of course."

"What about a job?"

"Well, yeah."

"Think you'd be good at selling stuff?" Sean continued.

"Maybe." Bruno pursed his lips.

Hayden sat back and smiled. Sean was getting through to Bruno.

"What area — clothes?"

Bruno sat a little straighter. "I know what looks good."

It was true. Bruno had a great sense of style.

"So maybe you could target clothing shops." Sean glanced at Hayden. "Can he drop off his resume at different places?"

Hayden smiled. "He sure can. I bet you'd be great at matching clothes together and showing customers what to buy. Maybe you can prove yourself by helping a customer when you leave your resume."

Bruno nodded. "I can do that." He smiled. "Thanks, man." He held out his hand for Sean to shake.

"No problem."

Bruno left the room. "You're a natural," Hayden said.

"I remember what it was like," Sean said. "How hopeless it all felt."

That was the one thing Hayden couldn't relate to. He squeezed Sean's hand. "Come on, the next group is in the living room." He gestured for Sean to follow him.

In one corner of the living room, half a dozen teenaged guys were lounging on the sofas, chatting to each other. Bruno had already wandered over and there were several other guys that Hayden had met before.

"What's up?" Deon greeted them both and slapped their hands.

"Who's that?" one of the guys asked, nodding at Sean.

"Sean's a friend from Ireland," Hayden said. "I thought you might like to hear his story."

"You gay too?" he asked.

Sean nodded. "My mam kicked me out of home when I was fifteen."

"Tough break," Bruno said. "How'd you get by?"

Sean told his story. Hayden took note of the questions the kids asked and kept an eye on Sean to make sure he wasn't anxious. But he didn't seem to be at all concerned about telling his story.

"What did you do about the perverts?" Deon asked.

Hayden frowned. "Perverts?"

"The old guys who offer you a twenty to suck them off."

Hayden's mouth dropped open. "That happens to you?"

All of the boys nodded as if it was no big deal.

"Why didn't you say something?"

"Whatcha going to do?" Bruno asked. "It's not like they hang around after they're done."

"Do you use protection?"

"They pay more if we do it bare," Deon said.

Hayden shook his head. "Guys, all sorts of diseases can be transmitted that way, including HIV. You've got to be careful."

"Sometimes you gotta do what you can to survive," Sean said quietly.

Hayden glanced at him. "What?"

"If it's a choice between eating and a place to stay, against the risk of a disease, sometimes you have to take the risk."

"You did it?" Hayden asked.

Sean shrugged, but didn't meet his gaze. "The farmer who took me in occasionally wanted extra payment. At least I was off the streets."

This was bullshit. He hated that these kids had to go through this, hated that Sean had had it bad as well. He was grateful his parents had been so supportive.

The discussion continued and Sean gave the boys advice. Hayden could see the hope come into the kids' eyes. When they finished the session the boys got up and headed for other areas of the shelter.

Sean looked at Hayden. "Are you disgusted?"

Hayden frowned. "About what?"

"About what I had to do to get by."

"Of course not." He pulled him close. "If anything, I'm furious at your mother, and all these kids' parents who haven't protected them when they should have. It's not right."

"No, but sometimes you don't get a choice."

Hayden knew that, but it didn't mean he had to like it. He wanted to give these kids a better choice.

***

The rest of the week settled into a nice rhythm. Sean spent his days hanging out with Zita or at Casa Flanagan, and he spent his evenings with Hayden.

Zita and Carmen were so enthusiastic. Sean explored Houston with them or spent time listening to stories about their lives.

For the first time in his life, he had family and Casa Flanagan began to feel like a home. He was one of the kids, and Carmen sent him out to the garden to pick vegetables for lunch or asked him to fix something that was broken. He was given tasks to do like anyone else who was living there.

He was happy.

And then there was Hayden. And wasn't that the icing on the cake? He was having a holiday romance, and it was absolutely exhilarating. They spent most of their evenings at Carly's apartment because Sean didn't want to risk being seen.

He kept the two sides of his life quite separate. Zita and Carmen realized he needed time to himself, and they didn't argue when he said it was time for him to go home.

They didn't know he was seeing Hayden every night.

On Friday evening, Hayden came over to Carly's apartment to collect all the things he'd left there over the past week. Carly and Evan were due home early on Saturday morning. Sean almost hoped the current hurricane warning would turn into a do not fly, and he'd get another night with Hayden while Carly and Evan waited it out in safety.

Sean scanned the living room, checking for anything that might reveal Hayden had been here. Together they had cleaned the kitchen, vacuumed and tidied the living room and made sure the sheets in both bedrooms were clean. Hayden even sprinkled rose petals over Carly and Evan's bed to welcome them home.

He was such a sweetheart. Always adding those little touches to show how much he cared.

Now it was almost ten. "I should go," Hayden said.

He was right, but Sean didn't want him to. What was he going to do now? He wouldn't be able to spend any more nights with Hayden. Tomorrow he was moving to Casa Flanagan to give Carly and Evan some space to enjoy their wedded bliss. There was no way he'd be able to sneak Hayden in. No way he could risk it. "Don't go yet."

"Honey, if you won't tell your family about us, I have to."

His heart convulsed. He didn't want that. The thought of seeing Hayden and not being able to touch him or be himself with him was painful. He'd grown used to it.

But he still couldn't tell anyone. He wanted to — he *really* wanted to — but the fear of rejection was ever present.

"One last time." He drew Hayden to him and kissed him as if it really was the last time. His insides squeezed together and the pain was sharp. He needed to block it out, needed to just feel Hayden.

Sean backed him down the corridor toward the bedroom, stripping off his own shirt and then Hayden's, touching him, trying to imprint the feel of Hayden's skin, the taste of his lips on his mind forever.

Tears sprang to his eyes, but he blinked them away. He wanted passion, not sorrow.

They bumped through the bedroom door and Sean pushed him onto the bed before stripping off his shoes and shorts. Hayden was doing the same, his eyes full of lust.

He needed him. One last time.

It was fast, frantic, rough. When they were done, Sean collapsed on the bed.

"Wow," Hayden said, breathing heavily. He reached for the tissue box. "We shouldn't have bothered changing the sheets."

Sean couldn't laugh. He wanted to gather Hayden close and hold on to him. He couldn't speak. He cleaned himself and then gave into the urge and pulled Hayden against him, holding him tightly.

"Hey, it's all right, honey." Hayden kissed him, running a hand across his chest.

"I'm not ready for this to end," Sean said, his throat sore.

"It doesn't have to."

He shook his head. In an ideal world, Hayden was right, but the world Sean lived in had never been ideal. He got up, not able to look at Hayden, and pulled his shorts back on.

It was then Sean heard voices.

Fuck. Carly and Evan weren't due home for another couple of hours. Who the hell was it? He searched for his shirt and then realized he'd stripped it off in the hallway.

Along with Hayden's.

He raced out, his heart pounding.

"Hi, McClane. Did you miss us?" Evan's voice, but Sean couldn't see him from the corridor. He bent to grab Hayden's shirt as Carly came into view.

"Sean, there you are."

He couldn't say anything. His brain was too frenzied to think clearly.

Carly's eyes fell to the other shirt on the floor and then seemed to notice Sean's half-dressed state. "Oh. I should have called to tell you we were catching the earlier flight because of the hurricane warning. I didn't want to risk missing Zita's bachelorette party."

"Sean, honey. What's wrong?" Hayden's voice and then a moment later. "Oh, shit."

Carly's mouth dropped open as she glanced between Sean and Hayden.

No. This couldn't be happening. This was his worst nightmare. His heart thudded a death toll in his chest. He didn't wait for the revulsion on her face. Somehow, he got his body moving, and he spun around and ran back into his bedroom.

"Ah, hi Carly," Hayden said behind him.

Sean blocked out the voices. This was it. This was where he would be kicked out. They'd tell him they didn't want to see him again.

He pulled on a T-shirt and dragged his backpack out from under the bed. He wasn't going to wait for the abuse. Quickly he pulled his clothes out of the drawers and stuffed them in, tears pouring out of his eyes, making it difficult to see. He'd ruined it all. If he hadn't been so greedy to have Hayden one last time… His stomach swirled. He was going to be sick.

He raced out of the bedroom, pushing past Hayden to vomit in the toilet. He heaved, his body convulsing as it tried to deal with the rejection.

"Sean, it's all right," Hayden said.

He shook his head, panting to get some air into his head. He was dizzy. He didn't have time to be weak. He had to get out of here before Carly demanded he leave.

Pushing himself to his feet, he wiped his mouth with the back of his hand and went into the bathroom to throw his things into the toiletry bag.

"What are you doing?" Hayden asked.

"Packing." He strode back into the bedroom and added the bag to his backpack. What was he missing? His eye caught the photograph Hayden had given him. His first family photo.

His heart spasmed. He would lose them all.

The strength left his legs and he slid down the bed and onto

the floor.
  He sobbed.

Chapter 10

"Honey, it's all right." Hayden's heart hurt at the despair on Sean's face.

There was no response.

"Sean?" He stepped forward, put his hand on Sean's shoulder. Sean shrugged it off as he threw more clothes into his backpack. Then he reached for the photograph Hayden had given him and wordlessly crumpled to the floor. "Sean!" Hayden shook him, but Sean was in full meltdown mode, sobbing, not acknowledging Hayden at all. Hayden hurried into the living room where Carly and Evan were.

"I'm sorry, Hayden. I had no idea you and Sean were together," Carly said.

"Don't worry about it." Sure, it was embarrassing that his friend and boss had caught him in an awkward situation, but it could have been a hell of a lot worse. They could have arrived five minutes earlier. "You need to talk with Sean."

"Is he all right?"

"No. He's completely freaking out, now that you know he's gay." Hayden paced, unable to sit still. The vision of Sean crumpling to the floor tore at his heart.

"Why?"

"Because he's sure you're going to throw him out."

She frowned. "But I don't care."

Hayden went over and took her arm. "You need to tell him that. Please. Before he's sick again."

"Of course."

She strode down the corridor to Sean's bedroom. Hayden

followed her, standing at the doorway to give them some space. Sean was sobbing, his knees pulled up and his head buried in his hands. Hayden ached for him.

Carly glanced around the room. "Why are you packing?"

There was no response.

Carly sat on the floor next to Sean and put a hand on his shoulder. "Sean, what's wrong?" Gently she lifted his head.

"What's wrong?" He stared at her as if she had grown another head. "I'm *gay*."

"Yeah, I figured that out," she said with a laugh. "So what's wrong?"

He shook his head. "I'm gay."

"So you said. I don't care if you're gay. I want to know why you're packing and why you're so upset."

He blinked, glanced at Hayden, obviously confused.

"Sean packed because he thinks you won't want him here because he's gay," Hayden said.

"But that's silly. I don't care who you sleep with. You're my brother. I love you."

Sean's eyes widened. "You love me?"

"Of course I do." She hugged him, holding him tight. "Your sexuality doesn't change how I feel about you," she assured him. Then she glanced up at Hayden and smiled. "Can I say that you have excellent taste in men?"

Hayden smiled at her, forming his hands into a heart so she could see how much it meant to him.

Sean sniffed, wiped his eyes. "Don't you think I'm an abomination? Don't you think it's a sin?"

She frowned. "Not at all."

"You really don't care?" The hope on his face was so tentative.

Hayden wanted to hunt down his mother and every other person who had been cruel to Sean in the past and slap them.

"No."

"What about Evan?"

"He won't care either. Neither will Mama or Zita or Bridget."

The sob that came out of Sean broke Hayden's heart. Sean buried himself into Carly's shoulder and cried.

Hayden let out a sigh of relief and left them. It would take Sean a bit of time to recover and he might want the privacy. He returned to the kitchen where Evan had the kettle on.

"Is everything all right?" Evan asked.

"It will be," Hayden said. "Sean's been terrified of you all finding out that he's gay. Worried you would reject him."

"He doesn't know the Flanagans very well then."

"No. He doesn't have faith in many people. His past has taught him that."

"So you've gotten to know him while we've been away?"

Hayden nodded. Was Evan going to judge him?

"I'm glad." Evan sighed. "I probably didn't help matters. When he first arrived, I asked him if he had a girlfriend. I was making conversation."

"It's a reasonable question," Hayden said. "Though next time you could ask if he was seeing someone — keep it open just in case."

"I'll keep it in mind. Want a drink?"

"Got any whiskey?" Sean could probably do with a shot of it in his tea.

"Yeah, there's a bottle around here somewhere." By the time he'd found it, Carly had returned.

"How is he?" Hayden asked.

"Exhausted. He's going to freshen up and then come out."

Hayden wanted to go to him, but he resisted. He didn't want to crowd Sean. It was going to take him some time to get used to being out.

The selfish part of him was relieved. He was tired of sneaking around, he wanted to tell everyone he and Sean were dating. Even though their relationship wasn't going to last long, he wanted to enjoy it in full for the whole time Sean was here. Now he didn't have to worry about accidentally touching him, or showing his attraction. He could be himself again.

"Are you going to tell your sisters?" he asked.

"Sean will. They're all coming around tomorrow to look at our honeymoon photos anyway, so it will be a good opportunity."

"They're not going to care, are they?" He was almost one hundred percent sure, but the thought of Sean being devastated again wasn't one Hayden wanted to think about.

"Of course not."

Sean walked out, gave a cautious smile to Evan.

"Feeling better?" Evan asked.

"Yeah. Thanks."

Hayden grabbed the tea he'd made Sean and took it over to him. "I put a bit of whiskey in it." He rubbed his hand against Sean's back.

Sean flinched, eyes wide, and then relaxed. "Sorry. Habit." He moved back and took the mug from Hayden.

Hayden pushed aside the hurt at Sean's reaction. He smiled and gestured to the sofa. "Why don't you take a seat?" He grabbed his drink from the bench and sat next to Sean, putting his arm around Sean's shoulder.

Carly and Evan sat across from them.

"So how was the honeymoon?" Hayden asked.

"Wonderful," Carly said. "I'm so relaxed. Was everything all right at work?"

"No work talk until Monday," Hayden said. Seeing the expression of concern on Carly's face, he relented. "Everything is fine though."

She smiled. "So what have you been up to?" She screwed up her face. "That is, I mean, what have you been doing when you've not been…"

Hayden laughed and even Sean cracked a smile. "Sean and I took some of the homeless teens to the baseball and we went to the shelter on Tuesday to help out."

"That's great. It's such a worthwhile cause."

"Zita's been showing me around Houston," Sean said. "I swear she knows half of the people who live here."

Evan smiled. "That's Zita. She adopted me when I moved next door."

"Oh, and we've been getting things ready for Bridget's wedding," Sean said.

"That's great. I want to hear all about it." Carly yawned. "But maybe we can wait until tomorrow. I'm tired. Do you mind if we head to bed?"

Hayden let Sean answer.

"Not at all."

"All right. I'll see you both in the morning." She kissed them on their cheeks and then she and Evan went into their bedroom. "Oh my! Thank you!" she called, obviously seeing the rose petals.

"You're welcome," Hayden called back.

The door shut behind him and Hayden turned to Sean. "How are you feeling?"

Sean placed his mug on the coffee table. "I'm a little shell-shocked. I keep thinking I'm going to wake up to find this was a dream."

"It's not." He squeezed Sean's leg. "They really do love you and accept you."

Tears welled up in Sean's eyes again and he brushed them away impatiently. "I'm tired." He hesitated, glancing at the closed bedroom door. "Do you want to stay the night?"

Hayden felt as if he'd won the lottery. "I'd love to."

He followed Sean back to his bedroom and curled up next to him. Everything was going to be all right.

***

Sean woke on Saturday morning and rolled over, drawing Hayden close to him. Then he tensed. He was at Carly's place and last night Carly had come home early, had discovered he was gay.

And she'd been perfectly fine with it.

He couldn't quite believe it, but he knew it had to be true because Hayden was sleeping next to him still. Slowly, he relaxed as Hayden turned to him and kissed him. "Morning, honey."

He went gooey at the endearment and at waking up to the man who'd changed his life in two short weeks. "Good morning."

Hayden stretched. "What time is it?"

"I don't care."

"Isn't the rest of the family coming for lunch?" Hayden asked.

With those simple words, Sean's peace was broken. They were and there was a chance they wouldn't be as accepting as Carly. He checked the time. Ten o'clock. "We should get up."

"There's still a bit of time," Hayden said, running his hand down to Sean's penis which was very happy to see him.

Sean twitched, but firmly moved Hayden's hand away. "I'm not getting up to anything with my sister in the next room."

Hayden pouted. "It's not really the next room. There are a few rooms between us. Besides, she's probably getting busy herself."

"Ew." Sean laughed and got out of bed to resist the temptation. "Do you want to take the first shower?"

"We could share."

Sean shook his head. "I'm not ready."

The teasing expression on Hayden's face vanished. "Of course." He grabbed a change of clothes. "I won't take long."

Sean let out a breath. He had to be careful not to get too carried away. Sure, Carly might not care about his sexuality, but he had to be respectful while he was in her home. She might not appreciate him showering with Hayden, she might not have appreciated it if Hayden had been female either. He didn't know. He'd assumed she had no problem with Hayden staying the night when she'd said she'd see both of them tomorrow. At least he hoped that's what she'd meant.

Maybe she hadn't.

His skin prickled and he focused on his breathing to prevent the anxiety from taking hold. It was too late now. When his pulse rate was back to normal, he got some clothes out of his backpack.

Hayden came back in, looking fresh and delicious. "Your turn."

Sean hurried past him into the bathroom. It didn't take long to shower and change and Hayden was waiting for him in the bedroom.

"Are you ready?" Hayden asked.

Sean nodded. It was just Carly and Evan.

They walked out into the living room, and Sean was two steps into the room before he saw Bridget and Jack greeting Carly. He stopped and Hayden bumped into him.

Bridget turned and said, "Morning Sean." Then she spotted Hayden. "Hi, Hayden. What are you doing here?"

Carly hadn't told her. *Feck.* That meant he had to say

something, and fast. The silence was dragging on. Hayden slipped his hand into Sean's and it gave him strength. "Um, Hayden's with me."

Bridget's eyes widened. "Oh, I didn't realize. Sorry." Then she slapped her hand over her mouth. "I didn't mean I'm sorry you're dating, I meant I'm sorry I didn't realize you were gay." She winced. "Sorry. I'll shut up now."

At his sister's obvious mortification the tension left him. He laughed. "It's fine." He glanced at Jack, but he looked back as if it was no big deal.

"The coffee's on," Carly said.

"Great." Feeling a little more confident, he and Hayden walked hand in hand into the kitchen.

"You OK?" Hayden asked.

"Yeah. You?" He kissed Hayden's hand, then let go.

"Yes."

Sean made them both drinks and they carried them into the living room where the others were chatting. He sat next to Hayden on the chaise lounge.

"I've been feeling so guilty for not being able to catch up with you this week," Bridget said. "Work had a shutdown, and I had to be there."

"It's all right, Bridge. I've kept him busy," Hayden said and winked.

Sean stiffened, but Bridget laughed. "Good, I'm glad."

He relaxed again. Maybe everything was going to be all right.

Someone knocked on the door and Evan got up to answer it.

Hayden bent his head close to Sean's ear and whispered, "I'm here for you." He pressed a kiss against his cheek.

"I knew it!" Zita's voice was like a gunshot and Sean leaped away from Hayden. He looked up to find her grinning at the two of them. "I knew there was something going on with you two."

Sean glanced at Hayden, not sure how to respond.

Zita took a step back. "There *is* something going on between you two, right?"

He nodded. "We're…"

"Dating," Hayden supplied.

"I thought so."

"How?" Sean asked. They'd been so careful and she hadn't said a thing.

Zita greeted the others and she and David sat down on the couch across from them. "Well, when Hayden picked you up last week, he seemed annoyed when I answered the door," she said. "Then he called to say you were staying at his place that night because you were going out partying." She ticked off two items on her fingers. "Then neither of you could tell me what you did that night and Hayden knew how you liked your tea."

"My tea?"

"Yeah. When you were in the shower, Hayden made you a black tea. He didn't need to ask how you liked it. So you must have had tea some other time together." She grinned, obviously pleased with herself. She clapped her hands together and got up and gave them both a hug. "I'm so happy for you."

Sean couldn't quite keep up. "So you don't care?"

"Of course not. Why would I?"

He shrugged. He didn't want to go into his past.

There was another knock on the door.

Carmen.

Bridget got up to answer as Zita asked Carly, "How was the honeymoon?"

Sean let out a shaky breath.

"It's going to be fine," Hayden said quietly.

Carmen walked into the room. "*Mis bebes!*" she cried and hugged her daughters and their partners. Then she turned to where Sean was still sitting with Hayden, waiting to be noticed.

She paused, arms out wide.

"Carmen, I'm gay." His tone was far harsher than he'd intended.

Carmen glanced between Sean and Hayden and Hayden squeezed Sean's hand. She shrieked and Sean flinched, but before he could move, she'd smothered the pair of them in a hug. "Yes! I have been trying to figure out how I can get this boy into my family, but he won't have any of my girls." She squeezed them again. "But he can have my boy!" She laughed with joy.

Sean sucked in a breath as his head went light. Carmen

kissed his cheek and then Hayden's.

"You can stay here in Houston and marry Hayden."

Sean shook his head, not quite believing what he was hearing. She wanted him to stay in Houston?

"Slow down, Carmen," Hayden said. "We're dating. Don't scare him with talk of commitment."

"Of course. My mistake." She mimed zipping her lips. She squeezed both of their hands and then turned to the others who were watching with varying degrees of amusement. "I want photos of the honeymoon."

***

Carly hooked up their camera to her television while Sean's thoughts raced. Carmen wanted him to stay in Houston, she was excited and *happy* he was gay. He pinched himself to make sure he wasn't dreaming.

"It's real," Hayden said with a laugh.

Sean slid his hand into Hayden's, amazed he could do this now, and no one was bothered by the gesture. In fact, each person was holding hands with their significant other. They didn't care he was gay. Never in his wildest dreams...

"What's going on in that head of yours?" Hayden murmured.

"Disbelief, shock, surprise."

"Happy?"

Sean smiled. "Yes."

"Good." Hayden kissed his cheek. "You deserve to be."

When they finished looking at the honeymoon photos, Carly said, "Sean, we thought while we were all together, you might like to go through the family photos and home movies."

His father.

He wasn't sure. After the emotion of the past few hours, was he ready for more tumult?

"We don't have a lot," Bridget apologized.

He couldn't say no. "All right. That'd be grand."

Carmen grabbed a bag she'd left on the table. When she returned she said, "I need all my children around me." She gestured for Jack and Evan to move off the largest sofa and then sat, patting the spot next to her for Sean.

Sean chuckled as he and Zita squeezed onto the sofa with Carmen, Bridget and Carly.

Carmen handed him the photo album.

"Take your time," Carly said.

He braced himself and opened the cover. The first picture was Carmen and his father on their wedding day. It was amazing how much he looked like Brendan. The strawberry-blond hair and blue eyes couldn't belong to anyone else. It was no wonder his mother hated him so much. He must have reminded her every day of the man she'd slept with, the mistake she'd made.

Carmen and Brendan looked so happy together. So much in love.

As he moved through the pages, Carmen told him who everyone was, explained where the photo was taken. When his sisters appeared in the photos, the expression of love and adoration on his father's face was beautiful. Would he have looked at Sean that way, if he'd met him? Or would he have been embarrassed by his mistake?

"Brendan loved his girls so much," Carmen said. "He would have loved you too. He had such a heart for loving."

Sean shut his eyes and took a long, steadying breath.

"There's one more thing," Bridget said. "If you'd like to see it?"

"It's a home movie," Zita said.

He nodded. He might as well see it all at once.

Carly set up her laptop and pressed play.

A wedding. Not just any wedding, but his father's and Carmen's. Brendan was grinning from ear to ear and speaking Spanish, but with an obvious Irish accent. At the end of the vows, he said, "I love you, Carmen."

The accent took Sean right back to Ireland, right to the region where he'd grown up. He wasn't sure what he was feeling inside. His chest was so full and his mind was whirling. He focused on controlling his emotions as he watched the rest of the movie — christenings, birthdays, and a day at the beach.

Carmen called out something in Spanish from behind the camera. His father jumped to his feet. "Last one in is a rotten egg," he said and raced for the water. The phrase and the accent had Sean catching his breath. He watched as Carly and Bridget ran to the water, with Zita trying so hard to catch up. But his father waited for her and let her beat him. She called out something to Brendan and tripped under the water. Brendan plucked her out, hugged and kissed her. "You sure did, *a leanbh*."

The words and the Irish endearment were too much. The pressure inside him needed a release.

He began to cry.

Chapter 11

As the Flanagans sat to go through photos, Hayden joined Jack, David, and Evan in the kitchen. They hadn't said anything about his relationship with Sean, and he wanted to make sure they weren't going to say something stupid that would upset Sean.

"Another drink, Hayden?" Evan asked.

"Yes, thanks." He glanced over his shoulder to check if Sean was all right. He seemed to be. He lowered his voice. "While I've got you all here, I need to ask you something."

"What's up?" David asked.

"Have you got a problem with me dating your brother?"

They all frowned and Jack answered. "Of course not."

"You don't have a problem with him being gay?"

"No," Evan said.

"Good." He hesitated. "Be careful with what you say over the next few days. He's a bit sensitive."

"Sure," David said.

He took the drink Evan handed him. "I'm glad we got that cleared up."

"Did he really think we'd care?" Jack asked.

Spoken like someone who'd never had to worry about fitting in in his life. Hayden nodded. "Of course he did. Hell, even I sometimes worry how people are going to react and you all know I've got no problem with who I am. There are always going to be ignorant people out there, and you're not just anyone. You're family."

"We should probably keep him away from my dad at the

wedding," David said.

Hayden groaned. "You're right." He hadn't considered David's father, but if there was ever a man to say the wrong thing at the wrong time, it was Bob Randall. He'd met him once when he went to their place to do wedding plans with Zita, and he'd seen the expression on Bob's face when he'd noticed there was a man helping with the planning. Distaste was a nice word for it. "I'll make a point of it."

"We're going to be busy keeping Bob to his side of the family," Evan joked.

David scowled. "Yeah. I'll have a word to my brother and sister. They might be able to keep Dad under control."

Hayden felt sorry for him. David was the nicest guy in the world, but his father was an opinionated, ignorant, mega-wealthy white man who'd known nothing but privilege. There'd been a few issues when David was dating Zita, and David and Bob had come to a tentative truce. Now any slightly controversial topic was taboo when Zita and Bob were in the same room together.

"Is there anyone else we need to worry about?" Hayden asked.

"There are a couple, but I don't think they'll say anything. They'll probably just scowl," David said.

Which could be just as damaging. "All right, well, I'll prepare Sean." He turned to Jack. "What about at your wedding?"

"I don't know. I don't think anyone would be so rude."

"All right. Good." Behind him, Carly had fired up her laptop.

"Better get some tissues out," Evan said. He left the kitchen, putting two boxes of tissues on the coffee table near the group and then sat on the arm of the sofa next to Carly.

Hayden frowned. "Why?"

"They all cry when they watch the movie," Jack said. "It has their father in it." He went and put a hand on Bridget's shoulder. She glanced up at him, smiled and squeezed his hand.

"Here it comes," David said, and went to stand behind Zita with both hands on her shoulders.

Look at those couples. They were perfectly in tune with each other. They knew what the other needed.

And between them were Sean and Carmen, alone.

Hayden moved closer and, as the movie ended, Sean broke down sobbing. Carmen pulled him into her arms and held him. They had each other.

And he was alone.

***

Sean wasn't sure how long he cried for, all he knew was his head throbbed and his throat felt raw. His hand held a bundle of soggy tissues and he wanted to crawl back into bed.

"It's all right, *niñito*," Carmen said. "You have us now."

His breath caught in his throat and tears threatened to fall again. He hadn't known he was capable of producing so many tears. It was like a river had burst its banks.

He had a family.

They knew he was gay and they loved him anyway.

He became aware that he was holding Carmen tightly, perhaps too tightly, and he relaxed. He couldn't recall a time when his own mother had hugged him like Carmen was doing now. She'd never soothed him when he was upset or told him everything was going to be all right.

He wanted to believe Carmen. He wanted to believe he'd found the acceptance he'd spent his whole life looking for. But the idea was terrifying. It meant he had so much more to lose than he ever had before.

"Lunch is almost ready," Carly said.

Sean sat up and smelled garlic in the air. The others were setting the table, getting drinks and generally preparing lunch. He blushed. How long had he been sitting there blubbering?

But no one was paying any attention to him. They'd all given him the space he'd needed.

He met Hayden's gaze, and Hayden blew him a kiss.

Sean smiled. It was all right. Everything was fine.

"Thank you, Carmen," he said.

"*Pfft*, there is no need for thanks," she said. Her top was a little bit damp from where he'd been resting his head.

"Damn, I'm sorry. I've cried all over you."

She waved off his attempts to dab at the spots. "It is no matter. It will dry."

Zita handed him a glass of water. "Thought you could do with restocking."

"Thanks." He drained the whole glass. His eyes were sore and his throat was raw. He wanted to curl up in bed and go to sleep.

"Go and splash water on your face and then you can have some lunch," Carmen said.

"Yes, ma'am."

Carmen's eyes widened and she flung her arms around him. "You called me mam." She nearly squeezed the breath out of him. "I'd been hoping you would, but I didn't want to push." She had tears in her eyes. "I was worried it might upset your mother."

Sean was at a loss for words. He didn't want to correct her, not when she was so happy. He couldn't quite believe she wanted to claim him for her own. His chest was about to burst. "Would you prefer Mam or Mama?"

"Anything. Whatever you want."

His sisters all called Carmen Mama. "How about Mama?" he said, trying it out.

She nodded.

He kissed her cheek. "I'll be back in a minute." He headed for the bathroom, swallowing hard, trying to get the lump in his throat to shift. He splashed water on his face and dried it, then looked in the mirror. His face was splotchy, his eyes red as if he'd been on a bender. He looked like shit.

But none of his family cared.

His family.

God, just the words warmed him, made him feel things he'd never felt before. He had sisters and a mother.

Hell, would these tears ever run out?

There was a quiet knock on the door and he glanced at Hayden leaning against the doorframe. "How are you feeling?"

Sean wiped his eyes. Hayden must think he was a complete basket case. "Exhausted, overwhelmed."

"It's been some day, huh?"

He nodded. "I'm so glad you were right." He turned to face Hayden.

"About what?"

"About how they would react."

Hayden smiled. "I've known them longer than you."

Sean wrapped Hayden in a hug. "Thank you for not running when Carly caught us."

"Why would I do that? We'd done nothing wrong."

"Past experience."

"Yeah, well it's time you got some new experiences." Hayden scowled. "I'm not running from you. If anything I'm running to you. Damn it, Sean, I like you a lot." He was fired up and so annoyed, but Sean glowed.

Hayden liked him. "I'm sorry." He brushed his lips across Hayden's. "Thank you."

"You're welcome." Hayden kissed him again, longer, deeper, more sensuous, and Sean was drugged.

"Lunch is getting cold," Bridget called.

Sean pulled away. "That's our hint to get out there."

"Yeah. You ready?"

He nodded. He really was.

***

At six o'clock that evening, Sean caught a cab with Hayden to David's apartment. It was David's bachelor party and Carmen had suggested Sean stay in town rather than go out to Casa Flanagan. Sean was more than happy to agree.

"Do you know what's planned for tonight?" Sean asked.

"No. David's friends organized it," Hayden said. "There's definitely going to be drinking involved." Hayden took hold of his hand. "Nervous?"

Sean shrugged. He didn't know David's brother or friends and wasn't sure what kind of reaction he'd get. Not that they'd know he was gay by looking at him, but he would be spending the night with Hayden and he wanted to be able to dance with him.

When they arrived at David's apartment, Zita was just leaving. She was dressed stylishly in a stunning, fitted, thigh-length red dress.

"Have fun tonight," Sean said.

"Will do." She waved and was gone.

Inside, Evan was lounging on a sofa with a few other guys.

David made the introductions — Garth, Lee and Colin were all college friends of David's, and Grant was his brother.

"Nice to meet you," Sean said.

When Jack arrived, they trooped downstairs to where a black stretch limousine was waiting. The limo was incredible. Sean had never been in one before, and it was big enough for all nine of them to fit with the seats stretching the length of the car. The bar was stocked, and while Garth spoke to the driver about their first stop, Lee and Colin started pouring drinks.

When Garth joined them, he said, "To David finding his love and joining us in wedded bliss."

"To David," everyone chorused.

David grinned. "Zita was worth the wait."

Sean exchanged a smile with Hayden. He was glad his sisters had found such great guys.

The first stop was dinner at a steakhouse. The atmosphere was relaxed and the food was good. Sean sat between Hayden and Lee, who was continually checking his phone.

The fifth time he did it, Sean asked, "Waiting for a call?"

Lee grimaced. "My wife is nine months pregnant. She could go into labor at any minute." He ran a hand through his hair.

"And if she can't get hold of you, she'll try all of us," Colin told him.

"It's our first," Lee said to Sean.

"Do you know the gender?"

"A girl. We're still arguing over names." He checked his phone again.

"If she goes into labor, we'll send you with the limo to pick her up," David called from the other side of the table. "It'll be fine."

Lee nodded. "I know." He adjusted the ringer volume so it was as loud as it could be.

Garth laughed. "Lee's going to be a bit distracted tonight."

Sean smiled. It was nice they were supportive and understanding.

Garth was sitting across from Sean. "What about you, Sean? Are you married?"

"Not yet."

"Girlfriend?" Colin asked.

"No." Was this where he was supposed to say he was in a relationship with Hayden? Was it easier not to mention his sexuality to people he was only going to see once more at Zita and David's wedding? Or was it the perfect time to try it out?

"So what are we doing tonight?" David asked. He gave Sean a small smile as he changed the topic.

In the past, it had been easy enough to deny the wife/girlfriend question that inevitably came up. But now he was dating Hayden. He risked a glance at Hayden, but he was paying attention to the conversation around them.

What was the etiquette? By not mentioning he was gay, did that make it seem like he was embarrassed by his relationship? Or did it make him sensible for not opening himself up for the potential bigotry?

He had no idea.

He'd have to ask Hayden later.

After dinner and a number of stories about what David and his friends had got up to while at college, they started their bar crawl. They were going to all the bars that held significance for the four friends during their college days. And at each bar they had to have a different drink.

It was going to be a rough day tomorrow.

By midnight, Lee's wife hadn't called and he had drunk enough to relax. There was music playing at Whitewash, the bar they were at, and the beat was great.

"I'm going to dance," Hayden announced, standing up. "Who's with me?"

Sean jumped up. "I'll dance."

The others shook their heads. "You'll look like a couple of fags if it's just the two of you," Grant joked.

Sean lost his breath.

Hayden grabbed Sean's hand and glared at Grant. "Well, then it's just as well we are."

Grant's mouth dropped open and Lee and Colin stopped talking and looked at them both.

Face burning, Sean allowed Hayden to pull him onto the dance floor. He'd been outed again.

"What an idiot," Hayden said.

Sean nodded, glancing back at the table. David was saying

something to his brother, and he looked annoyed.

"You're supposed to be dancing." Hayden grabbed his hand and pulled him around so he was facing away from the table.

Would the others treat him differently now? As Hayden started dancing, Sean tried to forget Grant's comment and ignore the way his stomach was twisting itself into knots. Tonight was about having fun.

Hayden's moves were sinuous and sinful and Sean stirred. No. This wasn't the place to get down and dirty. He looked around and there was quite a bit of space around them. In fact, they had this section of the dance floor to themselves. People were giving them a lot of room.

Hayden didn't seem to notice or care.

He caught a few sideways looks, a few frowns, and it reminded him of the danger of being gay in public. He'd narrowly missed being beaten up the last time he was in Dublin when two thugs had decided to take exception to him leaving a bar with another man. If they hadn't managed to run… "I'm going to sit down."

"Ignore them," Hayden said, taking his hand. "We're allowed to dance here too." He danced closer, but Sean shifted away. He couldn't. Not here.

"No." He shook his hand free and went back to the table. There was safety in numbers, in fitting in.

When he sat down, Grant turned away.

Feck. Was that how it was going to be? He rubbed his palm on his chest.

Colin moved to sit next to Sean. "I owe you an apology."

Sean braced himself. "What for?"

"I assumed you were straight. I didn't mean to make you feel uncomfortable."

Sean stared at him. "It's fine. You didn't mean anything by it."

"Yeah, but it's time we stopped assuming, isn't it? We need to start changing our default language."

Sean nodded as Hayden returned to the table.

"So are you seeing anyone?" Colin asked.

"I'm dating Hayden," Sean said. He reached over and squeezed Hayden's hand, hoping to make up for leaving him on the dance floor.

Hayden smiled.

"That's great." Colin got to his feet. "It's time we moved to the next club."

***

Hayden was stupidly drunk. Normally he didn't drink too much, but after Grant had made his "fag" comment, he'd decided he didn't care to be careful tonight. He was tired of the haters, of the small-minded jackasses who had no idea how much a comment could hurt.

Sean had physically recoiled at the word and hadn't been able to relax afterward. Not that Hayden was blaming him. He'd noticed the way people kept their distance on the dance floor, but he'd been too pissed off to care. Sean didn't have the same confidence or experience in being out as he did, so his annoyance when Sean scurried off the floor was short-lived.

It disappeared completely when he'd caught the end of Colin's apology about assuming Sean was straight. It took courage to acknowledge your words and the small apology had made Sean feel that much better. He'd have to thank Colin later.

The limo pulled up in front of Hayden's house. They'd already dropped off David and Evan. "Thanks for the ride," he said, carefully getting to his feet and following Sean out of the car. He was a little unsteady on his feet.

"See you next weekend," Garth called and Hayden waved.

Hayden grabbed Sean's hand and walked slowly up the front path. Sean's hand felt nice, comfortable, right.

At the door, he got his keys out of his pocket and promptly dropped them on the ground. He bent to pick them up and bumped his head on the door. "Ow."

Sean chuckled. "Let me." He picked up the keys and had the door open in no time.

"I like a man who can take charge," Hayden said, winking at him. "I like everything about you, actually." He walked in, switched on the light and squinted at the brightness. Behind him, Sean locked the door.

"This way." Hayden beckoned Sean and stumbled down the corridor toward his bedroom, stripping off his shirt and unbuttoning his pants as he went.

"How about we have a shower?" Sean suggested. He took him by the hand and pulled him gently into the bathroom.

Hayden frowned. "Why do you still have clothes on?"

"Because I'm not as drunk as you are."

"Don't you want me?"

Sean smiled and pressed him up against the bathroom wall. "Of course I do." He kissed him once, hard, but before Hayden had a chance to react, he stepped back. "But we could both do with freshening up." He stripped off his shirt and Hayden grinned, running his tongue over his lips.

Sean had such a nice body. Even though Sean was so pale as to be almost translucent, there was a strength and hardness to him. The man had subtle but glorious muscles. Together they were ebony and ivory. Hayden laughed to himself and started to hum the song. He moved forward to run his hands over Sean's chest. "Do you work out?"

"No. I do all the lifting at the bar."

"Mmm. It shows." He licked Sean's nipple. "Like vanilla ice cream."

Sean chuckled and knelt on the floor to untie Hayden's laces.

"While you're down there..." Hayden thrust his crotch toward Sean's face.

Sean nuzzled it and Hayden was instantly hard. "Oh, yeah, honey."

Sean dragged off Hayden's underwear and took him into his mouth.

Hayden swore and his knees almost buckled.

"Stay with me," Sean said, placing a firm hand on Hayden's butt.

He'd stay with him anywhere. Hayden watched as Sean sucked him and the view was so damn erotic. He was going to come.

Sean pulled back. "Shower first, I think."

What? Hayden's mind couldn't catch up. Why had Sean stopped? Sean ran the shower and quickly stripped naked. Then he held out a hand and Hayden took it, allowing himself to be pulled under the spray. His body throbbed as Sean ran his hands over his chest.

Sean kissed like a dream and Hayden willingly surrendered to the sensation.

"Now where was I?" Sean asked and went to his knees again.

Lord have mercy. Hayden braced himself against the wall as Sean took hold of him. Sean was on his knees, his mouth around Hayden's cock and one hand stroking his own penis. The image was too much. He came.

The strength in his legs gave out and he slid down the wall as Sean's hand moved faster over himself. The expression on Sean's face as he came was blissful.

Hayden pulled Sean over to him and hugged him. He was happy. He could stay here under the shower spray and be content.

A few minutes passed before Sean moved away. "Let's get you into bed."

"I'm fine right here," Hayden assured him.

Sean smiled that sweet smile again. "I'm sure you are, but you won't be by morning." He got to his feet, turned off the taps and then carefully helped Hayden to his feet. After making sure Hayden was steady, he grabbed a towel and began to dry him.

It was nice, Sean's firm hands running all over his body. His penis twitched.

"Someone's eager for more," Sean said.

"Hell yes." He couldn't get enough of this man.

Sean dried himself and then led Hayden into the bedroom. He pulled back the covers and gently helped Hayden onto the bed. Hayden reached for him.

"In a minute." Sean kissed him quickly. "Tell me where you keep your headache tablets."

"Have you got a headache?"

"No, it's for the morning."

Hayden frowned. Why was he saying that? He was fine. Barely drunk.

"The tablets?" Sean asked again.

"In the kitchen, above the fridge."

"I'll be right back."

Hayden watched Sean go. He had a fine ass. It had just the right amount of jiggle to it and he was hoping he'd be able to spread those cheeks sometime soon.

He smiled at the thought and his eyes grew heavy. Sean returned and placed a glass of water and a bottle of pills on the bedside table next to Hayden. Then he passed Hayden another glass of water. "Drink this before you go to sleep."

He wasn't thirsty.

"Drink it for me," Sean murmured, kissing his neck. "It will make you feel better."

Hayden complied, guzzling the water, and carefully placed the glass on the table. He'd do whatever Sean wanted him to do at the moment. He wriggled down the bed and Sean snuggled in close. It was so nice to be held like this. His heavy eyes closed and he fell asleep.

Chapter 12

A stabbing pain shot through Hayden's head, waking him instantly. He groaned.

"There's water and pills right next to you." Sean's voice was like a megaphone.

Hayden pulled the pillow up around his ears and the movement caused another wave of pain. He focused on breathing. What the hell had happened? He tried to get his brain to focus on the night before, but it was much too difficult.

A hand on his chest had him lowering the pillow.

"Sit up and take these." Sean's voice was a little quieter and Hayden cracked open one eye. It was very bright, but as his vision cleared, he saw Sean holding out two pills and a glass of water.

Very carefully, Hayden put the pills in his mouth and swallowed some water. Sean took the glass from him. "Lie back down and wait until they kick in."

Hayden's stomach rolled as the pills hit it and he paused for a moment to make sure it settled before lying back down. "Why aren't you in agony too?"

"I didn't drink quite as much as you." Sean left the room and came back with a cold compress, which he placed across Hayden's forehead. "Are you hungry?"

He tried to shake his head, but it hurt too much. "No."

"All right. I'll make you one of my hangover cures."

Hayden didn't answer. He wasn't sure it was possible to open his mouth and not be sick. How much had he drunk last night? He could remember beer and wine before they started on the spirits. Ugh, no wonder he felt like death warmed up.

In the kitchen, Sean was opening cupboard doors, obviously looking for something, but Hayden didn't have the strength to call out and ask. About five minutes later, Sean returned with some kind of yellow smoothie.

"Drink this."

"What's in it?" He carefully sat up and sniffed at the drink.

"A bit of this and that. My customers swear by it."

Hayden took a sip and could make out the banana flavor. It was quite nice. Slowly, he drank it, glad Sean wasn't looking for conversation.

When he was done, Sean took the glass from him. "Feel up for a shower?"

The mention of a shower sparked a memory. "We had one last night, right?"

Sean grinned. "We did."

Sean had given him a divine blow job. He smiled. "Are you going to wash my back again?"

"If you ask me nicely," Sean replied and pulled back the sheets.

Hayden took the hand he offered and slowly got to his feet. Damn, he hadn't had a hangover like this since college. Why the hell had he drunk so much?

Sean ran the shower and Hayden stepped in. The spray was like tiny needles on his head, and he moved so it ran down his back instead. "Thank you for taking care of me."

"My pleasure," Sean said. He lathered up some body wash and gently massaged Hayden's back.

It felt amazing. Hayden closed his eyes and let himself focus on the sensation. He loved what Sean's hands did to him. They soothed and stroked and made all of the pain go away. His head was more of a dull ache than a throb now. When Sean's hands dipped lower, Hayden sighed in pleasure.

"You like that?" Sean murmured in his ear.

"Yes."

Sean dropped the sponge and used his hand instead. "What about this?"

"Mmhmm." That was the limit of his speech right there.

Sean stood behind him, pressing into his back as he stroked

Hayden's cock. It was heaven. Hayden's head fell back as the steady rhythm built and his arousal climbed. He was at Sean's mercy, not able or willing to move as he let Sean do what he liked.

"Come for me, baby," Sean whispered in his ear.

The touch of Sean's lips against his ear, the words he spoke, combined with the increased speed and strength of his grip had Hayden tipping over the edge. He wasn't able to make more than a half groan as the pleasure rushed through him.

Sean bit his neck and Hayden jerked as the pain and pleasure mixed. He was floating.

"How's your head?"

"What head?" There was no pain now, just a beautiful feeling of contentment.

Sean chuckled. "Good." He turned the shower off and like last night, began to dry him.

Hayden's senses returned and he took the towel from Sean. "I can manage." He kissed him. "Thank you."

"Anytime." Sean grabbed the other towel. "How are you feeling?"

His head was free of pain. Whether it was the painkillers, the drink or the hand job, he didn't know and he didn't care. "I feel fantastic. Remind me to keep you around next time I decide to overindulge." They wandered naked back to the bedroom. Hayden glanced at the clock. It was midday. "Do you have plans for today?"

"Bridget is picking me up at one to take me to Casa Flanagan."

It was on the tip of Hayden's tongue to invite Sean to stay here for the rest of his vacation. The strength of his want surprised him. They'd only known each other a couple of weeks. Besides, there was no point — he was working all day, and Sean had come from Ireland to meet his family. Hayden didn't want to mess it up for him. "Then we've probably got time for a quick lunch."

Sean kissed him. "I'd like that."

The man was addictive. Hayden wanted nothing more than to fall back into bed with him and spend what little time they had exploring his body.

But he should be the sensible one. He had to show Sean some semblance of hospitality since he'd been out of it all morning.

"I'll see what I can find."

****

Sean sat at the kitchen table while his lover made him a sandwich. It was such a cozy experience to be cooked for.

He'd enjoyed taking care of Hayden. When he'd noticed Hayden's level of intoxication last night, Sean had cut back on his own drinking, knowing that Hayden was likely to have the mother of all hangovers.

Hayden had been so cute in his drunken state and Sean had been meaning to simply shower him and put him to bed, but he hadn't been able to resist him when he'd thrust his crotch in his face. He was too damn appealing.

Part of him wanted to stay here, to spend the rest of the day in bed with Hayden, but Bridget was due and he hadn't had an opportunity to spend much time with her. He admired Bridget's work ethic. When she told Sean about her job, she spoke with such passion.

He wanted to find something he was similarly passionate about. He'd never believed he could be anything but a bartender until he met his sisters.

His conversation with Zita and his visits to the shelter with Hayden had made him want more out of his life. He wanted to help the kids who were homeless. If he moved to Houston he could do that. He could be close to his sisters and to Hayden as well.

Could he dare to dream so big?

He would have to check if he was eligible for a visa, make sure his family really wanted him here. Carmen might not have meant it.

But there was nothing for him in Ireland.

Hayden placed a sandwich in front of him with a flourish. "Eat up."

Sean grinned and took a bite. It was a simple chicken salad with a spicy mayonnaise and it was delicious. After he swallowed, he said, "What are you going to do this afternoon?"

"As little as possible." He sipped his coffee. "Though I might visit the shelter."

"If you do, let me know how they all are. I want to catch up with Angela and see how she's going."

"You've taken a shine to her," Hayden said.

"Her situation reminds me of my mam," he said. "I don't want her to have the hardship Mam had and end up hating her child for it."

Hayden frowned. "Your mom hated you? I thought she just worked a lot."

Sean pushed the plate away from him, his appetite gone. Did he want to share his whole pathetic life story with this wonderful man?

"Sean." Hayden turned toward him. "What was your childhood like?"

"I told you about it already."

"I think you might have missed some detail." Hayden studied him. "Why do you think your mom hated you?"

"She never spent any time with me. When I was ten, I asked her if I could join the town musical society. She screamed at me and said real men didn't act, sing or dance, told me I wasn't normal, that I made her life hell." The memory still hurt. "She said it was just as well my father wasn't here – he'd be horrified by who I was. From then on, she barely tolerated being in the same room as me."

"Do you think she knew you were gay?"

"Maybe. She used to yell at me if she caught me singing or dancing around the house. I used to stay in my room and mime into my hairbrush, and in my head I was singing at the top of my lungs." He'd dreamed of being a rock star until he grew old enough to understand that dreams weren't meant for people like him.

Hayden wrapped his arms around him. "Baby, I'm sorry you had such an awful childhood."

He shrugged. "It was what it was." He'd learned to be happy in his own company. He collected their plates, taking them to the sink to wash.

"I can see why it was such a big deal when Zita contacted you." Hayden's voice was soft.

"Yeah, but the odds were high that she'd hate me, and my last hope of having a family would be gone." He shut his mouth with a snap. He hadn't meant to admit that.

Hayden came up behind him and wrapped his arms around his waist. "I can't see how anyone could hate you." He kissed Sean's neck.

Sean's heart was so full it could burst at any moment. That would be just his luck.

Someone knocked on the front door. "That will be Bridget."

Hayden kissed him again. "I'll get it."

Sean dried the plates and then turned to greet his sister. She hugged him and kissed both his cheeks. "How was your night?"

"We had fun."

She examined him. "Not hungover?"

"No."

"That was my issue," Hayden said. "But Sean has a great hangover cure."

Bridget glanced between them and grinned. "I bet he does."

Sean blushed and said, "It's a drink."

"I'll have to get the recipe from you," she said. "Mama might need it after the bachelorette party last night."

Sean's eyebrows rose. "Carmen?"

She grinned. "Yeah. She had a margarita or two too many during dinner. She doesn't drink much, and she's got to be suffering today."

"I'll make it for her when I get to Casa Flanagan."

"Great. Why don't you get your things and we'll head off?"

"All right," Sean said.

He grabbed his backpack out of Hayden's bedroom and followed Bridget to the door. After he'd put his bag on the tray of her pickup, he turned to Hayden. "I'll see you later."

Hayden drew him close and Sean glanced around to check if anyone was watching. Bridget got into the pickup to give them some privacy.

"If you're not busy, you could come to the shelter with me on Tuesday night," Hayden said. "You could stay over."

Sean smiled. "I'd like that." He didn't think anyone would mind. He kissed Hayden slowly. "I'll call you later." He got into the car and waved to Hayden as Bridget backed out of the driveway.

"So you and Hayden," Bridget said.

Sean nodded, waiting for her verdict.

"It looks pretty serious."

Did it? They were enjoying each other's company and bodies. "He's a great man."

"He is," Bridget agreed. "You know same-sex marriage is legal here."

He glanced at her. Where was she going with this? "It's legal in Ireland as well."

"Oh. Well, I thought that could be something to add to your pro column."

"Pro column?"

"Reasons to move to America," Bridget said. "Mama mentioned she wanted you to move here, and I thought you might be putting together a pro/con list."

He was almost scared to ask. "Do you want me to move?"

"Of course."

Sean was silent. "You don't know me that well."

"That's another item in the pro column." Bridget smiled. "We can get to know you better."

He couldn't prevent his responding smile. She was definitely optimistic. "What else should I put in the pro column?"

"Aside from your three gorgeous sisters and stepmother?" She grinned. "Well, there's Hayden now — I'm assuming he's a pro. And the weather's warmer here — though some might think it's too hot."

He was getting used to the heat and it was nice not to worry about rain all of the time.

"The economy's bouncing back, so if you buy a bar, it will have a good chance at success."

Zita had been telling her things. "Do you talk about me behind my back?" He wasn't sure whether he liked that.

"Of course. How else can we plot to win you over?"

He blinked.

"It's what sisters do when they want to help each other without being too obvious about it. You should have heard some of the conversations Zita and I had when Evan was wooing Carly."

"You really want me to stay in Houston?" He couldn't quite believe he was having this conversation.

"Of course. You're our brother and we like you a lot." She indicated to change lanes. "It sucks that Mama's family is in El Salvador and we don't get to see them. I don't want you to be across the other side of the world too."

"Ireland's not so far away."

"It might as well be. You can't pop back for our Sunday lunches."

He loved that she actually wanted him there. "I might not be eligible for a visa."

"You are. Zita and I checked it out yesterday before we went out. We're all naturalized citizens so we can apply on your behalf."

"And you'd do that?"

"We may have already printed the forms and started filling them out." She grinned at him. "But we didn't know if you'd want to leave Ireland. Your mom's there."

He swallowed his laugh. She wouldn't care, but he wasn't ready to tell his story to his sisters. "We don't see each other much anyway."

"So you're OK that we've been investigating it?" she asked.

"Yeah."

"Good. I was worried you might think it was a little creepy." Bridget tapped her fingers on the steering wheel. "We'll have to find you a job. Have you got any qualifications?"

"No. Never been anything but a bartender."

"All right. We'll work something out. Maybe Carly can find you something at Comunidad."

He couldn't quite believe they were discussing him moving out here. It was a bit surreal. But he wasn't going to be reliant on his sisters. "I can find my own job." He couldn't prevent the slight bite to his tone.

"Sorry, I wasn't suggesting you couldn't," Bridget said. "I get annoyed when people tell me to go to Carly for help because she's a billionaire. The assumption that I can't do it on my own irritates me. I shouldn't have done it to you."

"It's fine."

They pulled into Casa Flanagan and Zita's two dogs came

out to greet them.

"Mama's looking forward to Zita and David moving into their house," Bridget said. "They'll be taking the dogs then."

"Carmen doesn't like dogs?"

"She doesn't like the barking and the hair."

He got his backpack out and carried it in.

"You've got Zita's old room," Bridget said as she showed him upstairs.

He placed his bag on the floor of the very feminine room. The bedspread on the double bed was covered in bright, colorful flowers and the dresser and curtains were both purple.

"Is that you, Bridget?" Carmen's voice called from one of the other rooms.

"Yes, Mama. I'm with Sean." Bridget motioned for him to follow her into a bedroom. Carmen was lying in bed with a compress on her head. Sean swallowed his smile.

"*Mis bebes.*" She held out her arms for Bridget to hug her.

"*Buenos días.*" Bridget hugged her then stepped aside.

Sean hesitated before saying, "Hi Mama." The word felt so strange on his tongue, but Carmen beamed as she squeezed him. "How are you feeling?"

"I am never drinking again," she declared.

"Hayden said Sean has a great hangover cure," Bridget told her.

Carmen's eyes lifted hopefully.

"I can check if you have the ingredients," he offered.

"Yes, please. Bless you."

Sean followed Bridget down to the kitchen where Beatriz and Elena were gathered.

"Help yourself to whatever's available," Bridget said. She turned to the girls. "He's making something for Mama."

The girls giggled. "She's not been well," Beatriz said.

Sean grinned. "Let's see what I can find." The drink was made up of whatever was on hand that would help with hydration or had vitamin B. Then it was just a matter of making it taste nice. "She's had some headache tablets?"

Elena nodded. "That was the first thing she took. She was so hungover that Alejandra ordered her back to bed and she didn't argue."

Bridget raised an eyebrow. "Well, she must be ill."

He mixed up the drink and poured it into a glass. "I'll take it up to her."

On his way, he greeted Alejandra, who was in the living room with her baby, Julio. When he reached the bedroom, Carmen had her eyes closed. He tapped on the doorframe.

"Come in." She squinted at him.

"This might make you feel better," he said, handing her the glass.

"*Gracias.*" She cautiously took a sip. "It's lovely." She took another sip and then patted the edge of the bed. "Sit down. Tell me about your night. You were not as silly as me?"

"No. I left that to Hayden."

"Hayden was drunk?" Carmen asked.

"Yeah. He felt a bit rough this morning."

"I know the feeling."

Sean grinned down at the small woman. It wouldn't have taken much for her to be over the limit. She was barely five feet tall. "Can I help make dinner?"

"I haven't even thought about it. We might have to order takeout."

"I'll have a chat with Bridget." He wanted to help where he could. Be part of the family. He took the empty glass from Carmen. "Why don't you sleep for an hour?" he suggested. "Bridget and I will keep an eye on the girls." Not that they needed minding — aside from Beatriz and Julio, they were all teenagers.

"I think I might. I'll be a better hostess when I wake up." She slid down in the bed.

"You're not my hostess," Sean said, brushing a kiss on her forehead. "You're my mam." He went over to the window and pulled down the blind. Then he closed the door behind him and let out a deep breath.

He had a mother.

Chapter 13

On Tuesday, Sean caught the bus into the city to meet Hayden after work. His heart beat faster as he rode the elevator to the top floor of Comunidad. He couldn't wait to see Hayden again. As the elevator doors opened, Sean grinned. Hayden was at his desk, talking on the telephone and looked gorgeous in a charcoal suit with a pink shirt. He didn't notice Sean approaching.

When Hayden glanced up, a huge smile lit his face. Pleasure flowed all the way to Sean's toes.

"Let me check that for you," Hayden said. "Can I put you on hold for a second?" He pressed a button on the phone and moved his headset out of the way. "Hello, gorgeous." He got to his feet and kissed Sean. "I need to finish this call and I'll be ready to go. Carly's in her office if you want to say hi." He replaced his headset.

Sean stood there, his pulse still racing from the kiss and the fact Hayden had kissed him in public, where anyone could have seen them. He glanced around, but no one seemed to have noticed. His cheeks were warm as he tapped on the door and moved into Carly's office.

"Sean!" Carly grinned and got up and gave him a hug.

"Hi, little sister."

"What are you doing here?"

"I'm, ah, going out with Hayden tonight. We're going to the shelter together."

"Wonderful. Gil started work here the other day. He's a real whiz. It's not going to take him long before he's up to speed with some of the graduates we've got working here."

"That's great."

She nodded. "We still need to sort out his accommodation, but I'm sure we'll find something."

Hayden ducked his head around the door. "I'm done, boss."

"Thanks, Hayden. You two have a good night." Carly waved them off.

Sean left her office and Hayden took hold of his hand. "It feels like ages since I've seen you," Hayden said, pulling him into the empty elevator.

It did. He'd spoken to Hayden the night before, but it wasn't the same as seeing him in the flesh. Sean moved closer to kiss him when the elevator doors opened and a man walked in. Sean shuffled so he was standing next to Hayden and noticed the quick glance at their joined hands before the man stood on the opposite side to them. Hayden didn't seem to care.

"We'll stop at my place for an early dinner before we go to the shelter," Hayden said.

Sean smiled. Being alone with Hayden was an excellent idea.

The elevator stopped and Gil got in. He grinned. "Hi, guys."

"How's work?" Hayden asked him.

"It's awesome. I can't believe the cool stuff they have here." His enthusiasm was palpable.

"Carly mentioned you were good," Sean said.

Gil's eyes widened. "She did? Carolina Flanagan said I was good?"

Sean nodded. "She said it won't be long until you're at the same level as their college graduates."

Gil's eyes rolled back in his head. "Oh man. Someone pinch me. I gotta be dreaming."

Sean chuckled. "It's true."

Gil did a booty shake in celebration. "This is a great day." The elevator stopped at the ground level. "This is my stop." He went to leave.

Hayden placed a hand on the door to stop it closing. "Where are you headed?"

"I'm catching the bus to the shelter."

"Get back in. We'll give you a ride. We're heading over there this evening."

"Thanks. That'd be great."

Sean's alone time with Hayden disappeared, but he didn't mind. Gil was so pumped up and full of life. He was far different from the boy he'd met at the ballpark just over a week ago.

It was proof that someone's life could change so quickly.

There was always hope.

A couple of hours later, they pulled up at the shelter. Gil had had dinner with them and kept them entertained while he told them about his few days at Comunidad. The kid was in love with the company and his job. Now if he just had a place to live. Sean wasn't sure Casa Flanagan would work for Gil. It had taken him an hour and a half to catch the bus to Comunidad today, and many of the foster girls were still recovering from being assaulted by men, so he wasn't sure whether a teenaged boy — even if he was gay — would be welcomed.

Gil and Hayden greeted a few people and Sean glanced around for Angela. He still hadn't had the chance to tell her about Carmen's offer. He couldn't see her among the youths who were gathered in the social area. He wandered over to Alberto. "Is Angela here tonight?"

He nodded. "She should be. She's in dorm four." He pointed.

Sean hesitated. Was it inappropriate for him to go near the dorm? As he debated, Angela came out of the room, holding her back and slowly walking toward a sofa. Sean hurried over. "Hi. Need a hand?"

She smiled and her eyes welled up with tears. "I'm so big I could explode."

"How long have you got left?"

"Maybe three weeks."

"Is your doctor happy?"

She laughed. "What doctor?"

He frowned. "Aren't you getting regular checkups?"

"How would I afford that?"

Sean helped her onto the sofa. He'd forgotten about America's stupidly expensive medical system. In Ireland, she would have access to free medical care. "Haven't you had any checkups?"

She shook her head. "Alberto monitors my blood pressure, but I haven't had an ultrasound or anything."

"What will you do when you go into labor?"

She shrugged. "Women used to have babies at home all the time. Alberto knows a midwife who might come here if she's not working."

He couldn't believe it. This fifteen-year-old girl had had no medical assistance and couldn't even go to hospital without incurring costs she couldn't afford to pay. "I might have someone who can help." He told her about Carmen and Casa Flanagan. "Carmen wants to meet you. I could take you out there tomorrow if you want."

She frowned at him. "Why would you help me?"

"Because I wish someone had helped my mam when she was pregnant with me."

Hayden walked over as Angela burst into tears and threw her arms around Sean. Sean held her while she sobbed, and glanced up at Hayden.

"You told her about Casa Flanagan?"

"Yeah."

"If you drop me off at work tomorrow, you can use my car to pick up Angela and take her to visit Carmen."

"Thanks."

"The first group is about to start. Join us when you're free."

Sean nodded.

Angela was still sobbing and he patted her back. "It's all right. We'll work out something."

Her sobs lessened.

"I'll give you my number and you can call me if you need me," he said. "Tomorrow I'll pick you up at nine-thirty and take you to meet Carmen."

"Is she nice?"

"The nicest," Sean assured her.

"She's not going to think I'm a slut?"

"No. She's had a few girls who have been pregnant, including two who are still with her now. She supports them and helps them raise their babies."

For the first time, Angela looked hopeful.

Warmth spread through Sean. Would his own life have turned out differently if someone had shown some kindness to his own mother? He'd like to think so.

***

Angela was waiting for Sean when he arrived at the shelter the next morning. She had a backpack with her. Sean spoke with Alberto to tell him where he was taking her and then he helped her into Hayden's car.

For the first half hour she was quiet, and Sean was happy not to talk. Then she frowned and shifted in her seat. "Where are we going?"

"Casa Flanagan is on the outskirts of Houston," he said. "Don't ask me the suburb name, but Hayden's programmed it into the satellite navigation. It's not far now."

He'd be totally lost without the GPS. As it was he had to focus on staying on the correct side of the road.

He finally pulled into Casa Flanagan.

"Wow. This place is incredible," Angela said.

"Wait until you see the garden out the back." He helped her out of the car and stood in front of her when they got to the front door to protect her from being knocked down by Zita's dogs, who were barking inside.

Should he knock or go straight in?

Splitting the difference, he knocked and opened the door calling, "Mama, it's me."

"Come in," Carmen called back.

He pushed the dogs out of the way and led Angela through to the dining room where Carmen was working. He made the introductions.

"Sit down, Angela," Carmen said. "Sean, there's some horchata in the fridge. Pour a couple of glasses."

He did as she asked. When he'd called Carmen the night before she'd told him she wanted an opportunity to talk with Angela privately and so he took his time in the kitchen, cleaning the few dishes that had been left in the sink.

"Sean, where are those drinks?" Carmen called.

He smiled and took them in. Angela was a little pale.

"I'm going to call Angela's parents," Carmen told him. "She

can stay here for as long as she needs to, but I want her parents to know where she is."

"OK." He gave Angela her drink while Carmen went to make the call. "What do you think they'll say?"

She shrugged. "I don't think they'll be home. They always take a summer vacation at this time of year." Her tone was unconcerned, but her hands gripped the glass tightly.

Carmen came back in. "I've left a message." She smiled at Angela. "How about I show you to your room?"

Angela burst into tears and flung herself into Sean's arms. "Thank you."

Sean took a step back, holding on to her as Carmen nodded her approval. He patted Angela's back and gently pushed her away. "You're welcome. Let's see where you're staying."

Angela slipped her hand into his and they followed Carmen upstairs to a bedroom with a single bed in it. "This will be your room. The bathroom is down the hall and my room is across the corridor." She stepped outside and came back a moment later with a couple of towels. "You might like to freshen up. I've got some spare maternity clothes in the attic. I'll fetch them down in a minute."

"Why?"

"For you," Carmen said. "The girls don't need them anymore."

"Where are they?" Sean asked.

Carmen sighed. "Larissa got her driver's license. She's taken them all to the mall." Carmen crossed herself and lifted her eyes in prayer.

Sean chuckled. "I'm sure they'll be fine."

"If you've got any clothes that need washing, put them in the laundry basket in the bathroom," Carmen continued. "We'll leave you to get settled, and when you're ready, come down to the kitchen and I'll get you something to eat." She gestured for Sean to precede her and they walked downstairs together.

At the bottom of the stairs, Sean turned to Carmen. "Thank you, Mama." He hugged her.

She tisked. "There is nothing to thank. The girl needs help."

"She does. She hasn't been to a doctor since she got pregnant."

Carmen stared at him. "None?"

"No."

She hurried into the kitchen. "I'll make an appointment now. She can't be far off full-term."

"She's got about three weeks."

"You did the right thing, *hijo*." She made the appointment for Angela and Sean took a seat at the table. He wasn't sure what she'd called him. If he was going to stay in Houston, Spanish lessons might be a good idea. There'd been a few times over the weeks that the foster girls and his sisters had spoken in Spanish and he'd had no idea what was going on. He hoped it wasn't going to be a problem for Angela.

Carmen hung up. "She's squeezing us in this afternoon." She sliced up some fruit and pushed the plate toward Sean. "My Brendan would be proud of you helping Angela."

The words were bittersweet. He smiled. "Thank you."

At that moment the dogs started barking. "That must be Zita," Carmen said.

Sure enough, a couple of minutes later, Zita came through the door carrying a garment bag. "*Hola!*"

"You have the dress!" Carmen exclaimed. "Everything is all right with it?"

Zita nodded. "I tried it on in the shop to make sure."

Sean was curious about what kind of wedding dress Zita had chosen. She was the most flamboyant of all his sisters.

"I'll go hang it in my room," she said.

"Sean's room," Carmen corrected with a smile.

Zita laughed. "Sorry. I forgot. Is it all right if I hang it in there?"

"Sure."

She took his hand. "Come and help me."

He frowned, not sure why she needed help, but followed her into his bedroom. Zita hung her dress in the wardrobe and turned to him, clenching her hands together.

"Sean, would you walk me down the aisle, like you did for Carly? You and Mama."

God, his sisters killed him with their acceptance and love. He grinned. "I'd love to."

She beamed at him. "I have another request."

"Shoot."

"Hayden mentioned you play the tin whistle."

He nodded.

"Would you play something Irish at the wedding?" Her expression was so hopeful.

The wedding was only three days away, which didn't give him a lot of time to practice, but he couldn't say no. "Sure. Would you like a jig or something slow?"

She flung her arms around him and kissed his cheek. "I don't know. Whatever you think is best."

"We're reviewing the program tonight, aren't we? How about we decide then?"

"That would be great."

He dug into his bag and pulled out the tin whistle. "I'd better get some practice in."

***

Hayden was running late. His last meeting of the day had gone over and he raced back to his desk to turn off his computer. Carly and Evan were waiting for him. "I'm sorry."

"Don't worry," Carly told him. "They'll wait for us."

He was going to Casa Flanagan to do the final run-through for Zita's wedding on Saturday, but all he could think about was Sean. He grabbed his things and followed them down to where Evan's car was parked.

He took a breath to calm himself. Should he be worried about how excited he was to see Sean? Sean was only here for another three weeks; what they had was temporary.

Hayden had thought this could be a short-term fling, but he hated the idea of it ending. He was being ridiculous. It had to end — Sean didn't even live in the same country. Though Carmen had wanted Sean to move to Houston. Did Sean want to?

His cell phone rang as he got into the car. He smiled at the caller ID. "Hi, Mom."

"How are you, baby?"

"Great. I'm heading out to Casa Flanagan to go over the last details for Zita's wedding."

"When is it?"

"Saturday."

"Good, then you can come to dinner on Friday night." It wasn't a question. "Your sister's bringing her new boyfriend to meet the family."

"Sure." He hoped this one was better than the last. His mind flitted to Sean. "Do you mind if I bring someone too?"

"Ooh, are you seeing someone new?" The excitement in his mother's voice was clear.

"Yeah. I'm not sure if he'll be available, though."

"Invite him. What's his name?"

Hayden glanced at Carly and Evan in the front of the car. He didn't want to go into any detail here. "Sean. Listen, I'll call you tomorrow and we can chat."

"All right then. You have fun tonight."

"Love you, Mom."

"Right back at you, baby."

He hung up. Maybe he shouldn't have mentioned Sean. Maybe it was too much pressure on him. Meeting each other's parents meant things were serious. Didn't it?

"Carly, do you think Sean will freak out if I invite him to my parents' place for dinner?" He regretted the words as soon as they were out. He was used to telling Carly about who he was dating, but this was her brother. There were probably rules about this kind of thing.

She twisted in her seat to face him. "I don't know." She hesitated. "Are you two getting serious?" There was concern on her face.

He shrugged. "I thought since Jada's bringing her new boyfriend, I'd ask Sean."

"He goes home in a couple of weeks."

He nodded.

"What will you do then?"

He really didn't know.

"We're trying to convince him to move out here," she said. "Maybe you could help us."

"You mean immigrate?"

She nodded. "We hope he likes Houston enough to stay."

He smiled. It was a delicious thought, to have more of Sean, to keep him around and give them a chance to explore whatever this was between them. But would the idea of a real relationship scare Sean? "I'll do my best."

"Thanks."

They arrived at Casa Flanagan and as he walked in, Angela was coming down the stairs. "Angela, what are you doing here?"

She beamed at him. "Hi, Hayden. Carmen's letting me stay. She took me to a doctor this afternoon who says my baby is fine. I'm having a girl!"

"Congratulations." He hugged her and then introduced her to Carly and Evan.

"Welcome," Carly said.

"Do you know where Sean is?" Hayden asked.

"I think he's upstairs in his room."

Hayden glanced upstairs. He wasn't sure which room it was, and it wasn't a mistake he wanted to make.

"I'll show you," Angela said and she slowly climbed the stairs.

He was pleased that she was already feeling at home here. There was something about Casa Flanagan that was instantly comforting.

"This is my room," Angela said, pointing. "Carmen's already brought the cot down for when my baby arrives." Her enthusiasm was palpable.

"That's great." He was happy for her, but he wanted to see Sean.

"Sean's room is down the hall on the right."

"Thanks." He walked down and peered into a bedroom which had a double bed in it. Sean's backpack was at the foot of the bed, so this was definitely his room, but he wasn't here. He wandered over to the window and peered down at the garden. Sean was sitting on one of the garden benches alone. His heart jumped and he hurried downstairs. In the kitchen, he had to stop to greet the others.

"Sean is outside practicing," Carmen told him.

Practicing? "Thanks." He went out the back door and heard a wistful tune. Sean was playing his tin whistle. Hayden walked slowly toward the sound, enjoying the melody. When Sean came into view, he stopped.

Sean had his eyes closed and his fingers moved effortlessly across the holes of the whistle. The tune changed to one which was a little more hopeful and cheery and when it was done, Hayden clapped his hands.

Sean's eyes opened and he lowered his instrument. "Hey, I must have lost track of time."

"That was beautiful." Hayden walked closer, wanting nothing more than to kiss his boyfriend.

"Zita's asked me to play a song at the wedding. I'm not sure which one to play."

"I can help you decide if you'd like." Hayden sat next to him. "But first…" He pulled Sean close and covered his mouth with his own.

Sean hummed in agreement as Hayden tasted him. He'd missed Sean's taste, his lips, damn, he'd missed *him* and it had only been a day since he'd last seen him. He was falling fast.

Pulling back, he licked his lips. "Honey, you're going to make me forget where we are."

Sean glanced around and then sighed. "You're right. Though I happen to know a couple of those cabins are empty."

Sean was absolute temptation. Hayden swallowed. "Why don't I get Zita out here and you can play her some songs?"

Sean smiled. "All right."

Hayden hurried away, wishing for the first time that there were no weddings to organize.

A few minutes later he returned with Zita, Bridget, Carly and Carmen in tow.

Sean's eyebrows rose when he saw them all.

"They wanted to hear what you've got," Hayden said.

Sean swallowed. "All right." He looked at Zita. "I'll play you a couple of tunes and you can tell me which one you like best." He stood and gestured for the women to sit on the bench. Hayden found a seat on the garden wall.

The first tune was upbeat and jaunty, the type of tune that made Hayden want to dance a jig. Sean tapped his foot, and Zita's grin went from ear to ear. When he finished, everyone applauded. Sean flushed and gave a bow. Then he closed his eyes and began to play again.

This time the song was slow, hauntingly beautiful, full of

hope, passion and love. Hayden's heart ached as he heard the longing. When Sean finished and opened his eyes, no one moved. Zita was holding a hand to her mouth and her eyes were full of tears.

"I guess the first one was better," Sean said.

Zita shook her head and stood up. "No. I want that one, it was so beautiful. I want it to be my wedding dance." She hugged Sean. "Let me get David. He should hear this." She hurried away.

Sean glanced his way and Hayden managed to smile at him. He couldn't speak through the lump in his throat. Sean was so talented, and yet he'd said he could only play a couple of tunes. That was the understatement of the century.

Zita returned with David and the others left to check dinner. Hayden stayed where he was, not wanting to move as Sean played the song again. David brought Zita close to him, holding her as they listened. When Sean finished, David kissed Zita. "You're right. It's perfect."

Zita beamed. "Will you play it at the wedding?"

Sean nodded.

"Thank you." She hugged him. "Come on, dinner is almost ready."

Hayden intercepted them on the path. "I need a word with Sean," he told Zita and David.

"Sure. Take your time." She grinned and then they were alone.

He wasn't entirely sure what he wanted to say. He couldn't figure out how to express what he was feeling inside.

"Is something wrong?" Sean asked.

Hayden slipped his arms around Sean, pulling him close. "That was beautiful." He kissed him slowly, wanting to pour all of his emotions into the one kiss. Sean did so much to Hayden's equilibrium, shaking him up, making him feel so many things.

Sean ran his hand over Hayden's hair, gripping his neck with a possessiveness that was arousing. If he didn't pull away now, he wasn't going to be able to. Hayden broke the kiss, but still kept one hand on Sean's butt. Their eyes met and he could see Sean's desire which was surely mirrored in his own eyes.

"Come home with me." He hadn't meant to say that, but it

was too late to take the words back and he wanted Sean to say yes. "Spend your days here at Casa Flanagan, and your nights with me. You can use my car. I don't need it while I'm at work."

Sean hesitated.

Hayden swore inwardly. "Forget about it. I shouldn't be asking. You're here to be with your family." He turned to go back into the house.

Sean grabbed his hand and pulled him back. "There's nothing I want more than to go home with you," he said, running a hand over Hayden's cheek. "But I do want to spend time with Carmen and I'm not sure how she will react. Can you let me figure it out?"

"Yes." He'd agree to anything at this stage. "How about we start with Friday night? Your sisters will be staying here before the wedding, and there may not be room. You could stay with me, and come to my folks' house for dinner."

"What?"

It wasn't how he'd meant to ask him. "Mom invited me around for dinner on Friday night. My sister Jada is bringing her new boyfriend and I asked whether I could bring mine too."

There was uncertainty in Sean's eyes, and then he smiled. "I'd like that."

Hayden grinned, kissing him again, and took his hand. "We'd better get inside before I decide to explore those empty cabins with you."

Sean chuckled and together they went back into the house.

Chapter 14

Hayden wasn't sure who was more nervous on the drive to his parents' house — him or Sean. It wasn't as if he'd never brought a boyfriend home to meet his family before, but generally they'd been comfortable with their sexuality. Sean was still getting used to being out and that might cause some issues if his family made any jokes.

And Jada's boyfriend was a wild card. He'd called Jada yesterday to make sure her boyfriend knew Hayden was gay and she'd assured him he was fine. But she'd thought that with previous boyfriends before.

He pulled up at his parents' single story, brick and tile house. His father had been in the garden recently because the lawn was freshly mowed and the garden beds were free of weeds.

"Are you ready?" Hayden asked.

Sean nodded, though he was a little paler than usual. They got out of the car and Hayden took hold of Sean's hand. "My folks are really nice."

"They made you, didn't they?" Sean's smile didn't quite reach his eyes.

Hayden sighed. There wasn't anything he could do about Sean's anxiety. He knocked on the front door and walked in. The living room was the first room on the left and everyone was in there — his parents, brother and sisters, and Jada's boyfriend who saw them holding hands and his eyes widened.

Sean dropped Hayden's hand and clasped his own together.

This was a good start. Hayden sighed. Good one, Jada. He forced a smile on his face. "Hi, all."

His mother got to her feet as he made the introductions and came over to greet Sean. "Lovely to meet you. Can I get you a drink?"

Sean smiled and shook her hand.

"A couple of beers would be great, thanks, Mom," Hayden answered.

"Sure." She left the room and Hayden gestured for Sean to sit on the spare sofa. He turned to Jada's boyfriend. "I don't think we've met."

"Oh, this is Nick," Jada said.

Hayden reached out to shake his hand and after a moment's hesitation, Nick took it. Not everyone was immediately comfortable when faced with two gay people, but Hayden did not need this now. If Jada had just given him the heads up, it would have been far better for all parties. "Nice to meet you."

Nick nodded.

"We were talking about our vacations to Galveston when we were kids," Malik said. "Apparently Nick used to live there."

"It was always fun," Hayden said. He looked at the man, wondering whether they might have run into each other during that time. All the kids used to hang out by the beach. He did look kind of familiar. He took the beer his mother handed him and thanked her.

"He used to work at the Pleasure Pier," Jada said.

Hayden had a very pleasant memory of the Pleasure Pier. One summer he'd met a guy there who hadn't been sure if he was gay. Hayden had been happy to help him figure it out and they'd spent one night together exploring each other's bodies.

Nick glanced at Hayden, and Hayden's mouth dropped open as recognition sparked. Nick was that guy. He hadn't been shocked about Hayden and Sean holding hands, he'd been shocked to see Hayden.

Well, this was all kinds of weird. He'd slept with his sister's boyfriend.

"I can't believe we didn't meet back then," Jada said.

"Yeah, amazing, isn't it," Nick said weakly.

Hayden closed his mouth. He wasn't going to make things more awkward for Nick than they already were.

"What about you, Sean?" Malik asked. "Where did you go

for summer vacation?"

"We don't get much of a summer in Ireland," Sean said.

"Oh, you're Irish," Madison said. "When did you move over here?"

"I'm visiting," Sean said. "My three sisters are getting married."

Madison shot Hayden a questioning look. Hayden shook his head slightly.

"So how did you meet Hayden?" Madison asked.

"Sean is Carolina's brother," Hayden told her.

"Oh." This time the look was clearly *what the hell are you doing?* Hayden ignored her.

"It's time to start cooking," his mom said. "Abe, why don't you check the grill?"

His father got to his feet and headed outside. Hayden stood up. "We'll help." He gestured for Sean to follow him and got out of there.

It took until after dinner for Madison to corner him. Sean was chatting to Malik and Hayden had gone into the kitchen to get them both another drink.

"Hay-Hay, what are you doing?" Madison asked as she followed him inside.

"Getting a drink."

"You know what I mean. Why are you so serious about a guy who's only here for a few weeks?"

"What makes you think it's serious?"

She arched an eyebrow. "You brought him to dinner."

She was right and they both knew it.

"He might stay longer. The Flanagans are trying to convince him to immigrate."

She put a hand on his arm. "I don't want you to get hurt. You always fall hard."

"It's not love." He couldn't let it get that far, not if Sean was going home.

"If you say so." Her tone clearly said she didn't believe him. She kissed him on the cheek. "Take care of yourself." She left.

Hayden let out a deep breath and found the bottle opener.

Nick walked into the kitchen and stopped when he saw

Hayden. He turned to go.

"Wait, Nick," Hayden said. This was one thing he could fix. "I remember you."

Nick slowly turned back around.

"Does Jada know you're bi?"

"It's never come up."

"It might be something you want to tell her before you get too serious."

"I love her."

Ah, hell. "Does she love you?"

He nodded.

He had no idea how Jada would react. "I won't say anything to her," Hayden said. "But if it comes out later, it might be worse for you."

Nick swore. "I don't want to lose her."

"She's pretty tough. If she doesn't have a problem with your other exes, then she shouldn't have an issue with us. It was one night when we were teenagers." He remembered it as awkward and frantic, and all about the sex.

"I'll think about it."

"Think about what?" Jada walked in and kissed Nick. "Is my brother propositioning you?"

Nick gaped at her.

She frowned. "What's wrong?"

"That's my cue to leave," Hayden said.

"Don't move," Jada ordered.

Hayden paused.

Nick looked longingly at the door. This was his chance to tell her. Would he be brave enough?

Nick swallowed. "Can we talk somewhere where we won't be interrupted?"

Jada glanced at them both. She bit her bottom lip and nodded. "This way."

Hayden watched them go. He hoped his younger sister would understand. He didn't want to ruin things for Jada.

With a sigh, he grabbed the two bottles of beer and went back outside to Sean.

It was some time later when Nick came outside alone. He

walked over to Hayden and said, "Jada wants to talk with you."

"You told her?"

He nodded. "She's in her old bedroom." He didn't look happy.

"Back in a second," he said to Sean and walked inside. Apprehension settled on his shoulders and he approached the room. Jada was sitting on the bed. He tapped on the door and she looked up. "This is kind of surreal."

He nodded. "I didn't recognize him at first. When he looked at me funny, I thought he had a problem with gays."

Her laugh was sharp. "We don't have to worry about that."

"No." He sat next to her on the bed. "How are you feeling?"

She shuffled away from him. "Confused. I don't know what to think."

Jada was the most emotional of his siblings, and he didn't want to get her fired up. "It was years ago," he said gently. "One night where neither of us cared who the other was."

"I'm not sure that makes it easier." Jada closed her eyes. "I keep asking myself whether it matters that it was you he slept with rather than Madison. Either way, it would be strange."

Hayden wasn't sure what to say. "How much do you like him?"

She looked straight at him. "I love him. I thought he was the one."

Hell. "And now?"

She shrugged. "I don't know. I know he has a history — we all do — but he's slept with my brother." She sighed.

"Honey, I can't help you make a decision. He seems like a really nice guy, and he cares for you." He wanted to see her smile. "I can promise I have no desire to sleep with him again."

Her lips twitched upward and she poked him. "Hands off, he's mine now."

Hayden smiled. "Then there's your answer."

She nodded. "Maybe you're right."

Hayden pressed a kiss to her forehead. "I'd better get back out there before Mom wonder's what is going on."

Jada groaned. "That's the last thing we need. If she asks, make up some excuse."

He nodded. "Love you, sis."

"Love you too."

He walked back outside to the party.

He met Sean's gaze the moment he stepped outside and immediately recognized the anxiety on his face. He wandered over and took Sean's hand.

"I can go if it's an issue," Sean murmured.

"It's not," he said. "That was about something else. I'll tell you about it later."

He kissed Sean's cheek and rejoined the conversation.

***

Something was definitely going on. Hayden had disappeared with Nick and Jada several times through the night.

Did Nick have an issue with him?

Despite Hayden's assurances, Sean couldn't fully relax. When people began to talk about leaving, he breathed a sigh of relief.

"I hope we'll see you again before you go," Hayden's mother said as she walked them to the car.

"That would be nice," he said. He had liked them, but he doubted he'd see them again.

Hayden backed out, waving to his family as they drove off. Sean wanted to ask what had been going on, but it was none of his business. Not really. He stayed silent.

"That was weird," Hayden said.

Sean jumped. "What was?"

He chuckled. "Turns out I did meet Nick during one summer vacation," he said. "We had quite an energetic night of experimentation."

Sean's jaw dropped. "He's gay?"

"Bi. He recognized me straight away and freaked out. He hadn't told Jada he was bi and was worried I'd say something."

Sean shook his head. Of all of the problems he'd imagined, that was not one of them. "So what happened?"

"He asked me to keep it quiet and Jada walked in. She got him to tell her the truth."

"And how does she feel about it?"

"She's confused, but I think she's going to be OK with it. She loves him."

Sean let out a breath. "Well, that's good."

"Yeah. I'm sorry it was worrying you, but they don't want the rest of the family to find out."

"Fair enough."

"So are you all right?" Hayden asked. "My family didn't say anything to make you uncomfortable?"

"No. They were really nice." He shouldn't be surprised. Hayden had told him they were accepting of who he was.

Hayden pulled into his driveway and they got out.

"We can sleep in a little tomorrow," Hayden said. "Everything is being delivered, so we just have to go to the venue."

Sean smiled. "Extra time in bed. I'm sure we can figure out some way to amuse ourselves."

"I agree." Hayden took his hand and led him into the house.

***

Sean and Hayden had a very lazy morning the next day. Zita's wedding wasn't starting until three, and so it wasn't until after lunch that they showered, dressed and headed to the chateau where the wedding was taking place.

When Hayden drove into the grounds, Sean stared. The place was amazing. A huge French chateau with acres of manicured gardens. It was the very last place he pictured Zita getting married.

"Epic, isn't it?" Hayden said.

"Yeah. Zita didn't choose it, did she?"

Hayden laughed. "No, it was David's mother, Fay. Zita didn't want anything extravagant, but relations with David's family have been a little strained since the Garcia incident."

He could understand wanting to keep the peace. He grabbed his bag and followed Hayden inside. They were about an hour early, so Hayden could solve any issues that might arise. The entrance of the chateau was immense, and the staircase curved high above them. There was no one around. "Everyone will be upstairs in the suites," Hayden said, starting up the stairs.

The door of the first suite was open and the men were lounging on the furniture, dressed in shorts and T-shirts.

"It's time you got dressed," Hayden told them as he walked

in. "The photographer's going to want to take photos of you soon."

"Hi," David said as he got to his feet. "I was wondering when you'd get here."

Sean greeted David and his friends. Grant even managed a nod hello, so David must have had words to his brother.

"Is there anything you need?" Hayden asked.

"No. We've been hanging around so we don't mess up our suits," David said.

Hayden grinned. "No chance of that," he joked with a wink. "We'll go and check on the ladies."

Down the hall was another suite, this time with the door closed. Sean could hear feminine laughter from within. Hayden knocked loudly. "Are you dressed?"

Bridget opened the door wearing a light summer dressing gown. Her hair was a mass of curls and her face was already made up. "Sort of," she said, gesturing them in.

The room was packed. Aside from his sisters and Carmen, there were two other women in dressing gowns and what appeared to be every foster sister who had ever gone through Casa Flanagan. Way too many people.

"Is that Hayden and Sean?" Zita called from somewhere in the middle of the group.

"Sure is, honey," Hayden said. "Do you need anything?"

"I need music. Sean, have you got your whistle?"

He still couldn't see her, surrounded as she was by sisters and hairdressers. "Yeah."

"Good, will you play something cheerful?"

"Sure." He moved across to the window where there was some space and got his tin whistle out of his bag. He began to play.

The music soothed him and helped him to relax. He ignored the crowd as the photographer took photos of everyone, including himself. Carmen waved at him from where she was sitting having her hair done.

Not long after, Zita stood up and said, "It's time to get dressed."

He tucked the whistle into his inside jacket pocket and moved toward the door with Hayden.

"You two don't need to leave," Zita called. "Turn your back if you're uncomfortable. I want photos with both of you before the ceremony."

Sean hadn't met the other two bridesmaids, who might not be as comfortable having him there. "We'll wait outside."

She nodded, already turning her attention to the garment bag draped over the bed.

Outside, Sean took a deep breath.

"There's going to be about two hundred people at the wedding," Hayden said. "After the ceremony, you can hide in here when you want to be alone." Hayden wiggled his eyebrows. "Though maybe I'll join you this time."

He liked the thought. Hayden was looking particularly delectable today in a blood-red suit. Sean was wearing the same suit he'd worn to Carly's wedding, but he had bought a different shirt during the week. Hayden had insisted he buy a rainbow-colored pocket handkerchief as well. Sean wasn't sure whether he was comfortable with the blatant symbol of who he was, but Hayden had said to trust him.

Carly opened the door, absolutely gorgeous in a ruby red knee-length dress with wide straps. "You can come in now." She led them through the girls to where Zita and the rest of her bridesmaids were. Each bridesmaid had a different colored knee-length dress — red, blue, green and yellow. Carmen wore a very sophisticated purple gown which showed off her curves, but Zita was the real center of attention. Her gown was white and short at the front, falling in ruffles to a long skirt behind. There were satin roses in different colors across the bodice and around the back which added a flair of color, and pizazz. It was definitely Zita's style in every way. She grinned at him. "Your handkerchief matches us!"

Sean glanced at Hayden, who smiled. "That was Hayden's work."

She blew Hayden a kiss. "OK, let's do a few photos, and then get this show on the road. I want to get married."

He followed her directions and smiled in all of the photos. Zita insisted on having one with him and Hayden before having a combination of ones with her sisters and mother.

"I'll make sure the guys are downstairs," Hayden said. "I'll meet you there."

"Girls, go with Hayden and take your seats," Carmen said. "We will be down soon."

In very little time, he was left in the room with only his sisters, Carmen, and the two other bridesmaids.

Zita was twitchy, moving her hands about, and not able to sit still.

"Are you nervous?" he asked.

"No. I'm impatient. I'm so excited." She beamed at him.

"Take some deep breaths," Carmen advised.

She did as she was told and then said, "Can we go now?"

"I'll check everything's in place," Sean said, walking down to the men's suite. The room was empty, and as he went to the staircase he could see people moving into the room where he assumed the ceremony was going to be held. Hayden came out, spotted him and gave him the thumbs up.

"We're ready when Zita is."

Sean nodded and went to tell his sister the good news.

***

In almost no time, the ceremony was over and Sean was having his picture taken again. He hadn't had a chance to speak with Hayden, who was flitting around, making sure everything was organized and running on schedule.

Finally, the photographer called an end to the photo session. As he turned to go, Hayden was right there holding a glass of champagne.

"Thought you could do with a drink."

"Thanks." He took the glass and sipped as he scanned the crowd. This time the percentage of Hispanic to Caucasian was tipped in the favor of Caucasians, and the level of expensive jewelry was high. David came from a wealthy family who'd made their riches in oil, and the display of wealth was quite something to behold. He wasn't quite ready to wade through the crowd. "I might head up to the suite."

Hayden's smile was understanding. He kissed him quickly on the cheek. "I'll come and get you when they seat everyone for dinner."

Sean squeezed his hand and turned to go upstairs. A couple

moved aside to let him through, but there was definite disdain on their faces. What was their problem?

Halfway up the stairs, he realized they had seen Hayden kiss him. How would they have reacted if the kiss had been on his lips? That would have been truly scandalous.

He wished he had the courage to kiss Hayden in public, to show the world how much he liked him. But he didn't want to cause any problems at Zita's wedding. Not when relations between Zita's and David's family were already strained. But the idea was a lot more tempting than it had ever been before. Perhaps he was getting used to being out.

Sean sat on the chair by the window overlooking the well-manicured garden, sipping his champagne. He could hear the murmur of conversation from where he was sitting. The idea that he wanted to be openly gay was such a foreign one. For so long he'd been terrified of judgment, abuse and abandonment, but now, when he was with his family and with Hayden, he didn't fear those things. In such a short space of time, they'd made him comfortable with who he was, made it easy to be himself.

Was it simply easier to be gay in a big city than a small town?

Probably. Not everybody knew your business or who you were.

Was Houston where he was meant to be?

He did want to be close to his sisters and to Carmen. Then there was the question of Hayden.

Things had gone from zero to one hundred in the blink of an eye with him, and Sean was still reeling. Perhaps Hayden was so into him because there was a time limit to it. Another three weeks and he could move on to the next guy who caught his eye.

Sean scowled. He didn't like the thought.

He really liked Hayden — liked that he was comfortable with who he was, liked his caring nature, liked the way he was so organized all the time, and liked when he let loose and relaxed. Hayden was a friend, a confidant and a lover. Sean had never had that before. His lovers were one-night stands, enough to blow off some steam so he could climb back in his closet when he got home. He'd never hoped for more, but now he had it, he wanted to hold on to it. Hold on to Hayden.

That was scary in itself. He'd never had such strong feelings toward anyone before.

"Now that's a lovely silhouette." Hayden was standing in the doorway.

Every nerve in Sean's body did a little dance to see Hayden's casual elegance. He needed Hayden. He put down his glass and rose, crossing the room in a few strides. He pulled Hayden toward him and pressed his lips against his, slowly kissing him.

Hayden hummed in approval and wrapped his arms around Sean, squeezing his butt.

Sean's emotions went explosive in seconds and he fought the urge to press Hayden against the wall and devour him. He wanted intimacy, not sex. Finally, he broke the kiss.

He stared into Hayden's eyes as different emotions — joy, hope, passion, tenderness, love — coursed through his body. This was no holiday hook-up. Not for him. But he couldn't say that. He couldn't expose his heart. Instead, he said, "Is it dinner time?"

Hayden nodded.

Sean took his hand, wanting nothing more than to climb into bed with Hayden and show him how much he cared for him. "Let's go then."

Hayden was lost for words. He followed Sean out of the bridal suite and down the stairs. What had that kiss been about? That wasn't a kiss hello, that was a kiss which had rocked his socks off, that had touched him deeply. It was a kiss to say Sean cared.

Wasn't it?

Or was Hayden just hoping it was more because that's what he wanted?

As he walked into the ballroom, he bumped into someone. Excusing himself, he shook his mind clear of the confusion. Now wasn't the time to analyze. It was dinner and he had the opportunity to enjoy Sean's company. They were sitting next to each other at a table with Jack, Evan, Carmen and a couple of the women who had been foster girls in their youth.

"Wasn't the ceremony lovely?" Carmen exclaimed.

Jack smiled. "Yes, Mama."

"Don't my girls look beautiful?"

"Absolutely," Evan said, glancing over to where Carly was sitting at the bridal table.

Carmen patted both men on their hands. "You have such good taste in women."

Hayden smiled, content not to speak. He wanted to soak up the atmosphere and enjoy being with this family, in particular with the man next to him.

After dinner, there were a number of speeches. Carly and Garth both spoke as matron of honor and best man, then Bridget and David's sister spoke for each of their families. David and Zita had ruled out letting David's father speak because they had no idea what he would say. Then it was time for the first dance.

There was a tiny tremor in Sean's hand as he withdrew his tin whistle and moved to stand by the dance floor. David took Zita's hand and led her onto the floor, then Sean began to play. There wasn't a single sound in the room as the notes sang out clear and crisp. Both Carmen and Fay wiped their eyes as the couple danced, but Hayden's focus was solely on Sean. He stood tall, his eyes closed, and as the song progressed, Sean relaxed and opened his eyes, his focus on the dancers. Hayden couldn't draw his eyes away. There was such elegance, such depth to this man.

When the song was over, there was a huge round of applause, then the band started playing and others got up to dance. Sean tucked his whistle back into his jacket and walked out of the nearest door.

Something was wrong.

Hayden followed him outside into the garden where he was striding across the floodlit lawn.

"Sean!" Hayden called and trotted down the steps after him. Sean didn't stop, but he slowed his stride and Hayden caught up. There were tears in Sean's eyes.

"What's wrong?" Hayden stroked his arm. "You played beautifully."

"Do you think we'll ever have that?" he asked, brushing away the tears.

"Have what?"

"That acceptance. Everyone there loves and accepts Zita and David. They have no problem with the couple dancing together, they wouldn't flinch if they saw them holding hands, or kissing in public. Do you think one day gay people will have that same acceptance?"

Hayden's heart squeezed. "I don't know. I hope so. I have to believe that the more common it is, the more comfortable we become with public displays of affection, the better society will react." He took Sean's hand, ran his thumb over the back of it. "But if either of us got married, we'd invite people who would celebrate our union. Our wedding would be like Zita and David's." He'd phrased that wrong. He should have said our weddings, but the idea of marrying Sean wasn't scary. It was actually really appealing.

He was in way too deep, and it was too late to go back.

He loved Sean.

Joy clashed with concern. Sean wasn't staying.

He tugged Sean close and kissed him gently on the mouth. "We can help change perceptions. We can go in there and dance together like other couples do. We can help people get used to same-sex couples." He fully expected Sean to refuse.

"All right." Sean nodded. "Let's go dance." He took hold of Hayden's hand and together they walked back inside.

What had got into Sean? This wasn't a guy who was terrified of being outed. This was a guy who wanted to show the world who he was.

It was a complete turn-on. He followed Sean onto the dance floor and they were joined by Zita, David, Bridget and Carmen. At Carmen's request, the band played a salsa tune and she and Sean danced together. The man knew how to move his hips. He was sensual and sexy and Hayden longed to get him alone. He checked his watch. There were still a couple of hours until the wedding would be over, and he needed to stay until the end.

Damn it.

When the song finished, the band took it down a notch, playing a slow song. Couples took to the floor, holding each other tightly. Sean was still dancing with Carmen, gently leading her around the dance floor. Hayden wanted to cut in, but it wouldn't be right. This was time for Sean to bond with his stepmother, and Carmen had no one else to dance with.

They moved closer to Hayden and the music segued into another slow song. Carmen kissed Sean's cheek. "Thank you for the dance." She stepped back and gestured for Hayden to take her place.

He loved Carmen. Loved her acceptance, her kindness and her astuteness. He raised an eyebrow at Sean to make sure he was comfortable and in answer, Sean pulled him into his arms.

This was where he belonged. His arms wrapped around this man, as they danced so closely together. It was everything that was right in the world.

He gazed into Sean's eyes and the intensity in them took

Hayden's breath away. Sean had to feel the same way he did — didn't he?

Someone bumped into them, breaking the moment. Hayden glanced over to David's parents and tensed as he met Bob's eyes.

Bob scowled and turned away. He opened his mouth and Fay cut in. "Don't say anything."

Hayden didn't hear Bob's response as Bob moved away from them.

"Zita warned me about him," Sean said.

"Does he bother you?"

Sean shook his head. "Not tonight."

"Good." Hayden smiled.

The song came to an end and Hayden led Sean off the dance floor. Angela waved at him from where she was sitting with the current group of foster girls. She seemed to be having fun chatting with Alejandra. As Hayden watched, Alejandra picked up a baby monitor and held it to her ear. With a sigh, she excused herself.

Hayden wanted kids one day. Did Sean want them? He'd probably never thought about it, given that he'd never been openly gay. Hayden would have to ask him sometime, but not today. Sean was relaxed and happy, and Hayden wanted to keep it that way.

The evening wore on until finally Zita and David announced they were going. Everyone stood to send them off and then began to leave. Hayden was more than ready to get Sean alone. While Carmen and Fay said goodbye to the guests and thanked them for coming, Hayden and Sean went upstairs to pack up all of the things left in the suites.

"It was a fun night," Sean said as he folded dressing gowns and put them into the overnight bags the girls had brought with them.

"It was," Hayden agreed. "You were more relaxed than at Carly's wedding."

Sean smiled. "I'm getting used to being around people, and it's easier when I don't have to hide my attraction to you." He brushed past Hayden, squeezing his ass.

Hayden grinned. "When I showed you into that courtyard at Carly's wedding, I did fantasize about you grabbing hold of me and proving you were gay."

Sean flushed. "Hold that thought."

As soon as they had packed up, he could get Sean alone. He worked faster.

It was another two hours before Hayden unlocked the front door of his house. He was exhausted.

"I need a shower," Sean said, walking toward Hayden's bathroom. Hayden followed him, pleased Sean was so comfortable in his home. They took a quick shower together, both too tired to do more than wash each other's backs, before falling into bed. Hayden pulled Sean close to him.

"Good night," Sean said, kissing him.

"Night." As Hayden snuggled into Sean he knew this was what he wanted for the rest of his life.

***

The few days after Zita's wedding were relatively subdued. Zita and David were on their honeymoon, and Bridget and Carly were at work, so Sean spent his days at Casa Flanagan and his nights with Hayden.

Angela had settled in and spent much of her time with Alejandra, who was giving her tips about being a mother. She seemed happy.

Angela's parents hadn't called back, but Carmen kept leaving messages. It was a waste of time. If they were anything like his mother, they weren't going to respond.

Today, the house was quiet as Carmen had taken everyone except Angela, who was too tired, to the beach. Sean wandered into the kitchen, where Angela was getting a snack. "How's things?"

"Ugh," Angela said. "I can't wait until I get this baby out."

He smiled. "Won't be long now."

"Easy for you to say. You're not carrying around a basketball."

Thinking it wise not to comment, he went to the fridge. "Can I get you a drink?"

"Iced water please."

He poured her a glass and sat next to her at the bench.

She took hold of his hand. "Thank you, Sean." Her eyes welled up. "Thank you for bringing me here. I didn't know what I was going to do after the baby arrived."

He smiled. "I'm glad I could help."

Angela shifted in her seat. "That's better." She sighed. "I can breathe a little easier." She sipped her water. "Damn, I need to pee." She climbed off the stool. "Be back in a minute."

Sean grabbed an apple from the fruit bowl and took a bite. He was content here. He'd spent so much of his life keeping his head down trying not to attract any attention — too scared that if he did something wrong he'd end up without a job and back on the streets — and he wanted that to change. Helping Angela made him feel worthwhile. He glanced up as Angela came back into the room, her face deathly white. He got to his feet. "What's wrong?"

"I think my water broke."

"What?" His heart raced. He didn't know what to do.

"There was a lot more fluid than there should be. It wasn't just pee."

He slowed his breathing, not letting the panic take over. He knew nothing about giving birth. "Are you having any contractions?"

She shook her head. "My back's a bit sore though."

He helped her onto a chair in the dining room. "Let me call Carmen."

He dialed, but there was no answer. He left a message, trying not to sound frantic. "Did Carmen talk to you about going into labor?" He crossed his fingers.

"I've got a bag packed for the hospital in my room."

"I'll get it." He raced upstairs. Should he take her to the hospital? Hell, he didn't even know where it was. Grabbing the bag, he carried it back to Angela. "How are you feeling?"

"A little light-headed."

So was he. "All right, let's get you to the hospital just in case. What's its name?"

She told him, and he helped her outside. Thank God Zita had loaned him her car while she was on her honeymoon.

Angela got into the passenger side and he raced back inside to get her bag and scribble a hasty note to Carmen. He programmed the GPS with the hospital's address and drove.

Halfway there, Angela grabbed her belly and groaned.

He increased his speed. "Are you all right?"

She nodded, her face scrunched up in pain. "I think that was a contraction."

He checked the time. "Tell me when you have another one."

As he pulled into the hospital parking lot, she clenched her teeth. "Another one," she gasped.

Ten minutes apart.

They hurried into the emergency department.

"Identification and insurance," the nurse said.

Sean looked at Angela.

"I don't have ID and Carmen's got the insurance details."

He tried calling Carmen again. This time she picked up.

"*Hola*, Sean."

"Carmen, Angela's gone into labor and we're at the hospital. We need her insurance details."

"Pass me to the nurse, I'll tell her."

Sean handed the phone to the nurse and glanced at Angela. Her eyes were wide and she looked scared. Sean hugged her. "It's going to be all right. You're not doing this alone."

Her eyes glistened and she managed a smile.

The nurse handed the phone back to Sean.

"We're packing up now," Carmen said. "But it will be a couple of hours before I can get there. Will you be all right?"

"Yes. We'll be fine." He prayed he was right.

A surprisingly short time later, they were upstairs in a birthing suite. Angela had been given a hospital gown to wear and was waiting for the midwife to come.

"How are you doing?" Sean asked her.

She gripped his hand. "I'm scared. Don't leave me."

"I won't. I'll stay as long as you want me to."

The midwife came in, checked Angela's name and date of birth. Her eyes widened, and she flicked a glance between Sean and Angela. "Is there anyone you want me to call?"

Angela hesitated, then shook her head.

The midwife examined Angela. "This baby is in a rush. You're already eight centimeters dilated."

"Is that good?" Angela asked.

"Another inch and you can start pushing."

Angela's eyes widened. "I'm not ready. I don't want to do this."

The midwife pasted a smile on her face and said, "I'm afraid the baby's not waiting."

Angela started crying.

"Come now, you'll be fine," the midwife said. "When you're ten centimeters dilated, it will be time for you to push. I'll talk you through it so you don't need to worry. There are plenty of experts on hand. We'll make sure you'll be all right. Would you like an epidural?"

"A what?"

"It's for the pain. It goes into your spine."

Angela glanced at Sean.

He shrugged. "How much does it hurt?"

"It's painful, but not too bad," Angela said.

"It's going to ramp up, especially when you start pushing," the midwife said. "Some women prefer to go without, and others swear by it. It depends on your pain threshold. I'll need to arrange an anesthesiologist if you want one and that could take some time."

He didn't want to see her in pain. "I'd go for the epidural."

Angela nodded. "All right."

"I'll be back when I've arranged it," the midwife said and left the room.

Another contraction hit Angela and she screwed up her eyes as she rode it out. He took her hand. It was awful seeing her in so much pain. Sean had never considered the realities of childbirth before. Sure, he'd seen it depicted in movies, but that wasn't real and it didn't involve anyone he cared about. This looked like Angela was being attacked from the inside.

"I want my mom," she whimpered when the contraction finished.

Sean's heart broke. "I'll call her. What's her name?"

"Gabrielly — Gaby."

"What's the number?" He dialed and went to stand by the

door. He didn't want Angela overhearing what her parents might say.

A female answered the phone. "Hello?"

"Is this Gaby?"

"Speaking."

"My name's Sean. I'm a friend of Angela's."

There was a sharp intake of breath. "Is she all right?" There was concern in her voice. Sean felt a glimmer of hope.

"She's currently in labor and would really like her mom with her."

Angela was watching him closely.

"Oh my God. Where is she?"

He told her the hospital name.

"I'll be there as soon as I can."

Sean hung up and smiled. "She's on her way."

Angela burst out crying.

The midwife returned. "The anesthesiologist will be half an hour," she said. "Let me check you again."

Sean moved back to the side of Angela's bed, keeping his eyes on Angela's face. He didn't want to see what was going on below her waist. Angela gripped his hand and he winced at the pain as she had another contraction. He couldn't complain, she was going through far worse. He'd never imagined he'd be in this position in a maternity ward. He'd never thought about kids at all.

"Angela, this baby's in a real rush. You're fully dilated. We don't have time to wait for the epidural. Let me get some things and then you're going to start pushing on the next contraction."

Feck. Sean's heart pounded. Gaby wasn't going to get here in time. Neither was Carmen. It was just him and Angela. He squeezed her hand. "You've got this."

She nodded, her face determined.

The midwife returned with other nurses and the next half hour was a flurry of noise and activity as Angela gave birth. Before Sean knew it, the midwife was laying a wrinkly, gooey baby girl on Angela's chest.

Sean brushed the tears from his own eyes as Angela stared at the baby, wide-eyed.

There was a commotion in the hallway outside and a voice

said, "She's my daughter. I want to see her."

Then an older version of Angela rushed in.

"Mom?"

Both Angela and Gaby started talking at once. Sean moved away from the bed to give them space to reunite. One of the nurses took the baby from Angela so she could sit up.

"Is it a boy or girl?" Gaby asked.

"It's a girl," she said. "Her name is Shauna."

Sean glanced at her and she smiled.

"Is she named after her daddy?" Gaby asked, giving Sean a suspicious glance.

"No. It's my friend's name. He enabled me to have my baby in a hospital where we'd both be safe." She introduced them.

"You're the one who called me," Gaby said.

He nodded.

"Thank you for looking after my baby."

"I'm glad I could help." His phone rang. "It's Carmen," he told Angela. He stepped outside. "She's had a baby girl," Sean told Carmen. "And her mam's arrived."

"That's wonderful news," Carmen said. "We just got home, but perhaps I won't rush over there. Tell Angela we'll visit her this afternoon."

"Will do." He hung up and sent a text to Hayden. He wasn't sure whether he should go back in. Gaby probably wanted some time alone with her daughter. But he'd check to make sure the reunion was going well.

Mother and daughter were holding each other's hands. "I've missed you," Gaby said. "So many times when I went shopping and bought something fabulous, I wanted to show it to you. It's been awful only having your father and brothers around. They don't understand."

Sean frowned at the woman. Was she mad? Her daughter had been living on the streets for six months and all she cared about was not having someone to go shopping with?

"The whole time we were in Cancun these past two weeks, I kept thinking you must be due, and it wasn't a vacation without you. We should have been shopping together and working on our tans. You would have loved the place where we were staying."

"Does that mean I can come home?" Angela asked, her tone hopeful.

"Of course. We'll find a good adoption agency and have everything sorted before you know it. You don't need to worry about anyone finding out. Your father told everyone you were in England for the semester."

Sean winced as Angela pulled away from her mother. "He told them *what*?" She shook her head as if she couldn't believe it. "It doesn't matter. I'm not giving Shauna up for adoption. She's my baby. I'm keeping her."

"You don't know what you're saying." Gaby wrung her hands together. "It's so hard to have a baby, especially at your age. What will people think?"

"I don't care what people think," Angela said, her eyes wide and incredulous. "I've been living by myself on the streets for six months. *That's* hard. Now I have a place at Casa Flanagan where I have support and can keep my baby."

Sean loved her fire and her determination to care for her child.

Gaby shook her head. "Your father won't approve."

"If he can't accept me and my baby, I'm not going home." Angela was adamant.

"Of course. I'll talk with him. Make him understand."

The midwife came into the room. "It's time Angela rested. You can both return at visiting hours."

Sean nodded. He walked over and kissed Angela's cheek. "Are you OK?"

She let out a shaky breath and nodded.

"I'll be back with Carmen and the girls in a few hours. You call me if you need anything."

"I will. Thank you."

He left the room and Gaby quickly followed him.

"Do you think you could change her mind?" she asked.

He stopped and looked at her. "No." He clenched his fist. "She's had a lot of time to think about what she wants and how she's going to cope. She's had to grow up fast because you were more worried about what people might think than what your child might need." He was so angry. She was just like his mother – too concerned about herself to care for her child.

Gaby took a step back, her eyes wide. Her hand fluttered by her face. "Do you know what this Casa Flanagan place is?" she asked as she followed him to the elevators.

"It's a foster home for refugee children," he told her. "But Carmen has room for Angela and said she could stay."

"Could you give me her number?"

Sean rattled it off and took a breath to calm himself. "Carmen left a few messages on your answering machine," he told her. "She wanted you to know where Angela was in case you wanted to contact her."

"We had literally just arrived back from Cancun when you called. I didn't have a chance to check the messages," Gaby said. "How did she meet Angela?"

"Carmen's my stepmother. I met Angela at the shelter she was staying at and introduced them."

"She's happy to take on a teenager with a baby?"

He nodded. "She's done it before."

"It sounds like she has a kind heart."

"She does."

Gaby placed a hand on his arm. "You're right about what you said. I should have been thinking of Angela instead of myself." She paused. "Thank you so much for caring — for looking after my girl." She looked genuinely sorry.

"It was my pleasure," Sean said. He said goodbye, hoping Gaby would rethink her priorities.

Chapter 16

Hayden stared morosely at the calendar in front of him, but it refused to change. He had a four-day conference in New York next week. It was four days he'd be away from Sean.

He needed to convince Sean to stay.

"Why the long face?" Carly stopped at his desk on her way into her office.

"Just checking my schedule next week. I'm going to New York."

"Don't you want to go?"

It was an amazing opportunity. A whole host of innovators, entrepreneurs and government groups were getting together to talk about the future of technology. It was going to be really thought-provoking. It was a shame he couldn't take Sean with him. "Of course I do. I was making sure I've handed over everything."

"You said you had," Carly said. "Did you forget something?"

"Not really."

"Then what's wrong?" She gestured for him to follow her into her office.

He wandered in after her and took a seat at her table. How pathetic was he going to sound?

"Hayden." It was Carly's no-nonsense tone.

"I'd be thrilled to be going to New York if it was after Bridget's wedding."

"You don't need to worry about that. Everything's organized."

"I know."

She frowned. "This is about Sean."

He nodded. "It's only ten days until he goes home and I'm going to be out of the state for four of them."

"Do you want me to send someone else?"

He shook his head. "I've been looking forward to it for months." He sighed. "Have you had any luck convincing him to stay?"

"We don't want to push him for an answer." She examined him. "Do you want him to stay?"

"Yes. He's..." What word was big enough to describe Sean? "Amazing." It wasn't nearly good enough.

Carly smiled. "Have you asked Sean to stay?"

He shook his head. "We've not talked long-term."

"Maybe you should. We'll support Sean any way we can. I can buy him a house and car, and I'm sure we can find him a job somewhere."

"Do you think it will freak him out?" he asked. "It's only been five weeks."

Carly laughed. "You're talking with one of the three sisters who fell in love in about that amount of time. It's possible. Mama only took a day."

He hoped Sean took after his sisters. "I'll think about it."

"Good. You know I'm here if you ever need to talk."

"Yeah. Thanks, Carly." He got to his feet and returned to his desk. He'd not wined and dined Sean yet. Perhaps it was time he romanced Sean, showed him how much he cared. Pleased by the idea, he dialed Sean's number. "Do you want to go to dinner with me tonight?"

***

The idea of going out to dinner with Hayden was both thrilling and terrifying. It would be the first time they had been out, just the two of them, as a couple. He'd be telling the world, "Hey look, I'm gay."

He remembered the looks in the club at David's bachelor party, and felt a sliver of worry, but perhaps he was being too sensitive. Hayden wouldn't take him anywhere dangerous — surely a restaurant would be all right.

He sorted through his very limited supply of clothing. He

175

had either his suit or more casual jeans and T-shirt. It would have to be jeans; the suit was too much for a simple dinner date. Wasn't it?

He dressed, brushed his hair and trotted downstairs with his overnight bag. "I'm heading off," he said to Carmen who was in the kitchen preparing dinner.

She smiled at him. "Will you be back before you go to Jack's bachelor weekend?"

He nodded. "Hayden and David are working until three tomorrow, so I'll visit Angela and then come back here for a few hours."

"Any news from her parents?"

"Yeah. Gaby put her foot down and told her husband they were taking Angela back." He hoped that was a good thing for Angela. "She shouldn't need the room after all."

"That's wonderful," Carmen said. "I'll see you when you get back." She kissed his cheek.

Sean said goodbye to the girls in the living room and drove into town. Hayden had told him where he'd hidden a key to his house, and to make himself comfortable until he got home from work.

It was strange to let himself into Hayden's house as if he had a right to be there. He put his bag in the bedroom and wandered into the living room.

Hayden's place was really comfortable. The living room looked out onto the back deck and the garden was mostly lawn, with a couple of shady trees. The sofas were sleek, but comfortable and the television was epic. On every available surface, there were photos of friends and family and the one painting on the wall was a tasteful male nude. Hayden wasn't ashamed of who he was.

The whole house was a reflection of Hayden: stylish and comfortable. It was a home Sean could live in.

He paused. He *could* see himself living here with Hayden, and the idea was all his secret hopes and dreams rolled into one. But he had only ten days until he went home. There'd been no discussion about him staying, nothing that suggested this was more than a short-term thing.

He wanted to stay. Stay in Houston, stay with Hayden, stay

with his sisters and Carmen. He wanted to continue helping at the homeless shelter, buy his own bar.

But something was bound to go wrong soon. It had been going too well for too long. He probably wouldn't get a visa. He sighed and went into the kitchen to get a beer. He didn't want to be pessimistic, but optimism had never worked for him. Returning to the living room, he sat down on the sofa and took a sip.

Did he have a right to be happy? To hope for more from his life? He wanted to think so.

But it was so damn difficult.

He grabbed his laptop from his bag and fired it up. He'd played around with the idea of buying a bar for years, putting together a plan, taking notes of things that he liked or didn't like. Maybe if he moved to Houston, he could find investors — make it a reality. He could hire some of the kids at the shelter to be waitstaff or kitchen hands, and perhaps he could even give them a place to stay.

There was the sound of a key in the lock and he looked up.

"Hi, honey, I'm home," Hayden called.

Sean grinned shutting the laptop, and got to his feet as Hayden walked in and slung his satchel onto the table. "I wasn't expecting you for another hour."

"I sweet-talked my boss into letting me go early," Hayden said. "She's a pushover." He pulled Sean toward him and kissed him.

This was everything that was right with the world. The passion, the acceptance, the lust.

"I'll have to thank her when I see her next," Sean said when he could speak.

"Mmm," Hayden said, kissing him again.

Sean held him close, running his hands down Hayden's back. "You know, we don't have to go out tonight."

Hayden stepped away and smiled. "No. I haven't romanced you nearly enough. I'm taking you on a date." He kissed him quickly. "Let me take a shower and we'll head out. You stay here." He gave Sean a stern look. "You're too much of a distraction." Hayden strode out of the room.

Sean let out a breath. Hayden wanted to romance him. The

idea made him giddy. It was ridiculous. He didn't need romance. What was romance anyway? A three-course dinner, fine wine and candlelight? No. Romance was Hayden finding him a quiet spot to get away at the weddings, it was understanding he needed space. Or the brief touch of hands when they were in public to give him reassurance, but not long enough to draw attention. Romance wasn't the big gestures, but the little ones that showed he cared, to show he knew Sean well enough to know what mattered.

Hayden had already romanced him.

But what had Sean done to show Hayden he cared? Nothing. He'd been a pain in the ass any time they were out in public. He was the one who should be romancing Hayden.

Was he brave enough to hold Hayden's hand in public, to kiss him and declare their relationship to everyone who would listen?

He wanted to be. It would mean a lot to Hayden.

Hayden walked into the living room looking gorgeous in a pair of gray fitted pants and a collared shirt. All his clothes showed off his body in a way that made Sean want to rip them off him.

They also made Sean feel like the country cousin.

"You ready to go?" Hayden asked.

Sean glanced down at himself. "Do I look OK?"

"Of course. You look sensational." The way Hayden's eyes roamed Sean's body made him feel better.

"All right."

When they arrived at the Vietnamese restaurant, Sean joined Hayden on the pavement. With only the slightest hesitation, he slipped his hand into Hayden's. It wasn't far to the front door.

Hayden glanced at him and beamed, squeezing his hand as they walked into the restaurant together.

It wasn't so bad. No one looked twice at them.

The waitress showed them to a table and they picked up the menus.

"This place has the most amazing pho," Hayden said.

Sean scanned the menu to see that pho was a type of soup. After they ordered, Sean took hold of Hayden's hand across the table. "How was your day?"

"Pretty good, aside from one thing."

"What's that?"

"I have to go to New York next week for a conference."

The disappointment was instant. "How long will you be away?"

"Four days. I leave Sunday night when we get back from the bachelor weekend and return Thursday."

It was almost half the remaining days Sean was in Houston. He tried to smile. "What's the conference about?"

"Innovation and entrepreneurship," Hayden said. "I've been looking forward to it for ages, but now…"

"You don't want to go?"

"I don't want to miss out on the nights with you." Hayden watched him.

Sean's heart expanded. "I'll miss you."

The waitress brought their drinks over and her eyes widened when she saw their hands together. Quickly she dumped the glasses on the table and fled.

Sean resisted the urge to move his hand away. He wasn't doing anything wrong.

The waitress was talking with a waiter and gesturing toward their table. Sean sighed and turned his attention back to Hayden. "So what's happening this weekend?"

"I'm not sure. Jack's brother Hal arranged everything. He's hired a beach house and there was talk of fishing."

Sean screwed up his face. He'd never been fishing.

"I'm sure being out on the boat will be nice," Hayden said.

He'd have to pack plenty of suntan lotion, otherwise he was going to be burned to a crisp.

Their food arrived, this time delivered by the waiter the waitress had been talking to. He didn't so much as glance at their hands. He smiled as he served them and said, "Enjoy your meal."

"Thanks," Sean said.

"Remind me to give that guy a tip," Hayden said as they started to eat.

Curious, Sean asked, "What kind of reception do you normally get when you date?"

"Depends on where we go," Hayden said. "The gay-friendly

venues are well-known, and we generally don't have a problem. Other places, it's hit and miss depending on who is serving. I've never had a problem here before."

"So this is a favorite date spot for you?" Sean asked, slightly amused.

"No. I've come here with Max and other friends. No one seeing Max would ever think he was anything but gay."

That was true. So should he be worried that Hayden was taking him out to somewhere he went with friends rather than dates? His insecurity was pathetic.

He turned his attention to his meal. Hayden was right. The pho was delicious.

They chatted more about the weekend and about the homeless shelter before ordering dessert. The same waiter took their order.

When it arrived, Sean had a tentative taste of his jelly, bean and rice concoction. It was delicious. "You should try this." He held a spoonful out to Hayden who grinned at him and slowly took the spoon into his mouth.

Hubba, hubba. Sean's body woke up. He swallowed. "What do you think?"

"Divine," Hayden said. "Taste mine." He grinned and glanced down.

Oh, he was definitely going to taste something when they got back to Hayden's. He licked his lips. "I'd love to."

Hayden's eyes darkened. "Shall we skip coffee?"

"Absolutely."

They finished their dessert quickly and Hayden called for the check. The waitress rushed to bring it over to them. Sean reached for his wallet.

"It's my treat," Hayden said, placing his credit card down.

The girl scowled. "You're supposed to tip."

Hayden nodded. "I'll tip the waiter who served us."

The waitress spun on her heel and stormed off. She returned shortly after with the receipt.

"Shall we?" Hayden asked.

Sean got to his feet. As they walked to the door, Hayden stopped the waiter who served them and gave him a twenty. "Thank you."

The young man smiled. "Anytime."
Outside, Sean took Hayden's hand. "Let's go."

Chapter 17

The next day, Hayden picked up David on his way to Casa Flanagan. "How was the honeymoon?"

"Pretty darn good," David said. "Hawaii is gorgeous at this time of year."

"Did you see much of it?"

"Enough." David grinned. "Some days I have to pinch myself to remind me this is real, that Zita wants to spend her life with me."

"That's pretty special."

"Yeah, it is." David glanced at him. "I'm under strict instructions to ask how things are with you and Sean."

"Are you just?" Hayden smiled. "Zita's being nosy."

"Not nosy, just curious…and concerned. She wants Sean to stay in Houston and figures you're another reason for him to stay."

"The Flanagan sisters really do know how to love, don't they?"

"They sure do. Are you going to answer the question?"

"Things are great."

David raised an eyebrow. "Great's the best you can give me?"

Hayden knew how tenacious Zita could be. "Tell her if she wants more, she can talk with me or Sean."

"All right."

They kept up an easy conversation on the drive and pulled up at Casa Flanagan a little after four. Carmen answered the door. "*Hola, Mamá,*" David said, giving her a hug.

"David. Did you have a lovely vacation?"

"Yes, thank you."

Hayden kissed Carmen's cheeks. "You're looking as lovely as ever."

"You flatter me." She swatted him. "Sean's upstairs." She raised her voice. "Sean, Hayden and David are here."

A moment later, Sean came into view wearing green board shorts and a pale blue T-shirt. He was carrying his bag. "I'm right here, Mama."

He sure was. Hayden could look at him for days without getting bored. "Ready to go?"

Sean nodded.

"We'll be back for lunch on Sunday," David said to Carmen.

"Have fun. Take care of each other." She waved them goodbye.

It took them another hour to reach the beach house they'd hired in Galveston. Jack, Evan, Hal and Jack's father, Eric, had already arrived and had the grill fired up.

"David, you're bunking with me," Evan said. "We left the master bedroom for Sean and Hayden."

Hayden exchanged a glance with Sean. Was he going to be cool with that?

"Shouldn't it be for Jack?" Sean asked.

"I've got no use for a queen-sized bed this weekend," Jack said with a grin. "You two might as well make use of it."

Sean smiled. "Thanks. Which way?"

Jack pointed down the corridor.

Hayden followed Sean into the bedroom, his love for these men growing. It was no wonder the Flanagan sisters loved them. He dropped his bag inside the door. "Are you comfortable with this?"

Sean glanced at him. He slowly nodded. "Yeah. The others don't seem to care if we share a bed."

"Good. I'm glad. You know there aren't any other bedrooms down this side of the house, so if we make some noise…"

Sean smiled. "I didn't bring any lube."

"I did."

"Then we'll see," Sean said and took hold of his hand. "Let's see if they need a hand with dinner."

Hayden was happy not to push the point. It was a win that he could spend the nights next to his man.

Dinner was a nice, casual affair with them all sitting out on the deck in view of the bay.

"You boys think you'll be up for a six a.m. start tomorrow?" Eric asked. "The breeze is due to come in by midday, so the earlier we get out fishing, the nicer it will be."

"Whatever you say, Dad," Jack said. "I'm not planning on getting wasted."

"I am," Hal said. "I never had a bachelor party."

"That's because you eloped," Eric said.

"Yeah, best decision I ever made," Hal said.

"Did I ever thank you for that?" Jack asked. "Moving in with Bridget was the best thing that could have happened."

Hayden frowned. He hadn't heard the full story of how Jack and Bridget met. "What do you mean?"

"Hal married Bridget's roommate," Jack said. "She moved out and Bridget couldn't afford the place on her own, so I moved in with her because I'd been living with Hal."

"So that's how you met?" Sean asked.

"No. We met at a nightclub and then I discovered she was part of my new team at Dionysus."

"I never realized," Hayden said. "That had to be awkward."

"Sure was. She didn't want to be seen sleeping with her boss."

"I can imagine the office gossip." Hayden sipped his beer.

"Yeah, it was worse for her than me, but people stopped talking after she saved my life."

"What?" Sean asked.

"There was an explosion at the plant and I was knocked unconscious. When Bridget found me, she single-handedly carried me out of there before I was roasted alive."

Sean's eyes widened.

"Your sister's a badass," Hayden said.

Sean nodded. "So what happened after?"

"She got wise that Dionysus was never going to give her the opportunities she wanted." Jack glanced at David. "No offense."

"None taken. They were stupid not to recognize her passion."

"And she took a job at another refinery," Jack continued. "The incident made her realize she loved me and we've lived happily ever after since." He grinned.

"What would you have done if she hadn't got another job?" Sean asked.

"We would have made it work. I was determined not to let her go."

Hayden sat back. Was that all that was required? An absolute determination that things could work out? Could it be like that for him and Sean? Did he *want* it to be like that for him and Sean?

Absolutely, he did.

***

When Hayden's alarm went off the next morning, Sean groaned. Five-thirty was the earliest he'd been awake in years. He rolled over and pulled Hayden toward him. "We don't really have to go fishing, do we?"

Hayden's chuckle woke other parts of him. "No, but it's probably the right thing to do."

"You're right." He stretched. "Have a shower with me?"

"Sure."

They had an adjoining bathroom, and after a quick, but fun shower, they got dressed and headed to the kitchen where Evan and David were making breakfast.

"Aren't the others up yet?" Sean asked.

Evan laughed. "They're up, have had breakfast and are loading lunch onto the boat. I think they've got a routine."

Sean poured himself a tea and made Hayden a coffee while Hayden put two slices of bread in the toaster. Outside, the sun was shining and the heat could already be felt. He definitely needed to remember his hat and sunscreen.

Jack came back inside. "You guys almost ready?"

"Yep," David said.

Sean scarfed the toast Hayden handed him and hurried back to their room to get their things. In no time at all, they were at the boat ramp, putting Eric's boat into the water.

The sun already had a bite to it, so Sean got out the sunscreen and lathered up. He passed the bottle to Hayden.

"Thanks, I don't need much." Hayden tapped his dark skin. "Built-in protection."

"I'll take some," David said and Hayden passed it to him.

It was a beautiful morning. The ocean was flat and glassy, making the ride smooth. The boat was a little snug for seven grown men. There was a cabin area with wrap-around seating, and on the deck there was a seat in each corner. Sean took a seat at the back, out of the way.

Hayden came and stood next to him. "It's been a long time since I've been out on the bay."

"Is this where you used to come as a kid?"

He nodded. "Not far from here."

A beach vacation sounded like the ideal summer holiday, like something from a Hollywood movie. "Must have been amazing."

"I didn't appreciate it at the time, but it was." He turned to Sean. "What did you do in summer?"

"I worked mostly."

"So what about now?" Hayden asked. "Where do you go on vacation?"

"Houston." Sean smiled.

Hayden hesitated. "So do you think you'll come back?"

Should he tell Hayden he was considering moving permanently? He wanted to move even if this thing between Hayden and him was temporary. "Definitely." He waited for Hayden's reaction.

Hayden grinned. "That's great."

"You haven't got your fill of me yet?" Sean asked, keeping his tone light.

"Not even close." Hayden kissed his cheek.

The relief was instant.

"So have you done much fishing before?" Hayden asked.

"None," Sean replied.

"We'll have to get Eric to teach us."

They chatted until Eric slowed the boat, and both Jack and Hal prepared the fishing rods. There were only two, so they were going to have to take turns. Sean and Hayden moved to the front of the boat as Jack cast the first rod. Eric was still motoring slowly along.

"Are you going to drop anchor?" Hayden asked.

"No, we're trawling today," Eric said.

Sean looked to Hayden for a translation, but he was as confused as Sean. "Trawling?"

Eric laughed. "You boys haven't been trawling before?"

They shook their heads.

"Trawling's when you drag the bait behind the boat. If we're lucky, something big will grab hold. That's when it gets fun and we get to pull it in."

Jack moved over to them. "We'll give you the first turn if you want."

"Thanks," Sean said.

At that moment, one of the reels started whirring. "We got one!" Eric yelled.

"Come on." Jack beckoned to Sean and they went over to the straining rod. "You've got to play with it," Jack said, demonstrating what he meant before handing the rod over.

Sean started to wind the fish in, but it was difficult. Whatever was on the end was strong. His shoulders bunched as he struggled to turn the reel. The tip of the rod bent under the weight. The others gathered to watch the show.

"What is it?" Hayden asked.

Jack shrugged. "We get Spanish mackerel, tuna, marlin and snapper out here."

Sean's fantasy of sitting on the boat dangling a line over the side and drinking beer had been thoroughly destroyed. This wasn't the least bit relaxing. He had to fight to pull in whatever it was.

"Tell me if you need a rest," Jack said. "It can take twenty minutes to reel some of them in."

Twenty minutes? Hell, he couldn't keep this up for that long.

"I'll tag in when you're ready," Hayden said.

Hayden hadn't done this type of fishing before either, and probably wanted a go. "Absolutely." He handed the rod over.

"Hell, this is harder than it looks," Hayden said.

Sean stepped back as Hayden worked the reel. His muscles strained under his T-shirt and a bead of sweat glistened on his brow. He looked in charge and damn hot. Sean's lips turned up. Suddenly fishing was much more appealing.

"Check that out," Evan said, pointing to something at the back of the boat.

Sean saw a splash about twenty meters away.

"That'll be your fish," Hal said.

"Damn! How much line did you put out?" Hayden asked.

"Enough." Jack laughed.

"And here I thought it was going to be a nice relaxing day," Evan said. "I'm not sure I want to try that. It looks like hard work."

When Hayden tired, he handed the rod over to Jack, who pulled the fish in the remaining distance. Sean handed Hayden a bottle of water from the cooler.

"Thanks." Hayden held the bottle against his forehead for a moment before taking a big drink. "That was harder than my gym workout."

"You made it look good," Sean said as he followed him into the cabin and took a seat.

Hayden raised an eyebrow. "Really?"

"Mm. Shame we've got company." Sean ran his eyes over Hayden's body.

Hayden grinned. "You're going to make it uncomfortable for me to sit."

"Maybe later."

Hayden's laugh was loud, but the others were too busy talking about the fish to notice. "I'm glad we've got our own room."

"Me too."

"You two coming to see your fish?" Jack called.

Sean was happy where he was, but he should show some interest. "Sure." He got to his feet and offered Hayden his hand. "Let's see our spoils of war."

***

Hayden had to admit the mackerel was pretty impressive at

five and a half feet long. No wonder it had been so hard to reel in.

"We'll get some good-sized fillets from that," Eric said.

"We're not expected to do that, are we?" Hayden asked. The idea of cutting the fish open wasn't very appealing.

Eric laughed. "I can do it for you."

"Thanks."

Hal had already put the lines back out and Jack was passing around a bag of donuts. Hayden took one and bit into it. "So this is fishing." It was quite nice on the ocean with the hum of the engine and the gentle breeze. Good company, decent food and the occasional bit of excitement to break things up. He understood why so many people enjoyed the pastime. "Do you come out much?"

"Dad's out every weekend," Jack said. "I get out here about once a month."

"Do you ever bring Bridget?" Sean asked.

"I did once, but she wasn't into it," he answered. "We stick to scuba diving."

"That must be pretty amazing." Sean helped himself to another donut.

"It is. You should try it."

Sean chuckled. "I can't even swim. I'd be useless at diving."

Hayden frowned. "You can't swim?"

"No. There was nowhere to learn when I was a kid. Besides, it's not often swimming weather in Ireland."

One of the reels started whirring and Hayden moved to the front of the boat as Hal and Jack showed Evan what to do. Sean joined him and they moved into the cabin out of the way. "Do you want to learn to swim?" Hayden asked.

"If I move to Houston, I'd better. This heat is incredible."

"You're considering moving?" He tried to keep his tone casual. He didn't want to get his hopes up.

Sean hesitated. "Yeah. I'd like to spend more time with my sisters and Carmen."

No mention of him. "I'm sure they'd love that. Carmen's practically adopted you already." *Say you want to spend more time with me.*

"She's great."

Obviously, his mind-control powers were failing him today. Disappointed, he leaned back against the seat.

The boat began to rock. Hayden glanced outside. The swell had picked up. The motion was quite soothing.

Sean put a hand to his stomach. "I suddenly don't feel so good." His face had a decidedly green tinge to it.

"You should get some fresh air," Hayden said, helping him to his feet and outside. Eric took one look at Sean and said, "If you're going to puke, do it off this side." He pointed.

Sean moved quickly to the edge of the boat and vomited into the water.

Hayden grabbed a bottle of water and returned, rubbing Sean's back. "Feel any better?"

"No." Sean closed his eyes and took a sip of water. "I think I ate a dodgy donut."

"It's more likely seasickness," Hal said. "It's getting choppy."

Sean moaned. "Thanks for pointing that out." He hurled again.

Hayden winced.

"Try the front of the boat," Jack suggested. "Some people find the fresh air and being able to watch the waves helps."

Sean nodded.

Hayden helped him climb onto the bow and took a seat next to him. They both dangled their legs off the edge. He stayed silent as Sean took deep breaths and focused on the horizon. It was awful to see him so pale and miserable. "Do you want me to ask Eric to go back?"

Sean shook his head. "I'm not going to spoil Jack's bachelor party."

"Honey, if you're not well, you need to take care of yourself."

"I'll be fine. The fresh air is helping."

Hayden put his arm around Sean. "If you change your mind, just say the word."

They sat in silence.

"Sean, how you feeling?" Jack called.

"Tell him I'm fine," Sean said quietly.

"He's fine," Hayden called.

"Do you guys want some lunch?"

Sean groaned.

"I'll grab something later," Hayden told Jack.

Jack nodded.

Hayden turned back to Sean. "You want me to distract you?"

Sean nodded. "Tell me more about your family."

"Not much to tell since you met them all last week," Hayden said. "I called Jada yesterday to see how things are with her and Nick. They've worked it all out."

"That's good."

"Sure is. Mom and Dad raised us right."

"You're lucky." Sean managed to smile.

"I know. Do you ever see your mom?"

"No. I sent her my address and told her where I was working, but never received a response. That was twelve years ago. I've got no idea if she still lives in our old house."

It had to be difficult to be so thoroughly rejected by your family. Hayden couldn't comprehend not being able to call his mother once a week or chat to his sisters regularly. "Will you tell her if you move here?"

He shrugged. "I don't know."

Behind them, another fish was hooked, and the guys called encouragement to David as he reeled it in. Sean glanced over and smiled. "This has been such a bizarre holiday."

"How so?"

"I've met my sisters and they've been so welcoming, I've come out, and for the first time I've lived openly as a gay man, and I've had my first real relationship. When I arrived, the most I was hoping for was that my sisters didn't hate me and send me home."

"It's past time you set your expectations higher. You're a wonderful man, Sean Flanagan." He was everything Hayden had ever wanted in a partner, in a husband. Hayden had to tell Sean how he felt. He brushed a thumb over Sean's cheek. "I love you."

Sean's jaw dropped.

Hell. He shouldn't have blurted it out like that, while Sean was feeling like shit. It was the worst possible moment. He forced a smile onto his face, hoping Sean would say something, anything.

"You barely know me."

OK, so maybe not just anything. "I know enough." He squeezed Sean's thigh. "You don't have to say anything." But his heart sank at the fear on Sean's face. He had to get away. He got to his feet. "I'm going to grab some lunch. Do you want anything?"

Sean shook his head.

"Be right back." He moved to the back of the boat, wishing he'd kept his big mouth shut.

Chapter 18

It was a huge relief when Eric announced they were done for the day and heading back to shore. Sean hadn't vomited again, but his stomach was fragile. He tried to convince himself it was due to the seasickness and not a reaction to Hayden telling him he loved him.

He failed.

He'd been floored when Hayden had uttered those words, so taken by surprise that he'd muttered some inane response and the moment was lost. Now he didn't know what to say to Hayden to make things right. He'd never dared to hope that Hayden could love him and the idea terrified him. He'd mess it up for sure.

The boat pulled alongside the jetty and Sean disembarked.

"Why don't you head for the car?" Jack said, giving him the keys. "We've got this."

Sean glanced at Hayden, but he was busy getting things from the cabin. They hadn't really said anything to each other since lunch. Sean sighed and headed for the parking lot. The humidity cloaked him the further away from the ocean he went, and he was soon sweating.

Evan walked next to him carrying one of the bags. "How are you feeling?"

"Better," Sean said. At least that was partially true. The nausea had faded.

"Great. We're going to head back to the house and go to the beach. You up for that?"

He nodded and unlocked the car. The others soon joined them. Sean gave Hayden a tentative smile and Hayden smiled back. It was a good start.

When they arrived at the house, David said, "I'm hitting the water." He dumped the cooler on the kitchen table.

"Me too," Evan said, adding his bags to the pile. "You guys coming?"

"We'll be right behind you," Hayden said. "Sean needs more sunscreen."

Relief and nerves collided in Sean's stomach. Hayden wanted to talk with him. He headed for their bedroom to grab a towel, hoping Hayden would follow.

Hayden leaned against the doorframe. "If I'd known it was going to freak you out so much, I wouldn't have said anything."

Sean turned. "It's not that."

Hayden raised an eyebrow. "No?"

How could he explain? "It's more than that." He met Hayden's gaze. No, he couldn't do this with Hayden waiting so patiently, watching him with eyes that saw more than they should. He paced away. "I'm scared."

"Of love?"

He nodded. "No one's ever loved me before my sisters. I keep waiting for them to change their minds, to say they made a mistake. Then you tell me you love me and it's so unbelievable, like my wildest, most fantastical dreams are coming true and I'm waiting for it all to come crashing down."

Hayden stood up. "Like a dream, huh?"

Sean nodded. "You're the most amazing man I've ever met. You're sexy and funny and so kind and smart. How could you possibly love someone like me?"

Hayden walked toward him and Sean backed up, not trusting himself near Hayden. He bumped into the wall.

"Maybe it's because you've got those same traits." Hayden was standing only inches away.

"I don't know how I'd survive if you changed your mind," Sean confessed, feeling as if he was ripping his heart out of his chest and throwing it onto the floor.

"I won't." The love, the promise in Hayden's eyes was too much to bear. Sean closed his eyes.

"You need to ask yourself, how do you feel about me?" Hayden murmured.

Sean's chest was tight. It was hard to breathe. Could he risk it? Could he admit the truth? He opened his eyes. "I love you."

Hayden grinned. "That's all that matters. We'll work out the rest." He pressed his lips against Sean's in a promise and Sean allowed himself to hope.

***

Hayden was feeling pretty good about the world as they left the beach house and headed to Casa Flanagan for the family lunch on Sunday. The night before, they'd hung out with the guys, drinking, eating and telling stories, before heading to bed about midnight. He'd made sure to limit his alcohol consumption in order to prevent a recurrence of David's bachelor party.

Today they would have the final check for Bridget and Jack's wedding the following weekend and then he'd fly to New York, where he'd miss Sean for four days.

But it wasn't so bad now he knew Sean loved him. When he got back, he'd look into spouse visas.

Zita, Bridget and Carly were already at Casa Flanagan when they arrived. Zita flung her arms around David and kissed him. "I missed you."

"Missed you too," David said.

Hayden grinned. Love was all around.

Carmen clutched her hands together. "Come. It is time to eat. Did you have a nice weekend?"

"We did," Jack said as he walked into the dining room. "Though we were all a little jealous of Sean and Hayden."

Hayden frowned at him. "Why?"

"You had your significant other with you. The rest of us were missing ours." He kissed Bridget's cheek.

Hayden smiled and turned to Sean, whose cheeks had flushed red. "Being gay has its advantages."

The table was full, the food was plenty and the voices were loud. Hayden loved the Flanagan household. There was so much life here.

"The forecast for Saturday has a sixty percent chance of rain and with scattered thunderstorms," Carmen announced.

Bridget winced. "Really? It's been fine all month."

"We can always go to our backup plan," Hayden said.

"When do we need to decide?" Bridget asked.

"By Wednesday. That will give us time to tell the guests and to tell the venue we're going ahead." It wouldn't be too difficult because the catering had been organized and the decorations had been made. All they would have to do was set up on the day.

"OK. I can always hope the weatherman is wrong."

Hayden knew she had her heart set on getting married in Carmen's garden. "Contact me and I'll make the calls from New York."

"No. Leave me a list of numbers and I can do it," Bridget said. "I finish work on Wednesday anyway."

"All right."

Too soon, it was time for Hayden to leave. He had to pack and then get to the airport for an evening flight. Sean walked him to his car.

"I'll call you when I can," Hayden said, pulling Sean into his arms. "Conferences are usually full-on, so I can't promise what time."

"That's fine." Sean brushed his lips against Hayden's. "I'll be thinking of you."

"Same." Hayden's heart smiled. "I have some vacation time built up," he said. "After Bridget's wedding, I could take some time off. I hear Ireland's nice this time of year."

Sean hesitated. "I'm not sure that's a good idea."

"Why not?"

"No one knows I'm gay over there."

Hayden's stomach twisted. "You're not going to come out?"

Sean stepped back. "There's no point — not when I'm moving. It will just make the remaining months awkward."

"What about us?"

"What do you mean? We'll call and Skype."

"But I can't visit you because you won't want to know me?" This wasn't how it was supposed to be.

"Hayden, please. It's not that simple."

"Yes, it is. You're gay. You have a partner who loves you. It doesn't get simpler than that." His heart hurt.

"You don't understand."

"Then explain it to me." Hayden waited as Sean ran a hand through his hair. His patience ran out. "What are we going to do in the future? Are we to pretend we're just friends when we go somewhere new? Are you only going to come out to your family?" The idea made him ill. "That's not going to work. You have to come out time and time again and sometimes you're going to get a shit response. That's what being gay is."

"I don't know." There was pain on Sean's face, but Hayden had to be strong. This affected him as well. He couldn't be with someone if he had to hide who he was, if he couldn't hug Sean or kiss him in public, if he had to go to events with his "friend," not his husband. He wasn't ashamed of his sexuality.

He checked the time. He had to go. "Think about it while I'm gone," he said, getting into his car. "And tell me what you decide." He drove away, his heart sore.

***

Sean was miserable. It was stupid, he was used to being alone, had never had a problem amusing himself, but today Carmen had taken all of the girls to the mall and he missed Hayden like crazy.

He'd really messed things up. He'd reacted badly — instinctively — and he'd hurt Hayden. He hated himself for that.

He should have reminded Hayden that he'd lose his job if he came out, should have told him about his near miss with those thugs, but instead he'd panicked at the thought of losing Hayden and hadn't been able to convert his thoughts into words.

Of course, now that Hayden was thousands of miles away, he was able to think of logical arguments: He couldn't afford to be fired now, not when it could take several months for the visa to go through. He blocked out the little voice in his head that told him Carly could help him out if that happened. He didn't want to be reliant on his family. He had made it this far on his own, he could see it through.

The worst thing was that he couldn't call Hayden. He was going to be in sessions all day, and wouldn't have time to talk, to clear the air. Hayden had said he'd call when he could.

And he hadn't.

Not that Sean was sitting by the phone. He hadn't checked for missed calls in at least half an hour.

Disgusted with himself, he turned on his laptop. He'd check his emails just in case.

He frowned at the first email on the list, from his boss back in Ireland. Vinny hated using the computer. Sean clicked on the link and read the first line. He shook his head. *No. Not now.* His stomach rolled and he closed his eyes. Not when he was finding happiness.

He read the line again. *Your stepfather's been looking for you. Says your mam is ill and she wants to see you.*

Sean didn't know if he had a stepfather, but it was possible. But why the hell would his mother want to see him, even if she was sick? She'd never wanted him.

He read the rest of the email which was as brief. A name and a contact number.

What should he do?

He focused on his breathing. The guy probably had it wrong, had him confused with someone else. There was no way his mother would be asking for him. Sean should at least call and set him straight so he could find the right person. He checked the time. It would be late afternoon in Ireland.

Sean started Skype and dialed the number. A man answered the phone.

"I'm after Keiron Doherty," Sean said.

"Speaking."

Sean swallowed. "I got a message you were looking for me. My name's Sean Flanagan."

"Sean, thank the gods you've called me. I'm married to your mother, Ellen."

Sean opened his mouth to speak, but Keiron kept talking. "I know you and your mother haven't been close for a few years, but it's time to bury the past. When she rang you six months ago and told you she had cancer, the doctors thought they could cure it. But none of the treatments have worked and she's only got days, maybe a couple of weeks now." His voice broke.

Sean stared at the screen in front of him, not sure what to think, what to feel. He'd never received a phone call from his mother. "I'm not sure you've got the right person."

"Sean O'Connell Flanagan, son of Brendan Flanagan and Ellen O'Connell, lived at ten Church Lane until you ran away from home at fifteen." Keiron's tone was angry.

Ran away? "Did Mam ask to see me?"

"Of course she wants to see you. She's been missing you for fifteen years."

Sean hesitated. Keiron didn't know the truth. Not if he thought Sean had run away. "Where is she?"

"She's at home in Dublin." He rattled off the address and Sean wrote it down. "Will you come?"

"I'm in the United States at the moment." Did he want to go? Did he want to see his mother one last time before she died? Did he want to face her disgust again?

"I can send you the airfare." Keiron was obviously desperate to have him there.

"I'll let you know." Sean hung up.

He pushed his laptop away and breathed out. His mother was dying. If he'd heard the news two months ago, before he'd come to Houston, it might have hit him harder, but he knew what real family was like now. There was only a tiny part of him that wanted to go, to find out if she really wanted to see him.

He opened a web page and searched for flights to Dublin. There was one tonight. He could change the date on his ticket, but it would mean he'd have to cut his holiday short and miss Bridget's wedding. He wouldn't be able to afford to fly back.

Was he a bad person that he would prefer to go to his sister's wedding than his mother's funeral?

And what would Hayden think? Would they be able to resolve their disagreement online, or would this be the end for them? It would be several months before he got his visa sorted and would be able to come back.

Sean stared at the screen, all the potential reactions from his mother running through his head. At best she would say she was sorry and at worst, the sight of him would kill her.

Neither was comforting.

But if he didn't see her one last time would he regret it?

He wished he could call Hayden, talk with him about it. Hayden knew about his mother and what she'd done, his sisters didn't. If he told them Ellen was sick they would urge him to go back, they wouldn't understand why he was so reluctant.

Should he tell them?

A door closed downstairs. Someone was home.

Footsteps sounded on the stairs. He should close his bedroom door, but it seemed so far away and he couldn't get his brain to function with all the emotions swirling around inside.

Carmen ducked her head into his room. "I left them to it. Those girls can shop for hours." She frowned as she looked at him. "What is wrong *mi niñito?*"

The simple question, the fact she could tell something was wrong and cared enough to ask, was all it took. Tears flooded from his eyes.

Carmen hurried over and wrapped her arms around him, pulling him in for a hug as he wept. "There, there. Tell Mama what is wrong?"

He couldn't. He couldn't get the words out of his throat. He clung to her, wishing desperately that she had been his mother, that he'd known his father, that he didn't have to make a decision between his old family and his new.

She stroked his back as he cried, murmuring Spanish words that made no sense to him, but were soothing in tone.

Finally, he ran out of tears. He sat back, wiping his eyes, his face flushed not from the tears, but from embarrassment. He'd broken down again.

"Did you get some bad news?" Carmen nodded toward the laptop.

"Yeah."

"Do you want to tell me about it?"

That was one thing he loved about Carmen, she didn't push him to tell, she asked him. He took a deep breath. "My mother is dying."

"*Dios mío!* I am so sorry, my child. What has happened?"

"She has cancer."

"It has worsened since you've been here," Carmen guessed.

He nodded. He didn't want to tell Carmen the truth.

"When does your flight leave?"

There it was, the assumption he was going. How could he tell her he didn't want to go? They'd think him heartless. "Tonight. I'll probably miss Bridget's wedding."

"She will understand. You must go to your mother."

She was right. He needed to see his mother again if only to show her that he'd survived, that he'd grown up without her help and become a man. Part of him wanted to tell her he'd found his own family, people who loved him for who he was.

He sighed. He hated the idea of leaving without speaking with Hayden, but he had little choice. He had to hope Hayden would understand, that they could work everything out over the phone. With his heart pounding hard in his chest, he booked his flight home.

Chapter 19

The next few hours happened in a blur. After Sean booked his tickets, he called Keiron to tell him he was coming and then packed. Carmen dropped him off at the airport, and before he boarded the plane, he tried to call Hayden, but couldn't get through. He didn't bother leaving a message, or sending an email. He didn't want Hayden to be worried. There wasn't anything Hayden could do to help anyway.

Now it was early morning, and he was in Ireland, studying the terraced house in front of him. The small front garden was tended and the grass had been mowed. The whole house was in good repair. It was far different from the place where he'd grown up. He wished Hayden was with him, which was ridiculous. He'd told Hayden he didn't want him to come to Ireland, but the truth was Sean would feel better hearing his voice. He checked the time. Hayden would still be asleep and Sean didn't want to wake him.

He sighed. He could do this. He was used to doing things alone.

Bracing himself, he walked up the front steps and knocked on the door.

A dark-haired man answered, his face drawn and his eyes red.

"Keiron?" Sean asked.

"Sean." He shook his hand. "I'm so glad you made it. Come

in."

Sean walked into the narrow hall. "How is she?"

"She's sleeping," Keiron said. "Let me get you a cup of tea." He walked down the hall and Sean followed him.

"Does she know I'm coming?"

Keiron shook his head. "I didn't want to get her hopes up."

That wasn't good. He could imagine the horror on his mother's face when she saw him. "You should prepare her."

Keiron hesitated. "Why?"

"How long have you known my mother?"

"We've been married three years. She was so disappointed when you didn't come to the wedding." There was such censure in the man's eyes.

Should Sean tell him the truth? Was it fair to reveal his mother's lies when she was dying? Did he want to soil this man's memory of the woman he clearly loved? "I didn't get the invitation."

Keiron frowned. "I saw it myself. It was addressed to the bar where you work."

Sean didn't comment. Defending himself wouldn't help. "How did you meet?"

Keiron blushed. "She worked for me. I swear it was love at first sight, but it took me six months to convince her to go on a date with me and another six months to talk her into marrying me. She'd been burned so badly by your father."

Sean wasn't going to ask what she'd said about Brendan. "I'm happy for you both." He took the mug of tea Keiron handed him.

"I wish you'd called your mother back when she first got sick, I wish you had more time to make things right with her, but the truth is she's only lucid some of the time now." Keiron's voice was thick with emotion. "She's only got a day or two left." Tears shone in his eyes.

Sean tried to feel something at the news, but he was numb. He understood why Keiron had called him, why he wanted Sean there, but it was all under false pretenses. His mother didn't want him here, she hadn't asked for him, she'd lied about her past. He didn't want to go upstairs and see the disgust in his mother's eyes. He didn't want to cause her any stress in these last moments of her life.

"I shouldn't have come." He pushed his chair back and stood up.

"Sit down!" Keiron slammed his hand down on the table. "Don't you dare walk out now. She's *dying*." His voice broke. "She deserves to see her son one last time, even if you've been a worthless shit for years."

The words hit him, and he lost his breath. He shook his head, clutching on to his control. This man didn't know him, he didn't know the truth.

From upstairs he heard a bell ring.

"She's awake." Keiron got to his feet and stared at Sean. "I'm going up there and telling her you're here. Don't leave." He didn't wait for a reply.

Sean sank into the chair and put his head in his hands. This wasn't going to end well. Not for any of them. He should go. He stood up, undecided, and glanced through the back window into the garden.

Part of him wanted to look at his mother, see what kind of woman she'd become, see if she still held on to her anger. Was his closure more important than Keiron's happiness?

No. However badly his mother had treated him, it wasn't right for him to reveal their relationship to the man who'd loved her for four years. He turned to go and found Keiron waiting at the doorway. "What did she say?"

"She wants to see you."

That made Sean pause.

Keiron frowned.

"What's wrong?"

"She's a bit confused. She kept saying I told him not to come back."

Sean gazed at the man. "Perhaps it's the drugs she's on."

Keiron nodded. "Come with me." There was determination in his eyes.

There was no way he could leave now. He followed Keiron upstairs to a bedroom. There was a large window open to let in fresh air, but it didn't hide the scent of sickness.

Sean barely recognized his mother. She had shrunk. Her skin was pale and fell loose on her body, her eyes were sunken into her head and her cheekbones showed clearly. She was sitting up, her brown hair brushed back, and she was wearing a cotton nightgown. He met her gaze and there was fear in her eyes.

Why was she scared of him?

"Hi, Mam." He kept his tone gentle.

"God, you look so much like your father." Her voice was soft, raspy.

He took a few steps toward her.

"Why don't you take a seat?" Keiron said, indicating the chair next to the bed. "I'll let you two catch up." He left.

Ellen waited until his footsteps faded before she spoke. "Why did you come?"

"Keiron said you wanted me here."

"He doesn't know the truth."

Sean sighed. "I gathered that."

"Please don't tell him," she begged.

"I won't."

"Thank you." Her relief was clear.

He nodded. He couldn't hold on to his anger while she lay there two steps away from death's door. There was no point. He was at a good place in his life. He had a new family and a man who loved him. He didn't need love from the woman who'd given birth to him. "How have you been, Mam?" It seemed a stupid question to ask after fifteen years, but he didn't know what else to say.

"Good," she said. "Things got better after I moved to Dublin and met Keiron." She hesitated. "You fared all right?"

"I've got a good job." He debated briefly as to whether to tell her more. "I found out what happened to my father."

Her eyes widened. "Brendan?"

"Yeah. He died over twenty years ago, but he had three daughters. They live in Houston and they've welcomed me into their family."

"I'm glad. Really, I am. I tried to love you, but I couldn't."

"Why not?" It was the one thing he'd never understood.

"You ruined my life."

The words didn't hurt. Not anymore. He thought about Angela and how she'd embraced her child and was determined to love her. "No, Mam. You chose to let my existence ruin your life." He was done with feeling guilty, with feeling worthless and unwanted.

She gasped, and coughed, before nodding. "Maybe you're right, but it's too late now for regrets."

It was the longest conversation he'd ever had with her. He wanted to know more. "Do you regret kicking me out?"

She shook her head. "I regret not giving you up when you were born."

The breath left him. "Why didn't you?"

"You were my penance."

"You couldn't see me as your gift?"

She looked confused.

He didn't push the point. There was really nothing else to say. She didn't love him, she didn't miss him, she didn't want to see him. "I'll leave now." He got to his feet.

"I wish you well," she said.

"As I do you." Sean walked out. He would never see his mother again. There was no sadness there, only relief. There was nothing he could have done to make her love him. It didn't matter who he was, gay or straight, rebel or choir boy, she hadn't had it in her to love her mistake.

He found Keiron in the kitchen. "I'm going now."

"Is she all right?"

"Yeah."

"Will you be back?"

"No."

"Why not?" Keiron was hesitant, like he was afraid of the answer.

"Mam knows why, and if you want to know, you'll have to ask her."

Keiron stared at him for a long moment and then nodded. "Thank you for coming."

"Thank you for letting me know." Sean walked out of the house and down the quiet street. He breathed deeply. It was a sunny day and he needed fresh air. The heat here was so different from Houston. Here a sunny day was a cause for celebration. The buildings were different too, all centuries older than the modern metropolis. Hayden would love it.

Sean smiled. He'd love to show Hayden around Ireland. The

fear of being gay was no longer there. It wasn't his sexuality that had caused his mother to hate him, it was his existence, and there was nothing he could do about either. He'd been trapped by the fear for so long, held back from moving forward in his life, and he'd hurt Hayden because of it. If Vinny fired him, he would find another job, or perhaps he could stay in Houston while his visa was being processed. He'd make it work.

He walked into his hotel and checked the time. He had to talk with Hayden. If he called now he might be able to catch him before the conference started for the day.

Getting into the elevator, he dialed Hayden's number.

"Sean!"

At first Sean thought Hayden had picked up the phone, but it was still ringing in his ear. He turned around as Hayden ran across the hotel lobby. His heart jumped. The elevator doors began to close and Sean threw his hand out to stop them.

***

Relief flooded Hayden when Sean stopped the elevator from closing. He hadn't been sure about how Sean would react. He entered the elevator, panting. "I'm so glad I caught you."

"What are you doing here?" Sean frowned, touching Hayden as if he wasn't sure he was there.

"I missed your call yesterday and tried to call you back. When you didn't answer, I called Carmen and she told me about your mother." Hayden paused as the elevator doors opened on Sean's floor. "I caught the first flight out of New York." The thought of Sean having to face his mother by himself had been too much.

Sean opened his mouth to speak, but Hayden cut him off. "I know you don't want me here, I know you don't want to be outed — I'll stay here in the hotel if you want — but I couldn't let you go through this alone." He glared at him, daring him to disagree.

Sean opened his hotel room door and gestured Hayden inside. He wasn't speaking, but he didn't seem upset. Hayden put his bag on the floor and waited for Sean's reaction.

Sean wrapped his arms around Hayden. "You're wrong. I do want you here." Sean rested his forehead against Hayden's. "It means so much to me that you would come, especially since we fought. I was just thinking about how stupid I've been, and how much I want to show you around Ireland."

Hayden's brows lifted. "Really?" The hope was so full in his chest. Did that mean he was going to be open about his sexuality?

Sean nodded.

"You're not mad I came?" He looked into Sean's eyes, trying to figure out what he was feeling.

"No, I'm really glad." Sean smiled.

Hayden relaxed. "Have you seen your mother?"

"Yeah, just now." He told Hayden about the visit. "She'll never love me and I'm OK with that."

"Honey, I'm sorry about your mom, but I'm glad you're all right." He pulled Sean closer, needing to touch him.

"I'm better than all right with you here," Sean said. "I missed you." He stepped back. "When's your flight back to Houston?"

"I haven't booked one." His heart ached. "Do you want me to go?"

"No." Sean ran a hand through his hair. "I thought if you've got time before you leave, you might like to come to my place."

Hope bloomed in Hayden's chest, but then he frowned. "When are you returning?"

"I'm not," Sean said. "I had to change my ticket, and I don't have the money to fly back."

"But you'll miss Bridget's wedding."

He nodded. "I had to choose, but I'm glad I came back. It's given me closure."

Hayden was glad too, but there was no way Sean was going to miss Bridget's wedding. "I'll book you a ticket." He spotted Sean's laptop.

"I can't ask you to do that."

"You didn't," Hayden said. He turned on the computer.

"Hayden, I can't let you buy me a plane ticket. It's too expensive."

"No, it's not." He glanced up at the indecision on Sean's face. "Please, I want to do this for you. It took incredible courage to face your mother." He was going to do it no matter what Sean said, but it would be better if Sean didn't feel bad about it.

"I'll pay you back."

"Sure," Hayden said easily. They could argue about that another time. "The next flight out is tomorrow morning." He booked two tickets.

Sean smiled. "That gives me enough time to drive home so I can pick up some different clothes. Will you come with me?"

Hayden wanted to make things clear. "You're inviting me to your house?"

"Well, it's an apartment, but yes."

Hayden reined in his excitement. "Will you introduce me as your friend?"

Sean took his hand. "As my friend, my lover, my partner. You're everything to me Hayden, and I'm not scared anymore. I'm gay, and I have the most amazing man who loves me. I don't want to hide that."

Love filled Hayden's heart. "Are you sure?"

"Absolutely," Sean said with conviction.

Hayden smiled. "When do we leave?"

***

It was just after midday when Sean unlocked his apartment door. He glanced around. His place felt empty, soulless. There were no photos or pictures on the wall, the sofa was old and functional — the only thing that showed any personality was his small bookshelf full of books. He turned to Hayden. "Welcome."

Hayden looked around. "Nice place."

Sean shrugged. "No, it's not." He walked through to his bedroom and dumped his backpack on the floor. There was nothing comforting about coming here, it wasn't a homecoming at all.

Hayden came up behind him and wrapped his arms around Sean's waist. "Are you all right?"

Sean turned to face him. "Yeah. I just realized how lifeless this place is."

"Kind of symbolizes who you were before coming to Houston."

Hayden was right. He had been lifeless. He didn't want to

hang around here. Sean took Hayden's hand. "Let's get something to eat."

"Where do you want to go?"

Vinny could try to fire him, but Sean would fight it now. "Let me show you where I work."

Sean pushed open the heavy wooden door to the bar. The nerves that tickled his skin were barely a prickle. The lunch rush was over, so there weren't many people in there. Vinny's wife, Niamh, was behind the bar. She looked up as the bells on the door chimed and grinned. "Sean! What are you doing here? I thought you weren't due back for another week."

Sean crossed the room with Hayden next to him. "I came back to see me mam, but I'm leaving again tomorrow."

Niamh placed a hand on his arm. "I was sorry to hear about her." She glanced at Hayden. "Who do we have here?"

Sean braced himself. "This is my boyfriend, Hayden."

Niamh's eyes widened, but she automatically took the hand Hayden held out.

"Pleasure to meet you," Hayden said.

"Likewise," Niamh said faintly.

"Any chance we can get a couple of beef and ale pies?" Sean asked. So far, so good. She didn't seem upset, just surprised.

"Of course. Let me tell Vinny. Take a seat." She hurried out the back.

Hayden leaned closer and murmured, "That wasn't so bad."

Sean nodded, smiling. "Come on, let's grab a table."

Sean was about to sit when Niamh called, "Sean, Vinny wants a word out the back."

He exchanged a glance with Hayden. This was it. He walked around the bar into the kitchen, feeling calm. He could deal with anything they said.

Niamh stood with her hands on her hips, glaring at him. "Why didn't you say anything?" she demanded, smacking his arm. "I'm so embarrassed. I've been setting you up with girls for years."

He stepped back in surprise. "I needed the job. You fired Angus for being gay."

Niamh huffed. "Angus? Who's Angus?"

"The bartender who was working here when I started."

"Angus Murphy was fired for pilfering from the cash register," Vinny grumbled. "Not for being gay."

Sean stared at him. "He told me it was for being gay."

"Well, he would. He was a liar and a thief," Vinny said.

Sean shook his head, not able to believe it.

"So you kept it a secret all these years, because you thought we'd sack you?" Niamh asked.

He nodded.

"Well, that's an insult for sure," she said. "You should know us better than that by now."

She was right. He'd been scared his whole life. "I'm sorry." He took a breath. "You should know I'm moving to the States. I don't know how long the process will take, but you might want to start training someone new."

Niamh softened. "The visit with your sisters went well?"

"Yeah, and there's Hayden too."

She walked over and hugged him. "I'm happy for you. You seem different, more relaxed."

"I am."

"Good. We'll be sorry to lose you." She kissed his cheek. "Now go join your boyfriend and I'll bring the pies out shortly."

Sean smiled and walked into the bar. He nodded a greeting to one of the regulars and scanned the room.

This place represented his past, a place where he'd hidden who he was, where, like his mother, he'd just existed, scared of the world. He wasn't going to simply exist anymore. He wanted to live. He wanted to embrace life, love his family, build a life with Hayden, have his own dreams. Ireland was his past. Houston was his future.

He met Hayden's gaze, who had one eyebrow raised in question. His heart filled with love and he smiled.

Hayden was where he belonged.

Epilogue

The day of Bridget's wedding dawned bright and clear. The weather gods had heard their prayers and the day was forecast for sunny with a minimal chance of rain.

Sean and Hayden arrived at Casa Flanagan early on Saturday morning, and Carmen rushed into the living room to greet them. "Why did you not tell me about your relationship with your mother?" she demanded. "I would have gone with you."

Sean glanced at Hayden. How did she know?

Hayden winced. "Sorry. It slipped out when I found out you'd gone by yourself."

He didn't mind. Turning to Carmen, he said, "It was something I had to do, but I wasn't alone for long. I had Hayden."

"Thank goodness." Carmen hugged Hayden. "Thank you for taking care of my boy."

Sean's heart still jumped when she called him her boy. That alone showed him he'd made the right decision about leaving Ireland.

"It's always my pleasure, Carmen."

She beamed at him. "Come, we are putting up the decorations."

They followed her outside to the back of the garden where there was a large expanse of lawn. All of the foster girls were at work setting up chairs and hanging bunting and lanterns.

Bridget was directing everything and Carly and Zita were decorating the arched entrance.

Bridget looked up. "You're back!" She strode toward him and at her shout, Carly and Zita hurried over. Before Sean could brace himself, he was surrounded by a group hug. He didn't think he was ever going to get used to it, but he was looking forward to trying.

"We're so sorry about your mother," Carly said.

"Thanks."

"We're here for you if you need us," Zita added.

It meant the world to him. "I know." He smiled. "Now what jobs have you got for me to do?"

By mid-afternoon, Sean was once again in his suit and ready to walk his final sister down the aisle. "I'm getting to be a pro at this," he joked.

"Next time will be at your own wedding," Bridget said with a smile.

He paused. He'd never thought about marriage before he met Hayden. Same-sex marriage had only just become legal in Ireland. Now he couldn't imagine anyone else he wanted to spend his life with. He wanted to make that commitment. He shook his head. From in the closet to thinking of marriage in six short weeks. Discovering his sisters had changed his life.

After the ceremony, the family gathered for a photograph — Carmen, Carly and Evan, Bridget and Jack, Zita and David, and Sean.

"Wait a second," Sean said to the photographer. "We're missing someone." He dashed over to where Hayden was chatting with Alejandra. "I need you for a minute."

"Only a minute?" Hayden asked after he excused himself. "That's not really talking yourself up."

Sean grinned and took his hand. "We're having a family photo."

Hayden's steps slowed. "But I'm not family."

"Yes, you are. You're my family." He glanced over.

Hayden's eyes were wide.

Feck. He'd assumed Hayden was on the same page as him. "If you want to be." He ran a hand through his hair. "I mean, if you want to spend your life with me." Shit, he'd messed this up. Hayden was staring at him as if he wasn't making any sense. He had to do this properly. Sean took Hayden's hand and got down on one knee. "We haven't known each other for long, but you've changed my whole life. I love you so much and I want to spend my life with you. Will you marry me?"

Tears sprang to Hayden's eyes. "Do you mean it?"

"Yeah."

Hayden nodded. "Yes. Yes, I'll marry you."

Sean's heart leaped as he got to his feet and Hayden flung his arms around him. "I love you."

"Oh my God!" Zita yelled. "Did you just propose?"

Sean turned, his arm around Hayden's waist. His whole family was staring. He'd forgotten about them. "Yes, I did, and he said yes."

Carmen screamed the loudest, but not by much. He and Hayden were engulfed by a mass of bodies, all hugging and congratulating them.

Sean came face to face with Bridget and suddenly he realized he'd inadvertently stolen the spotlight. "I'm sorry. I should have waited until after the wedding."

"Hell no. This is way better." She hugged him. "Told you you'd be next."

Zita pushed her aside. "My turn." She squeezed him tightly. "Now you're definitely staying."

He nodded and Carly took her place.

"I'm so happy for you both," she said. "You deserve each other."

Carmen squeezed in. "One more wedding!"

Sean bent over to hug her. "Will you walk me down the aisle, Mama?"

Carmen burst into tears. She nodded.

Finally, Sean found himself next to Hayden again and pulled him into his arms. "Are you all right?" Sean murmured.

"More than all right. I'm perfect."

Hayden was right. He was perfect, *this* was perfect. He was where he belonged.

ACKNOWLEDGEMENTS

This book could not have been set in my home country of Australia for one simple reason — same-sex marriage is not legal there. It saddens and befuddles me that politicians are too afraid to do what is right and grant the LGBTQI community the basic human right to marry who they want, regardless of gender. Everyone deserves the opportunity to have the happily-ever-after that Hayden and Sean received.

As a heterosexual woman I was worried about writing a male/male romance, concerned I wouldn't do it justice, but I so wanted to write Hayden's story. My sincerest thanks go to Dan for running his fabulous writing workshop and for beta reading Place to Belong. Dan, your feedback was invaluable.

Producing a book involves many people and so I'd also like to thank my critique group, Anna, Juanita, Susy and Teena, for all their feedback, as well as Ida from Amygdala Design for the gorgeous cover, Julia Knapman for editing and Brooklyn Ann for proofreading.

About the Author

Claire Boston is the best-selling author of The Texan Quartet. In 2014 she was nominated for an Australian Romance Readers Award as Favorite New Romance Author.

Her debut contemporary romance novel, What Goes on Tour caught the attention of Momentum's Joel Naoum when her first scene was read aloud at the Romance Writers' of Australia (RWA) conference in 2013. This led to a four book contract for The Texan Quartet series.

Claire is proactive in organizing social gatherings and educational opportunities for local authors. She is an active volunteer for RWA, as a mentor for aspiring authors and the reader judge coordinator.

When Claire's not reading or writing she can be found in the garden attempting to grow vegetables, or racing around a vintage motocross track. If she can convince anyone to play with her, she also enjoys cards and board games.

Claire lives in Western Australia, just south of Perth, with her husband, who loves even her most annoying quirks, and her two grubby but adorable Australian bulldogs.

Claire loves to hear from her readers. You can find her at her website, www.claireboston.com, on Twitter, @clairebauthor, and on Facebook www.facebook.com/clairebostonauthor. You can also join her reader group at http://eepurl.com/Z4-4z.

Break the Rules

The Flanagan Sisters # 1

Bridget Flanagan knows how to assess risks, but are the consequences of exposing her heart too dangerous?

Bridget has a passion for safety and in the world of oil refineries that makes her great at her job. So when her big promotion goes to someone else, she heads out on the town to forget her troubles. Jack Gibbs seems like the perfect man to distract her.

At least until Monday morning when she discovers Jack is her new boss. There's no way she's going to keep seeing him, no matter the connection between them. She's been burned before.

Jack can't understand why Bridget's so against their relationship. They positively sizzled during their one night together. He knows he has to be careful now she reports to him, but she tempts him in every way.

Can Jack convince Bridget to give him a chance, or is the risk too high?

http://www.claireboston.com/books/break-the-rules/

Change of Heart

The Flanagan Sisters #2

Software billionaire Carly Flanagan has an abundance of everything except time.

With everyone wanting a piece of her, or more accurately, her money, she spends her days trying to live up to her company's motto of Community, Sharing, Support. Having always been so focused on responsibility, success and supporting those less fortunate than her, Carly's forgotten to consider what she wants for herself in life – until she meets Evan.

Evan Hayes is an artist and free spirit, and when they meet at a local art exhibition, he is immediately intrigued by Carly. He sees through her public persona, realizing she is not the person she portrays. Evan's the type of man who doesn't have a lot, but is perfectly comfortable with who he is. A man who knows what he wants – and he wants Carly.

Carly is sure Evan wants something else from her. Everyone does. All Evan is asking is the chance to get to know her, but will Carly let him in? Or will a lifetime of protecting herself prove too hard to overcome?

http://www.claireboston.com/books/change-of-heart/

Blaze a Trail

The Flanagan Sisters # 3

They're from the opposite ends of town but they're worlds apart.

Zita Flanagan wants more. She wants to help more Central American refugees and make more of an impact. But her family comes first and fulfilling her own dreams seems impossible.

David Randall leads a privileged life and knows nothing about refugee issues. When he meets dynamic, sexy Zita, it seems like the perfect opportunity to learn. Zita's passion for helping those less fortunate and her selfless devotion to the girls her mother fosters brings David's life sharply into perspective.

Zita soon realizes that David is so much more than a rich boy. She begins to trust him with her foster sisters' stories, and her own hopes and dreams. But when David's father announces he's running for governor and the focus of his campaign is the 'refugee problem', Zita has grave concerns for her sisters' safety. Then David's betrayal exposes secrets, and it becomes a race against time to save lives.

Can David convince Zita to trust him again, or will his mistake put the life of the woman he loves in jeopardy?

http://www.claireboston.com/books/blaze-a-trail